St. Nick's Journey

St. Nick's Journey

Suffering Souls of Awahso

KEITH MAYHEW-HAMMOND

Foreword by Charles A. Coulombe

RESOURCE *Publications* · Eugene, Oregon

ST. NICK'S JOURNEY
Suffering Souls of Awahso

Resource Publications
An Imprint of Wipf and Stock Publishers
199 W. 8th Ave., Suite 3
Eugene, OR 97401

www.wipfandstock.com

PAPERBACK ISBN: 978-1-7252-8282-7
HARDCOVER ISBN: 978-1-7252-8283-4
EBOOK ISBN: 978-1-7252-8284-1

Manufactured in the U.S.A.   12/04/20

To my dearest Emmanuel,

God with us, the Divine Child of the Cross, the Infant of Prague, born to us on Christmas Day, the consolation for all those of goodwill, and the hope of those of us who are imperfect, without whom the hope of Christmas would not exist, I dedicate this novel to You and Your Holy Family. For love of us, You humbled Yourself to become a lowly child, that we might become adopted as Your brethren, sons and daughters, and Your most intimate and affectionate and preferential companions. May the hope of Christmas that You sparked in the world all those years ago continue in the hearts of men each and every moment of every day and into eternity.

To Saint Nicholas,

Bishop of Myra, Lover of Truth, Patron and Protector of Children and Travelers, it is fitting that I dedicate this work to you and the One you so faithfully aided in life and continue suit and service to now in the Cloud of Witnesses. For love of God you have been spreading charity and inspiring good works for many centuries. By love of Christmas you have enkindled my faith for as long as I can remember.

To my Good Shepherd Church Family,

With special mention to Arthur Bousfield; Scott, Kellie, Justin, Noah, and all the members of the Walsh family; Eric Alcock; Bill Marchand; Rowan, Kevin, and Noel Willis; Irene and Jackson Tait; Valarie and Donald Richard; Tony Brooks; Liliane Mariza; Katharine Mahon; Peter Chin; the Rev'd James & Violet Tilley; and all the members of Good Shepherd, I dedicate this story to you. Each of you, in your own unique and special way, as dear and close companions, have greatly assisted and inspired me to grow in faith, hope, and charity as we continue on this pilgrimage together towards Heaven. God is the only one who can fulfill us; and yet, this known truth only makes the gift of friendship more valuable and precious; because love is not finite, and only grows when shared. May God grant that we may all grow in love of him and neighbor, until safely sealed in Heaven's kind embrace.

"But in all these things we overcome, because of him that hath loved us. For I am sure that neither death, nor life, nor angels, nor principalities, nor powers, nor things present, nor things to come, nor might, nor height, nor depth, nor any other creature, shall be able to separate us from the love of God, which is in Christ Jesus our Lord."

—Romans 8:37–39 Douay-Rheims

"There, if thou wilt have recourse to the Lord thy God, if thou wilt but have recourse to him with all thy heart, in the bitterness of thy tribulation, thou wilt find him again."

—The Book of Deuteronomy 4:29 Knox Bible

"Two are better than one, because they have a good reward for their toil. For if they fall, one will lift up his fellow; but woe to him who is alone when he falls and has not another to lift him up. Again, if two lie together, they are warm; but how can one be warm alone? And though a man might prevail against one who is alone, two will withstand him. A threefold cord is not quickly broken."

—Ecclesiastes 4:9–12 Revised Standard Version Catholic Edition

"Bear ye one another's burdens; and so you shall fulfil the law of Christ."

—Galatians 6:2 Douay-Rheims

Contents

Permissions

For Whom the Bell Tolls, by John Donne/written in 1624/public domain/a paraphrased line from the prose, Devotions Upon Emergent Occasions (Meditation XVII) and Several Steps in My Sickness, is used in Chapter 1, when the dark figure speaks to Tom in his dream before sending him to his death.

Call of the Wild by Jack London/published in 1903/public domain/referenced as a book that Tom was currently reading in Chapter 2.

A Christmas Carol released in December second, 1951/directed by Brian Desmond Hurst/fair use/referenced in Chapter 15 with Tom mentioning where he learned the word "Walk-er" from.

Ecclesiastes 4:9–12 Revised Standard Version Catholic Edition/used for epigraph in front matter/copyright permits use of under 500 verses

Galatians 6:2 and Romans 8:37–39 Douay-Rheims/used in for epigraph in front matter/public domain

Deuteronomy 4:29 Knox Bible/used in epigraph in front matter/fair use

Foreword

In *St. Nick's Journey,* Keith Mayhew-Hammond takes us on a strange and magical journey through a land as close as down the street, and as far as imagination can conceive. Reminiscent of Shirley Jackson's ability to make an unusual point of view seem normal to the reader, Hammond gives us a taste of the horror and wonder that his Aspergered and OCD'd hero perceives in a way that makes the reader wonder if he himself is losing something not having those conditions. But he does so in such a way as to make it all seem very natural. Moreover, while both the protagonist's handicaps and youth might, in less deft hands, be used to explain away the enchantment and numinosity of the journey the four friends undertake, Hammond uses them to create a breathtaking Christmas masterpiece.

Charles A. Coulombe, contributing editor of *Crisis Magazine* and author of *Vicars of Christ; Puritan's Empire; A Catholic Quest for the Holy Grail.*

Acknowledgments

The author wishes to express his gratitude to the following, who generously offered their time, inspiration, encouragement, advice and editing assistance: a special mention of Arthur Bousfield, who put in countless time and effort to help make this project a reality; Rosemary Campbell; Jeff Clement; Charles Coulombe; Katharine Mahon; Shawn Mayhew-Hammond; Noel McFerran, Dr Alexander Roman; Garry Toffoli; Dr Richard Toporoski; Dr Scott Walsh; Matthew Wimer, George Callihan, Savanah Landerholm, and the whole team at Wipf and Stock Publishers who helped with this project. Without their kind support this story would never have been written and completed. Any failings of the author in telling the story remain his own.

The author would also like to give thanks to all his family, Good Shepherd Church, patrons and protectors, benefactors, friends, enemies and those who are indifferent towards him, for all his experiences of life both good and bad which have helped in forming who he is today.

To his loving Creator and Preferred Friend, the Most Holy Trinity to Whom he owes all his talents, graces, inspiration, love and life itself—to him and all his faithful companions, especially the Holy Family, he gives his eternal thanks.

Abbreviations

OCD   Obsessive-Compulsive Disorder
PTSD   Post Traumatic Stress Disorder

Introduction

Contemporary literature too often scandalizes people, polluting their minds by promoting ill-will and disbelief, glorifying questionable morals and making heroes out of villains. To entertain people while also edifying them, *Keith Mayhew-Hammond* feels that there is a need for more stories that promote faith, morality, charity and goodwill. In that spirit he has found a fulfilling call in writing such works.

Since early childhood, struggling with Obsessive-Compulsive-Disorder (OCD) symptoms, Asperger's, Acute Anxiety and Depression intensified for Keith his crippling religious doubts and worries regarding time and death. The experience of attempting to control these through his faith, as well as struggles with bullying, gave him insight and inspiration for writing his first novel, *St Nick's Journey: Suffering Souls of Awahso*, in which such themes are prominent.

In his early youth Keith sought God by the practice of Evangelical Protestantism. After a long journey of looking at different Christian sects he eventually found the fullness of faith in the Holy Catholic Church, founded by Christ, and is now a member of the Ordinariate of the Chair of St Peter, and lector and altar server at Good Shepherd Church.

Chapter 1

Shortbreads, Carols, and Coffins

Standing tall in my living room, the beautiful but tackily decorated Christmas Tree—far too many colors on it—was supposed to be a symbol of eternal life. That hoary belief stemmed from an evergreen's ability to keep its color during all seasons. Yet the very notion that we had killed this sign of endless life itself became a symbol of doubt of eternity.

Not that I disliked Xmas Trees or wished to doubt the immortal soul. On the contrary I loved the Xmas Tree. And I hated my doubts about Heaven. But then, I always tended to think too much about the contradictions of our breathtaking customs; conflicting my soul by causing the perpetuation of my doubts. Plus, I felt bad for killing the tree. I knew trees had no souls yet my emotions told me otherwise.

Anyway, there was no point in letting such petty ideas keep me from enjoying Mom's Xmas cookies.

In the dining-room I took the biggest bite of the shortbread I could without choking. With half the cookie melting on my tongue, I had no choice but to chew as fast as possible to avoid spitting it out in a fit of uncontrollable laughter. Nathaniel, like a typical younger brother, had been waiting patiently for me to take a bite to try and amuse me with the silliest dance he could come up with. He stuck his tongue out as far as he could and moving both eyes back and forth like a ticking clock, attempted to do the robot.

I was familiar with his tactics. Nathaniel—sometimes called, Nate, for short—knew upping the game was the only chance he had of getting me to laugh before I could swallow. From the pain of holding my laughter in, a lone tear rolled down my cheek, and down I went on my knees, chewing as quickly as I could. But as soon as I was safe from choking, I crouched on the floor laughing my hardest, hoping at the same time not to humiliate myself completely.

Only my brother and I were in the dining-room. Mom and Dad, talking away as they were in the adjoining kitchen, did not seem to notice our antics. Since it was only family, I should not have felt embarrassed; though, even around them I could still be very self-conscious at times.

Catching my breath from all the laughter, I inhaled a sweet-scented mix of shortbread and pine, my two favorite smells in the world.

Nate was always trying to lift my spirits. Knowing my recent melancholy, he redoubled his efforts. My brother was the opposite of me. He was always trying to make people happy and bring out the best in them. Fitness and causing others to smile seemed to be his favorite occupations. Thinking back, I realized it was rare for him not have a smile on his face.

I more often looked sad and angry. I would never have guessed that. It was only because others told me that I knew. That and the fact that my school pictures always turned out badly, even though I thought I was smiling when they were taken. My parents actually punished me for spoiling them. They thought I did it on purpose.

Once I stood up, Nathaniel reached up his hand and patted me on the shoulder. He was very short and not simply because he was only in grade four and two years my junior; seeing him even amongst his peers you would not have guessed he was their same age. "Tried my best to get you on that one, Tommy," he proclaimed, looking up at me with a sparkle in his eye. "I really put my all into it!"

That was something we shared. Not the sparkle, but the same blue-green eyes. But my eyes, unlike his innocent-looking puppy dog ones, always looked spaced out, even when fully present.

Patting Nathaniel on the head and tousling his short light brown hair a little, I reassured him. "You'll get me next time Yobro. Almost had me this one." Why did I encourage him? I could have choked from that prank, and had now basically told him to try harder next time.

"Don't call me that!" my brother exclaimed. "You know I hate it!"

"That's right Nate, I'm sorry," I apologized. "I always forget somehow. Just so used to it you know."

I do not recall at what point I began calling Nate by that nickname, but for whatever reason I did, he despised it. Perhaps finding one thing that really bothered him was why I kept it up so long. After all it was not even clever. 'Yobro' was just short for 'younger brother'. Regardless of why I started it, I really wished to give the habit up, not wanting to annoy the one person trying so hard to help me feel better.

That moment, when Nathaniel and I were standing by the dining-room table, was the very second the sensation of glimpsing a shadowy looking figure, which dashed by us into the living room and behind the Christmas tree, struck me. Startled, I suddenly felt very warm. Overcome by the impression of heat I began to sweat intensely. Did I imagine what I thought I saw? What could it have been? There was only one way to find out.

Mustering the much-needed courage, I took a gulp and proceeded towards the tree. Nate stopped me, however, after only a few steps and pointed me back to the goodie-filled table. I saw with surprise that he had fear in his eye and was shaking subtly. Had he seen the figure too? Or was it something else that was bothering him?

Nate consumed a lot of protein powder to try and improve his running. From not having enough carbs and fat, his nutrition at times got off balance and made him a little shaky. It would hit him suddenly then go away as quickly. Should I have asked him whether he saw what I did, or ignore it as simply an illusion?

If he had not seen the shadowy figure, I did not want to scare him over what was likely only my imagination. He was a little sensitive too about the protein issue, so I hesitated to bring it up. Knowing how strong my imagination could be, I concluded the appearance must have solely been another trick of my fitful mind.

When I was really tired my mind would frequently play tricks on me. A spec on the floor turned into an insect squirming menacingly around, for instance. So far, this susceptibility was known only by me. I should've told my parents about it but I had a fear of being institutionalized. As long as I knew the figure that I thought I saw was not real, I would keep it to myself.

Mom and Dad came into the dining-room from the kitchen and asked if we wanted to go to a carol service. Filling with glee at the prospect, I looked at Nate in hope that he would like to go too. He nodded yes. I tried to hold in my excitement. There was nothing I loved more about Xmas than the carols. They were joyful, full of hope, and brought people together. I always paid special attention to the lyrics which constantly reminded me of the Heaven that lies beyond this life.

We got our coats on, went out the door and climbed into our dark blue Malibu Chevrolet. I knew of course that my family could not possibly be as excited as I was at the prospect of the coming treat, so I masked the joy I felt the best I could.

Though it was snowing, it had not been for very long, and so Dad reversed out of the driveway without needing to clean off the car. Just as he started to switch from reverse to forward, I felt a terrifying presence emanate from outside our house. Summoning up the little courage that lay dormant inside me, I whipped my head in that direction, forcing myself to see, before Dad hit the gas pedal, if I could catch a glimpse of what, if anything, it was.

Even though it was dark, I could distinctly see a black shadow-like figure exiting our driveway. Almost as if it had waited for me to see it, the figure dashed towards our car just as the Malibu accelerated forward. I jumped so quickly from fear, and not even my seatbelt prevented me from whacking my head on the car roof.

My parents pretended not to notice. They probably thought that it was merely Tommy being weird again. I was glad they did not ask me about it though. How does one explain to one's parents that he was experiencing vivid hallucinations? Speaking of which, where did the figure I saw disappear to? Was it under the car? No, it must have left my field of vision when I was distracted by the head pain. Why was I experiencing these random night visions? Was it from too many cookies, or was it going to be an ongoing problem?

Whatever the truth, I tried to be nonchalant about the sudden bump on the head, though it did not seem to fool my brother. "You don't have to hide your excitement on my account," Nate said with his usual smile. "If holding it back makes you hurt yourself, what good is it?"

Ah, that was better! My brother did not seem to have noticed my fear. He knew how much I loved Christmas carols, and attributed my odd behavior to that excitement.

"I won't make fun of you for loving Xmas carols more than other songs," Nate continued. "It's awesome that you like something that much! You should be proud of it. You don't see me pretending not to like sports, do you?"

That was true. Personally though, I thought Nate should tone down his passion for sports. At least a little. But how could I tell him that after his pep talk to me? "Thank you for understanding." I laughed. "You always see right through me!" This time though it was a lie. And I hoped he would stay blissfully ignorant of my current dilemma. It was bad enough that he knew of my depression.

After we arrived at the church, I still could hardly wait to hear and take part in one of the closest things to Heaven on earth. Not seeing any statues, I assumed that we were in a Protestant congregation. There was nothing unusual in that. Protestants tended to offer more carol singing services than Catholic parishes, since carols developed through folk singing, unlike the hymns created for Mass. It was permissible for us as Catholics to attend Protestant services as long as we did not take their communion. I only hoped there were as many carols as possible—especially my favorites.

We took our seats in the loft. I preferred it because there were often fewer people up there. The atmosphere was noisy from all the chatter and whispering, yet the environment still felt sacred. Trying my best to avoid the irritating smell of mixed perfumes and colognes, I let my eyes wander around the room while I admired the gorgeous decorations. Holly, tall evergreen trees with showy ornaments, and glistening Christmas lights of multi-colored bulbs, were catching my attention in almost every corner. I did not mind the gaudiness at all. Any reminder of Xmas was a good thing to me.

The noisy voices stopped abruptly as the organ began to enchant my ears with the tune of God Rest Ye Merry, Gentlemen. We joined everyone in standing up and I fumbled to get my booklet to the right page. After three beautiful carols, it seemed the rest of the night would go perfectly.

But as my favorite Xmas carol started (O Come, O Come, Emmanuel—though technically an Advent hymn), my brother tapped me on the shoulder. I continued singing while I looked over at him, making sure to show, by clear facial expressions, how upset I was at him for the distraction. Noticing that Nate was pointing in awe at the clock on the wall, I looked in the same direction and stared in wonder too. The hour hand was moving faster than it should be and was gaining speed. Soon it was going so fast that I could no longer even see the hands.

Unable to withstand the increased speed the clock began shaking. What was going on? If my brother was seeing it too it could not be an hallucination. Or could it? Was it mass hysteria? Maybe some trickster put hallucinogen in the air! Part of me was angry at whoever was causing this disturbance on so wonderful a night, while the remainder wished only to continue singing. I did not desire to be the one to break up such a wonderful song.

Finally, the clock shook so hard it fell off the wall. "Look out!" I shouted to warn those down below in the regular pews. So much for not interrupting the carol—but I couldn't be selfish. Saving someone's life was more important than my feelings. Thank God the clock did not fall on anyone. It crashed down onto a closed dark brown coffin. Why did I not notice the coffin before? A casket is an odd Xmas decoration. Was there a funeral earlier in the day? How sad if someone died so close to Xmas.

With the fall of the clock the music, alas, stopped. And an eerie silence had crept over the whole congregation. Then, out of the silence, a random bell started ringing. One of those large ones from bell towers, though I did not realize this church even had such a bell.

Suddenly, a terrifying voice spoke out loudly and clearly in what was somehow also a mere whisper. "Ask . . .," the voice slowly muttered. Shaking beyond control, Nate and I turned around in unison as speedily as caution and reluctance allowed. "Ask . . . not . . .," the dreadful sound continued in harmony with the bells. It was the frightening shadow figure, that had dogged us from home, now speaking to us. Able to take a closer look, I saw the figure resembled a human made out of smoke—but no face was discernible.

And whatever it was, it was coming nearer. In no time it seemed so close it was hugging my parents, who were sitting between Nate and me, from behind their chairs. ". . .Ask not . . .. for whom . . .," the horrifying tone went on, solemnly, as I panicked in terror at what it could want with us.

With an alarming cry, Nate made his way around our parents and hugged me tightly, grabbing my hand. I wondered if he was okay until I gave my parents a closer look and saw their faces were shrunken and ghastly pale, their hair and clothes covered in dust. Dead! They were dead. How could this be? They must have died only moments ago, yet they appeared as though they had been dead for centuries past.

The intimidating voice grew louder. "Ask not for whom the bell tolls . . .," it droned on. Forgetting my fears, I embraced my brother more tightly as I yelled at the awful creature, no longer able to hold back my tears. "Murderer!" I shouted at it. "Murderer!"

"Ask not for whom it tolls . . .," spoke the strange being in a manner so bone-chilling that I was recalled to our perilous situation. My accusation seemed not to phase the apparition at all! What was I to do? I needed to get my brother away from that thing!

"Listen Nate," I whispered desperately into his ear, "when I say go, we run down the stairs as quickly as possible. Okay?"

Nate did not answer. I dared not look at him. I knew what I would see. His body had become stiff. Drawing on the last bit of reason left in me, I tried as carefully as possible to sit my dead brother down beside my parents. But in doing so, I tripped and accidentally dropped him on top of them. Quickly I looked away, not bearing to know if my clumsiness had desecrated my family's remains. I felt dead inside knowing that now I was all alone.

Terrified still more at the peril of my situation, I gulped and accepted my fate. I stared defiantly at the personified smoke, as if to let it know that I had made whatever peace I could with my impending doom.

But the cold being seemed to care nothing for my reluctant and imprudent bravery. It finished its sentence—in grammar as well as in the judgement which it passed upon me. "The bell tolls for you!" Not a second after uttering this, the misty terror rushed straight towards me.

Frightened out of my wits, I ran backwards and tripped over the bal-cony. As I fell, the coffin opened its mouth wide, showing it could hardly wait to swallow me whole. I knew there was no getting out of this one.

Falling, time seemed to slow down for me and I pondered every detail of what was going to happen. How badly would the impact hurt? Would I remain in pain and die slowly or at once? Would I be lonely in death or would God let me into Heaven with my family? What if there was no after life? Shut up! This was not the time to question such things. May God have mercy on the souls of my family and mine.

As soon as I hit the ground I woke up in a dreadful sweat, screaming. Why does falling in dreams always feel so real, even if you have never had the experience before? In any case, thank God it was merely a dream. And yet, it was not. Dreams could have a funny way of reminding us of the cur-rent state of our minds.

When it was still fresh in my head, I decided that it was a good idea to record my dream in my journal before it faded from memory. In case I wanted to reflect on it later. I was so glad to be alive to be able to spend at least one more Xmas with my family!

TOM'S JOURNAL:

December 13/1997/Morning.

I had the most dreadful nightmare last night. My pajamas are still soaked in an ocean of sweat, making sure that I do not forget how scared I was. During the terrifying night time vision, some dark being, perhaps the Grim Reaper, killed my whole family while we were caroling, and then ended my life the moment before I woke up. I suppose one good thing about experiencing such petrifying terror is that it puts things into perspective, reminding me how glad I am to be alive for at least one more Xmas.

I've been having a lot of nightmares lately. I should only be having joyful dreams so close to my favorite time of year, yet I guess I cannot control the dream world. Anyway, the crazy vision inspired me to write this little entry. What's the point in having dreams if you don't reflect and write about them? That's obviously a rhetorical question. I would clearly use any excuse to write more. Anyway, here is my reflection:

> *Childhood is fleeting, life itself is a vapor. Growing up is like car-rying your own coffin in a funeral procession. You never know at what point the journey is going to end but you have the ever-growing feeling of its imminence.*

Should I really be comparing the adult world to death? It is unhealthy, but I cannot help it. Both remain a terrifying mystery for me. How can a person be ready for a world he does not yet understand, especially without even having a grasp of the current world? Which is worse? I suppose that cannot be known until it is reached. The chance of death coming before high school is slim to say the least, yet I cannot rule it out. After all, no one knows the day or hour in which he will meet his end.

How ridiculous it is to be speaking so grimly only a few weeks before Christmas. The holidays will fix everything. They always do. I have been waiting and preparing for Xmas all year, so this will be the best one yet. Knowing that only a few more holidays remain before high school gets here, I must try my best to enjoy every moment of them. Speaking of which, I smell my favorite shortbread cookies baking in the oven. I should go and assist so that I can justify testing them to Mom.

Good day journal.

Chapter 2

Are My Parents Felons?

DECEMBER 13/1997.

When I arrived home in the late afternoon today, my parents pulled me aside to have a talk. If ever I have kids, I must remember not to use such ridiculous phrasing. Every kid knows he is in trouble when an adult tells him he needs to sit down for a chat. It's not subtle in the least.

Not knowing how much trouble I was in, I needed a glass of juice in case my throat got scratchy. I went into the kitchen to pick out a mug from the cupboard. My hand immediately went to my favorite Xmas mug, which had a picture of a snowman on it. Yet seeing the surrounding cups, I felt that they were calling to me to take pity on them, since I had not used some of them for a few days. Their jealousy radiated from where they stood, hoping that getting me to feel sorry for them would make me more likely to switch choices. They knew me so well. I was at an impasse. I wanted to use my favorite cup so badly, yet I did not want to treat the other mugs unfairly by showing favoritism. Not wanting to keep Mom and Dad waiting any longer, I needed to decide fast. I made a mental resolution to make sure to use one of the other cups next time, but to then stick with the one in my hand.

Placing my cup of ice-cold apple juice on the well-worn wooden coffee table, I took my seat on the couch while Mom and Dad sat on either side of me, putting their arms around me. At that point I knew something terrible must be up, for my parents were not ones to initiate affection at random. For

9

them, fondness was usually more of a formality—kissing me good night at bed time as well as on other specific occasions. Not that I minded scheduled hugs, but unscheduled affection made me suspicious of their motive.

I rested my hands on my knees to try and hide my sweaty palms, but my unease was more obvious then, for when I did, I clenched my knees with my fingers. I could smell Dad's after shave lotion. It irritated my nostrils, though I could never muster up the courage to tell him it did. There was an awful taste in my mouth, which caused me to want to leave the room even more, so that I could find a mint. I knew though that they would never believe such a lame excuse.

Waiting patiently for Mom and Dad to begin lecturing me, all I could really think about was that they were keeping me from getting back to reading my book. The *Call of the Wild* it was, and it was quickly becoming a favorite read of mine, one which I could hardly put down. But I realized I had to stay focused. I did not wish to show disrespect to my parents by ignoring them entirely.

As Dad pondered how to start the talk, the silence and wait were killing me. Well, it was not complete silence—it rarely is. I could hear the distant but seemingly ever louder buzzing noise of the electricity traveling through the lights. How easily distracted I was.

When Dad pulled out a letter from the chest pocket of his worse-for-the-wear blazer and slapped it down gently on the chestnut coffee table in front of me, my anxiety escalated to the extent of being hardly bearable.

The impulsive thoughts racing through my head urged me to touch the letter to distract me from my worries. But how could I without Mom or Dad noticing? Apparently, I was already in trouble and I did not wish to cause my parents more distress. Yet I had not hidden my obsessive need to touch things that well, so surely, they must have noticed it. The eerie feeling came over me, harassing me with the fear that if I did not touch the letter, both my parents would die.

How ridiculous. It could not possibly be true yet how can one reason with an impelling feeling of impending doom? The more I ignored the notion the stronger it got. The more I argued against it, the thought only grew in obnoxiousness and distastefulness. Unable to stand it any longer I reached for the letter, reluctantly accepting the consequences. I could only hope they were not the nut-house.

As my finger reached the envelope, I finally went for it—just one touch, maybe two, but no more than three for sure. And three touches it was. That was my cut-off point. What relief came from such an absurd notion.

Hoping that neither parent had noticed my horrendous display of restraint, I grabbed the letter to hide the true reason for why my hand was there. After picking up the envelope however, my relief turned quickly into grief and intense panic, with, I am ashamed to say, no little degree of resent-ment and anger.

It was a personal letter that I had written and given to Dad to send in the mail to St. Nick only a few days earlier. Why did Mom and he have it? Did Dad not send it, or worse, did he read it? My hands shook nervously as I pulled my letter out of the envelope, which I saw had been opened, so that I could make sure that it was the same one.

TOM'S LETTER TO ST. NICK:

December 10/1997.

My dear St. Nick,

I hope you and yours are doing well, especially the reindeer. As always I will be sure to leave a carrot and apple for them beside your milk and cookies. I only mention this so you don't think I am trying to force you into eating more fruits and vegetables. I may even leave a bowl of oats to see if your companions like them. I will not be offended if they turn it down—I know better than most about the importance of routine.

This year I am in grade seven and am 12 years old. I am really getting up there. It saddens me so much that most if not all my peers no longer believe in you, and it must break your heart even more. I am glad that I still believe.

Sadly, I sometimes have crippling doubts about God's existence and of the after-life. I can hardly function when such thoughts overwhelm me. The consequences of no Heaven would mean eternal loneliness, without ever seeing my family and friends again. What a terrible and unfortunate fate it would be to experience love in a home and then lose it all as if it had never existed in the first place.

So many, who don't believe in God, tell me it would not matter, since, if we did not exist, we would have no thoughts at all. Perhaps it would be simpler if we had never existed. But to have life and then be deprived of it all—what would be the point? It would seem more like a cruel joke from an evil creator rather than just God not existing at all.

I have you to thank for stopping my doubts. Whenever doubt infiltrates my mind, I remind myself that since you exist, God must also exist. You have been spreading charity and love of Xmas for centuries and such a miracle could only be possible if God was the one behind it. So, thank you for inspiring my faith in Christmas and in God.

Enough of my annual emotional rant. I am sure you have more important things to do than read long-winded fan letters.

I tried to be good this year but likely failed miserably. If by chance I have made it on your nice list, please send me a book that you think I would like. As you know I enjoy reading and trust your judgement.

Have a good Xmas St. Nick!

Yours truly,

Tommy Jolmen

P.S. I want to put in a good word for my brother, Nate, too. He is always good but has been especially kind to me this year.

Oh no, it *was* my letter! My parents must've been upset at me for doubting God. That would explain this meeting. But why did they read my letter? How could they?

Looking a little sorry for having invaded my privacy, Mom pulled a card out of her pocket and gave it to me. It was a number for a tollfree children's helpline. Likely that one because a free therapy service such as it would be more affordable than what most of them charge. But being free makes it no less insulting and humiliating.

Unable any longer to hold back my boiling tensions, I stood up and screamed, "That was a private letter! You were supposed to send it not read it! That's a felony!"

I took the card and threw it as hard as I could across the room, but to my embarrassment it fell like a feather right beneath my feet. Pretending what just happened did not happen, I continued my shouting rant: "And now you subtly imply that I belong in the nut-house with this piece of garbage?"

Feeling bad for the card, I picked it up and passed it back to my Mother while whispering an apology to it. Whenever I over reacted, I immediately regretted it. It was so against my nature. Usually I kept all my emotional turmoil inside to avoid inflicting a burden on others. I tended to keep very quiet and argue with myself more than with others. Yet every once in a while, I could not seem to help letting my frustrations burst out at the surface.

My parents sighed in unison, as if they wanted to say something but could not bring themselves to do it. I have always had a paranoid thought that one day I would end up in a mental institution, so I concentrated on attempting to prolong my freedom. Any suggestion of therapy made me a nervous wreck because I knew that one appointment would be enough for sufficient data to be gathered to send me away.

I waltzed angrily into the kitchen to fetch a stamp and tape the open envelope closed. Then I marched out the front door and slammed it shut. Knowing how badly the guilt of such behavior would trouble me later. I walked back into the house to give my parents a hug. I hated leaving bad impressions on those I cared most about. Because I knew full well that they or I could die at any time.

I said a few gentle words of reproach to Mom and Dad as I embraced them, which may seem contradictory, but I needed to make sure that they knew my affection by no means justified their actions. Walking out through the door again, I closed it as softly as I could. Feeling bad for having slammed it shut earlier, I awkwardly gave the door a quick apology kiss, once I was sure no one was around to see. I knew it would bother me all day if I did not do so. Having done that, I walked off to mail the letter, deciding from then on to mail all my letters personally.

Heading toward the mail box to post the letter to St Nick, I slowed the pace and began worrying about my parents. What did they have to say but found that they could not? Were they going to tell me that St Nick was not real? It couldn't be. What would they have to gain by making up such a fable? Unless the story of St Nick was simply concocted as bribery to make kids behave. But how could they do that to me? Surely, they would not. If it were all a lie, would that mean that God was not true either? Or Heaven and the afterlife?

There had at first been no wind, so I thought I did not need a coat, but the deceptive air betrayed me, sending a light breeze my way. Shivering for a moment, I crossed my arms over my chest. Since the wind was so slight, the betrayal seemed trivial. It was the principle of it that bothered me. If the weather tricked me with something small, how could I not doubt it over bigger matters?

Realizing that I should have worn my overcoat, I picked my walking speed back up and took a detour. Though I was cold I did not wish to return home yet, and was becoming hesitant about posting the letter. If St. Nick were fake who would receive it? Was this an ongoing joke with someone laughing behind my back at reading letters not addressed to them? There's no way. That would be a crime for sure.

I walked over a long wooden bridge which crossed a small lake. The bridge was narrow and lonely with not a soul in sight. In summer there was often a nauseating odor of garbage at this point which ruined the beautiful view. But not today. The cold air must have killed the stench. But alluring though the prospect was, the lake seemed sad somehow, as if it were abandoned. A lone sheet of ice covered a small portion of the surface, happy on the one hand to have become unique from its peers, yet sad that it was now no longer able to flow with the rest of the water. Did the surrounding water even notice or care that the ice felt left out?

Although still a little cold, I stopped at the center of the bridge to gaze at the water. Do lakes get scared? Did this one fear the future? If so, I knew how it felt. I had yet to figure out childhood. How on earth could I ever move on to high school? It's too big a change. And how would I survive if I lost my faith in St Nick and God? They both had to be real. They must be. But what if they were not? I could not bear the thought.

As I stared out at the watery abyss which was surprisingly still today, I continued to ponder life and death. The chill in the air could not stop my palms and back from breaking into a sudden sweat, something common to me when I thought too much.

A Christmas tune popped into my head as I wiped my sweaty palms on my jeans. Such songs often made me feel better, reminding me of the things of God as well as happy memories of times with my family. Lost in my own head, I began to hum, O Come, O Come, Emmanuel, my all-time favorite musical piece. Entranced by the melody, I forgot where I was for a moment and the gentle hymn turned from humming into singing—quietly at first, then continuing to grow until it reached full volume.

As if hypnotized, I felt my worldly cares absent just then. Perhaps I was finally connected to God. Would this awe-inspiring experience last for long, perpetually even?

"How beautiful!" I heard a voice say in a well-mannered and elegant tone. "I love that hymn. It's so solemn and enchanting."

Immediately I froze. Scared even to look to my left where the voice seemed to come from. How did I not see or hear someone approaching? How humiliating. I should've ran for it before whoever it was saw my face. But I couldn't. So shocked was I by my choral outpourings being overheard by a stranger, I became as stiff as a board! What to do? I panicked.

"Please don't stop!" continued the friendly stranger. "It really was lovely. I should not have interrupted it, but couldn't help but compliment you on your voice."

Maybe I did not need to dash after all. Though I was embarrassed, the stranger showed no sign of making fun of me. Perhaps he was harmless. A person as gullible as I am, however, should never trust his gut instinct on such matters. Notoriously bad at judging character, I needed to postpone hasty conclusions. Delaying judgements provides greater opportunity for perceiving falsehoods.

After what felt like an eternity, I gulped and turned awkwardly to my left. Well, apparently, I was blind. It was a kid. Seeing him sitting down with his back against the bridge railing, I realized he had clearly been there longer than I had. How could I not have noticed this guy, who appeared only slightly younger than I was, seated there with his legs hugged against his chest, barely a meter from where I stood?

"Sorry if I startled you." the lad apologized in a calm and serene sounding manner. He was plainly dressed in khakis, bulky partially zipped jacket and a white buttoned shirt, all seeming oversized and looking as though they were hand-me-downs from his Dad. Large though his clothes were, they did not hide how skinny he was. Honestly, until I saw him, I thought I was the scrawniest kid around.

A backpack sat closely beside him but fell over as he stood up. He grabbed my hand like a gentleman to remind me of his good nature. As I accepted his assertive yet weak handshake, I felt assured that he was human. I didn't mean to be insulting, but he was so ghastly pale that I might have mistaken him for a ghost.

"My name's Brendan Mascent," said the young man whom I was now certain was quite harmless. "And yours?"

"Well it's Tom Jolmen," I answered, nervously running my hand through my hair. I was actually very jealous of Brendan's hair. His straight blond locks stayed perfectly combed even as they were blown around by the wind. My hair was always all over the place. Then again, as I did not really use a comb, what did I expect?

Realizing how formal my reply sounded, I added, "But my friends call me Tommy." Why did I say that? The only one who ever called me Tommy was my brother. To everyone else I was, Tom. I guess I wanted to brag about how many friends I had, though for some reason none of them hung out with me. Having no cause to impress this odd stranger, I could not understand why I felt the need to show off to him.

"I guess I'll call you Tommy then," Brendan responded quite forwardly. That felt awkward. This kid must have no friends since he was coming off so desperately. But how should've I responded without hurting his feelings. I would just need to ignore it for now.

Though he tried to hide his red eyes with a friendly smile, the attempt was vain. Not seeming the type to hang around with the bad crowd, it was safe to assume his condition was not from drugs. He had obviously been crying. I was hesitant to bring it up, but decided that it was the right thing to do. "Not having a good Christmas so far, eh?" I asked in hope that he wouldn't think I was prying.

"What do you mean by that?" Brendan responded looking a little puzzled. He must have been oblivious to the appearance of his red eyes Oh no! I was going to have to be direct. Why did I ask that? I guess I would just have to get it over with. Wait a second. I figured out a way to be more subtle. I explained, "Well, lots of people are having bad Xmases these days. I assumed you might be one of them."

"Well," Brendan stated, looking less confused about what I was asking, "regardless of how you or I, or anyone else is feeling, Xmas is always good, never bad. It never bends to the changing emotions of men. It's always joyous, you know."

Wow! I could not help but be impressed by such a heartfelt response explaining my favorite holiday in a way that was always true yet had never crossed my mind before. I could ponder that for a long while. At the same time, what did he mean by it? Though a beautiful reflection on the timelessness of Xmas, it completely avoided the question. Perhaps he was very smart or something. And was he also implying by his statement that I looked sad? Did I look upset and not notice? Putting all that aside for a moment, I felt this guy must have loved Xmas as much, if not more, than I did to have made such a claim.

Curious and excited to have met someone in love with my favorite holiday, I had to make sure. "That's very poetic. You must really like Xmas!"

"Of course," Brendan responded without hesitation. "Not only is it my favorite holiday, but it is mankind's only hope. It is even naturally celebrated in winter to remind us of its being a light in the darkness."

Delighted by our mutual love of Xmas, I felt as though I had completely misjudged Brendan's character. The one time I showed caution about opening up to someone, I ended up finding him a completely trustworthy person.

Looking over at Brendan's partly open bag on the ground, I saw that it was overflowing with books. "It looks as though you share my love of reading as well as of the holidays."

"Yes," Brendan replied eagerly, going to take a book from the bag. "I've finished all of them but this one." He brought the book over to show me. It was, *My Locked Basement,* from the *Frightful Sight* series. "I love *Frightful Sight* books. I've finished all of them in the last few days but could not complete this one since . . ."

My new friend paused in mid-sentence and then continued, "What about you? I'm a bit of a nerd I'm afraid."

If he was a nerd, did that make me one too? It couldn't be. *Frightful Sight* books and Xmas are cool, so he must've merely been insecure. "I love them too! My favorite is the one with the haunted Halloween costume . . . I hope I didn't ruin it for you."

"No," he answered, "I've already read that one. It is good, though."

Wait a second. Why did he pause and not finish his sentence earlier when speaking about why he was unable to complete, *My Locked Basement*?

Did he start to reveal something and then realize he should not? I had to know or it would bother me for days. And why did he have so many books in his bag?

Brendan suddenly began to wobble a little, moving back and forth unsteadily as if he were going to faint. He grabbed the bridge rail and leaned on it, acting as though he was doing so by chance, rather than to prevent himself from falling over. Was he sick?

"What were you saying about why you were unable to finish the book?" I asked.

Taking his hands off the railing, Brendan took his book from my hand to put back in his bag, pretending he did not hear my question. At least he tried to take it back. My left hand would not let go of it. I needed to hold on to the book a moment longer so that I could touch it three times before letting it go. But if I did that, he would know I was a freak. He must've thought so already because I grasped it so tightly to prevent him from prying it from my hand.

"You can borrow it after I'm done," Brendan laughed, thinking my reluctance to let go meant I really wanted to read the book.

That means it's not too late. I can still back out of it. What's the worst that could happen? Actually, best not to think of it. Too late! "I'm sorry!" I shouted as I poked the book with my index finger three times before finally releasing my grasp. "But I only did it to save your life." Yikes! Why did I tell him that? I knew that thoughts of touching an object being able to save someone's life were nonsense, so I tended to keep them to myself—yet my big mouth had now exposed me as neurotic. What would he think of me now?

"What are you talking about?" Brendan laughed, taking his book back, perhaps thinking that it was some sort of game I was playing. How could I tell him that it seemed that he would die if I did not obey the command inside my head? How could he understand when I could not even get it myself? Then, suddenly I realized, this was my opportunity to find out his secret.

"Listen, Brendan," I reluctantly requested. "This is going to sound really weird, but you seem like a trustworthy guy. So, I will tell you my secret if you tell me yours."

Brendan looked down at the ground for a moment, thinking it over. "Alright," he agreed at last rather shyly, "but you go first."

Though I was a fairly open person in general, a characteristic which got me into trouble often, this was one thing I had never talked to anyone about. So finally, having found someone to confide in, I told him everything. I don't know what came over me, but I went on for about half an hour

The obsessive-compulsive behavior, the depression, all my doubts about St. Nick, Xmas and God, I let everything come out into the open.

And though I was afraid of his response, not knowing if he would take me to the madhouse or not, it still felt wonderful to get it all off my chest. Who needs therapy after all? Perhaps all I required was to talk to someone who would listen.

"Wow!" I said, self-consciously trying to recover my dignity. "Where did all that come from?" Not able to bear waiting to hear Brendan's response, I hurried on. "Just kidding. It was a joke. You can forget I said all that stuff!"

Without saying a word, Brendan awkwardly gave me a long bear hug, and would not let go until I hugged him as well to show that I accepted it. Although I felt very uncomfortable, not being used to hugging anyone but family, I appreciated the gesture a lot. He had shown me that he accepted me and my faults in a way words could never fully express.

Perhaps I did not really tell him all my secrets simply so that I could find out his. Maybe I was only looking for an excuse to unravel my mind. There also seemed to be something special about Brendan that made me feel as if I could tell him anything, an innocence of soul I could somehow sense. But then again, I was a bit delusional.

As Brendan began to walk back towards his bag, he stumbled, but caught his step just in time before he fell. Rushing over to clutch his arm and make sure he was okay, I helped him sit down by his bag. As he leaned back against the rail of the bridge, I sat down next to him.

"Are you alright?" I asked.

He nodded, a glazed look in his eye. Perhaps he had cancer or something. Now wanting to know more than ever about him, not merely out of curiosity but from concern, I reminded him of his obligation. "It's your turn now."

Brendan smiled, hoping perhaps that I had forgotten. "Well," he started, "I could not get far through the book because I began to feel very dizzy and could no longer read the lines properly." He paused as if finished and hoping that I would be satisfied with such incomplete detail. I wasn't, and gave him a look to show that I needed to know more.

"The truth is," he continued, "I packed all these books and have been sitting here reading for three days, minus the nights,"

"Go on."

"I haven't really eaten much so I think hunger caused my fainting spells."

"You didn't go home all that time? Aren't your parents worried?"

"Don't remind me," he sighed. "They must be by now. At least I hope so."

This guy was full of surprises. Maybe he hung out with the bad crowd after all. Was there some secret nerd rebel group that I was unaware of?

"What do you mean?" I inquired, listening intently.

Brendan shrugged his shoulders then started to rock back and forth as if to distract himself from his guilt. "It's really stupid. You see, I was watching this movie a while back. The kid in the film is captured and the crisis brings the whole family back together to help find him. When they finally do find the kid, they pay attention to him—a lot of attention."

At last he blurted it all out and began to cry. "I thought maybe if I ran away, my Dad would come back and my Mom would pay attention to me. But they never came looking for me because they think I'm nothing but an attention-seeker. And now I'm afraid to go home. I'll be in such trouble."

I could hardly believe my ears. I put my arm around him to try and console him as he continued to cry. Never would I have imagined there was someone like this, an innocent, having such big family trouble.

After about five minutes of sobbing, he wiped his eyes and caught his breath. "Sorry for the waterworks. Please forget all that I just said. It was only attention-seeking, so you don't have to trust any of it."

"Don't worry," I reassured him, "your secret is safe with me." I could hardly believe that someone who wore so constant a smile could cry so much at one sitting. It was almost as if he had two distinct personalities.

With that, Brendan's smile suddenly returned and he patted me on the shoulder. "Enough of that! And thank you for understanding. Now let's get that letter mailed for you."

I was surprised how quickly he was able to move on from so emotional an outburst. It was impressive. I stood up and said, "You can help me deliver my letter to the mail box if you let me walk you home after. You have to go home at some point."

Brendan looked at the ground for a moment and then got up, saying, "Alright then, I guess you're right about that." As he made sure his bag was secure, he continued, "It doesn't matter so much if your parents believe in St. Nick you know, as long as you still do."

"I guess that's true," I told him, handing him my spare granola bar. "But I wish I could know for certain. To quench all my doubts would mean everything to me."

"We'll figure something out," he reassured me as he opened the snack.

We posted my letter then walked towards his house. He did not let me come to the door with him, which seemed strange to me; but it must only have been because he was worried about my seeing him get grounded. I watched from the opposite side of the street, sitting on the curb for a minute to make sure that he actually knocked on the door and went in.

TOM'S JOURNAL:

December 13/1997/Evening.

I have both marvelous news and bad news. In that sense, today was both great and terrible at the same time. I guess I should start with the bad news. Mom and Dad read my letter to St. Nick instead of posting it, then tried to suggest that I needed therapy. I am extremely peeved and disappointed in them. I'm pretty sure that opening others' mail is a crime, but I'm obviously not going to report my own parents. I would not want them to get in trouble. I just don't know why they would do that to me. And now they probably think I'm crazy—that would explain the suggestion of therapy.

Now for the good news. In my anger, I went for a walk to blow off some steam before posting my letter. I met someone on the bridge. He seemed a bit eccentric, was pale as a ghost, and was even skinnier than I am. But he was very kind. Sharing many of the same interests, we connected very well and became instant pals. My new friend is apparently as strange as I am and he actually wants to hang out with me again. I am one grade older than he is, so I hope his parents won't mind that.

In the end I opened up to him telling him about all my problems. It was not my intention to do so, but it just sort of happened. To be honest, it felt great, finally, to be able to tell someone all my secret woes. He seems trustworthy. I hope he is, because if he tells anyone what I said, they will institutionalize me for certain.

I look forward to seeing Brendan again—that is his name by the way. Apparently, he ran away from home to try and get attention. I hope he did not get into too much trouble when he got home.

Now I'm finally going to read a few chapters from, Call of the Wild, *and then head off to bed. Goodnight journal!*

Chapter 3

Wrapped in Doubt

Journal and pen in hand, I flicked on the light switch at the entrance to my dark bedroom. Though the promised glow should have brightened the room's despairing mood, it only highlighted the gloom. As I stepped in and gently guided the door to a close, it seemed to sigh in unison with me. I turned the knob three times then leaned against the rough wooden frame a few moments before mustering up motivation enough to go and sit down and write. Doing so offered consolation yet risked making me feel worse.

Drudging my way over to the bunk-beds which were set up horizontally against the near wall, I was disturbed by the untidiness of the top berth. How upset I became every time that I saw it. How could anyone sleep in a bed that looked like a natural disaster? I would have tidied the messy unmade sleeping quarters myself, but if I did Nate would think his rights had been violated. I could only be grateful that bunk-beds saved me from such unsightliness while sleeping. Were the beds placed beside each other, I would have had to look disdainfully on the terrible site much of the night.

It was good though to remind myself how grateful I should be to have my brother still with me. However much his chaotic bed annoyed me, I would not replace it with a perfect one if it meant losing Nate. One day we would both grow up; he would move out to start his own life and I would be left all alone. What a cruel joke growing up can be.

My soft and neatly folded sheets on the bottom bunk presented a warm welcome to me as I sat down on them, but they could offer me no relief from my current melancholy. Reluctantly I opened my journal and began to write:

TOM'S JOURNAL:

December 25/1997.

Christmas came and went, and much too quickly. What a disappointment it was. I had put so much hope into the aesthetics of the day itself, building it up in my mind to be the salvation of my whole year that there was no way it could possibly have lived up to my expectations. I must have known this would happen but somehow could not help myself from thinking of it in such a way.

There was nothing wrong with the day for the most part, but the astounding feeling of magic I used to get when I woke up each Christmas morning for as long as I could remember was nowhere to be found. Could adulthood really be so boring and miserable? A state where all of life is merely a redundant sequence of events with nothing interesting ever happening—one thing following after the other until our end?

A terrible thing did happen though that I have tried not to think about too much, but it is of course inevitable that it haunt my mind. When getting ready to open up our presents this Christmas morning, I could not help but notice that all the gifts from St. Nicholas had the exact same wrapping paper and tags as the ones from my parents. What are the chances of that being a coincidence? Was it like that every year and I simply never noticed? If so, how could I have been so blind? I am trying my best to think of reasons still to believe that St Nicholas is real, but I am running out of them—fast. Perhaps I am in denial from trying so hard to crush my doubts, but I cannot lose my faith in him. It is my foundation for everything—my world-view, my hope for life after death, the certitude that I will see again those who die before me, and even my belief in God himself. If I give in to my doubts, I am convinced that it will be my ruin.

I am going to meet Brendan tomorrow and accept the incredible idea for a trip that he mentioned previously. It is probably a bad scheme, but it is the only way I can think of either to quench my doubts for good, or else if I have been lied to for the whole of my childhood, then be crushed by the truth once and for all.

I wanted to write a poem about today. This is what I composed:

ON THE VERGE OF DESPAIR

I feel the need to vent,
Since Xmas came and went,
And put not even a dent,
In my saddened sentiment.

All my hope was in Xmas day,
Anticipation demanded its pay.
Yet now inside dead I lay.
Hope, return to me, I pray.

What should I do now?
To defeat should I bow?
Though my heart cries "Ow!,"
I never must, I trow.

For the sake of those I love;
And for the chance of those above
To descend like a dove
And assist me thereof.

Who have good will,
To them he will fulfil.
Removing of every ill
To bring peace eternal still.

With all my pouts
And all the doubts
My wits I must keep about
And avoid the risk of selling out.

Regardless of how I feel,
May I never forget to kneel
Please God to me reveal
If Heaven indeed is real.

P.S. I forgot to mention the awesome Xmas gift Nate gave me. He got me the Ronald Knox translation of the Bible which has a very poetic style. I am so grateful to him for it. I've never owned my own Bible, so I will make sure not to take his present for granted.

It was about a year ago I think that I first felt the desire to read the Gospels to learn more about Christ. My interest came from watching one of those old Easter movies—'The Robe', maybe. So, I started borrowing Nate's Bible, not realizing that I would get in trouble for using it. It was a souvenir for his Baptism, kept in a beautifully colorful and tightly fitted gift box. Apparently, it was not meant for reading. But no one ever told me so. How was I supposed to know? Though Nate did not seem to mind, my parents had a fit when they caught me reading it—well it was mostly Mom who did, but Dad did not disagree with her.

Nate was nice enough to go with me to the library to take out a Bible for me to read. Now, thanks to his getting me this Xmas gift, I will no longer have to keep re-checking the library copy out.

Goodnight journal.

Thud! I closed my journal. For a moment I stared at it. Realizing it was close to being full it came to me that I needed to get a new one soon. I should probably have asked for one for Xmas. Getting up to place the journal in my padlocked treasure chest, I accidentally knocked my head against the bunk-bed above me. Thump! Though I knew the top bunk was there, for some reason I often forgot to be careful when getting off the lower bed. My forehead throbbed, adding to the pressure my head already felt from thinking too much. After opening the storage box, I rubbed my brow with my hand.

Putting my journal away, I returned to my bed and knelt in front of it, hoping to complete my evening prayers, ignoring the dizzying pain torturing my head. My vivid imagination distracted me. It would not allow me even a few minutes peace to focus. A three-minute prayer turned into ten minutes of apologies for every unwanted thought that hijacked my mind. Intense images of attending funerals of all the members of my family and their presence at mine haunted me. Unwanted and distasteful thoughts refused to go away. Hard as I tried, I was not able to eject them from my thoughts. The constant disturbing interruptions made me feel terribly irreverent. I am an easily distracted person, but this was too macabre and terrified me.

I sat back down on the bed while my mind wandered aimlessly into space. Perhaps this year was a dud. It did not mean that I would never enjoy Xmas day the way I used to again. But what if that were the case? Xmas is the most joyous part of the year. Without its gladness to reinvigorate me, how could I possibly tolerate the rest of the year? Maybe all my best years had already passed and the rest of life was to be redundant misery. How did adults stand it?

Trapped in my own little world, I did not notice that Nate had come in to our room. But I came back to consciousness when he called my name.

"Tommy!" he said, startling me out of the dungeon of my mind.

I jumped and bumped my head again against the bottom of Nate's bed. "Ow," I said as I massaged my crown, noticing that a large lump had formed. "You scared me."

"Sorry," Nate said, rubbing the top of his own head as if he could, by merely witnessing it, share the same pain that I felt. "I wanted to ask you if you enjoyed our Xmas this year?"

Not wanting to dump my woes upon my optimistic runt of a brother, I tried to be as cheery as I could. "Yes. I especially enjoyed the gift you got me. I'm sure I will get good use out of it."

"Glad you liked it," Nate said with pleasure, his usual big smile increasing to an even greater degree. Then he added, "I know how much you like Xmas caroling. Would you like to sing a few carols before we go to sleep?"

I was not in the mood for carols though they did cheer me up when I was feeling low. But right now, I felt they would make me feel worse; perhaps because they would remind me of the joy Xmas ought to bring, yet had not given me this year—making me wonder why my heart had closed itself off to the happiness of Xmas. Nate however was no idiot. If I told him 'no', he would certainly figure that something was very wrong with me. Yet if I told him 'yes', there was only so much faking that I could do, and he would see through it. My only chance was to agree to it. My refusal would be a guarantee of his figuring it out, while going along with it would at least increase my chance of his not seeing through my mask.

Realizing that my hesitation itself was a plain giveaway, I overcompensated with a regrettably bizarre over-the-top enthusiasm. "Absolutely!" I said.

Nate frowned at me. I could only hope he had not already figured out that I was only pretending. He took a couple of carol books from the open shelf, which from so many chips of paint having fallen off, almost begged us for a fresh new coat to restore it. He handed a copy to me as I stood up from my bed, cautiously avoiding hitting my head a third time the same night.

Nate stood beside me and suggested, "How about 'All Through the Night' since it's a fitting hour?"

I thumbed through the pages to find it:

Sleep my child, and peace attend thee,
All through the night;
Guardian Angels God will send thee,
All through the night.
Soft the drowsy hours are creeping,
Hill and vale in slumber steeping,
God his loving vigil keeping,
All through the night.

While the moon her watch is keeping,
All through the night;
As the weary world is sleeping,
All through the night.
Through your dreams you're swiftly stealing,
Visions of delight revealing,
Christmas time is so appealing,
All through the night.

You my God, a babe of wonder,
All through the night;
Dreams you dream can break asunder,
All through the night.
Children's dreams cannot be broken,
Life is but a lovely token,
Christmas should be softly spoken,
All through the night.

That was one of my favorites, one of a dozen or two. I liked them all so much. Nate and I loved the tune so greatly that for fun we even added several extra verses of our own.

Jesus' love is so compelling,
All through the night;
Angels guide us to his dwelling,
All through the night.
Drawn to thee born in a manger,
Is the lost remorseful stranger,
Fleeing each deceptive danger.
All through the night.

Keep our hearts from ever freezing,
All through the night;
Making us to God more pleasing,
All through the night.
Like as in the Gospels written,
Angels now proclaim this often:
Peace on earth, goodwill towards men,
All through the night.

Angels bow before the New-Born
All through the night;
May our human hearts adore him;
All through the night.

Now for those whose lives are ending,
For their last fight come defending,
Sending Angels, them befriending,
All through the night.

Unfortunately, the carols I loved the most could bring me down all the more for they would remind me that I was not in happy unison with their wonderful melodies. "Sure! It's one of my favorites," I replied.

"I know," Nate acknowledged. "Mine too."

No matter how badly I felt, I wanted to give the song my all. It would be a disservice to the carol if I did not, and I had to for the sake of my brother, who was attempting to do me such a kind service on Xmas day. I could not let him down. Nor did I wish to push Nate away, fearing to lose him altogether, which would be causing the very end I wished to avoid.

We sang the song together in marvelous harmony, something that I did not realize we were capable of. As we raised our voices, my heart tried to hide from the lyrics, but to no avail. At each line and each verse, the beauty and meaning found me and pierced my soul. Wounded by it, I would run and attempt to hide again, yet was weakened more and more by every minor injury and potentially fatal blow. By the last verse my soul no longer had the strength to run or even walk, but could only crawl. The final line finished me off.

The song was over and I could not move. One step and Nate would know. My facial muscles tightened to try and prevent what seemed inevitable. Nate was as silent as I was, sensing my unease.

Finally, he broke the silence. "That song never gets old. Thank you for singing it with me."

I said nothing. I wanted to answer, but knew if I spoke a single word, my voice would betray my position. Yet not saying anything would be almost as obvious. My hand went out to pat Nate on the shoulder to show solidarity with what he had said without using words. In doing it I did not look at him and my co-ordinates were slightly off. I ended up patting him on the face instead.

Nate laughed.

Thank God, he thought it was a joke. He went to put the carol books back on the shelf. I panicked. He might not have noticed from the side view but as soon as he turned around and saw my red teary-eyed face, he would figure me out. So, I turned and faced the beds, realizing as soon as I did it how weird it looked to have my back towards Nate.

Nate approached me, tapped me on the shoulder and asked, "Is everything alright?"

Realizing that there was no way to hide it now, at least that I could think of, I turned to face him and get it over with.

"What's wrong?" Nate asked me.

I took him in my arms, burst into tears and held him as hard as I could without crushing him. "I don't know," I sobbed, not even understanding how to explain it to him or to anyone.

"You know you can talk to me about anything. Right?" he demanded doubtfully of me.

"I can't put it into words," I whimpered.

"It's alright," Nate stated in consolation, "I'm here for you—always."

That's just it. He could not always be there for me nor I for him. One day we would lose each other and everyone else. Our childhood was nearly over and I dreaded the thought of being without him. But how could I tell him that? I did not know how.

As I continued to cry on his shoulder, soaking his shirt with my tears, he gently interrogated me, asking me different questions to see if he could figure out what was wrong. After I said 'no' to all of them, he gave up asking, accepting that he was not going to figure it out at that moment.

"I'm sorry," I said as I finally started to calm down and let go of my brother, if only because my reserve of water for tears was running out.

"For what?" asked Nate sincerely.

"For ruining your Christmas with my silly waterworks."

"Don't be silly," he said, softly chastising me. "You could never ruin my Xmas. Don't ever apologize for being sad. I want your company no matter how you feel—as long as you're not being a jerk."

We both laughed.

"Don't isolate yourself out of some ridiculous worry about ruining my day, okay?" he added, "I'm your brother."

"Sometimes, Nate, I think you are actually the elder brother. You're so much wiser than I am. But don't let that go to your head."

"Nah," Nate jested. "My brain is so full of wisdom that nothing else could possibly fit in there—don't worry about it going to my head."

I laughed. "Well good night, Nate. Thanks for being there for me. And Happy Christmas."

"You're welcome. Glad I could be there. Merry Xmas and good night to you too. Are you sure you'll be alright though?"

I nodded.

"Okay," Nate said, then added pretending to be Mom, "Well I don't want any mischief from you tonight!"

"Nor from you," said Mom to Nate. She had sneaked up unnoticed.

Nate froze on the spot, probably feeling like an idiot for imitating Mom right in front of her. "Since it is Christmas, I'm going to pretend that I didn't hear you mocking me right now," Mom said.

After we got ready for bed Mom and Dad tucked us both in and turned off the light. I thought my tears had dried up, but perhaps being kissed goodnight by my parents triggered them again. I hid my face under my pillow to try and keep my crying as quiet as possible. I did not wish to prevent Nate from getting to sleep, and wanted him to believe that I felt better. My tears exhausted me and I soon went off to sleep, hoping that Nate did not notice any of it from the top bunk.

Chapter 4

Ornaments and Episodes

PART I

January 4/1998.

Taking a tacky bright gold bulb off our Christmas tree, I breathed in the luscious scent of spruce. During the holidays the house always had that smell, but the aroma was strongest when you were really close to the evergreen. I wanted to enjoy every moment of it while I could. As each decoration was yanked off, it inevitably became closer to the dreadful moment which came every year—the trashing of our wonderful Christmas tree.

I felt the gentle touch of the needles between my fingers as I evicted another ornament from its home. I always preferred spruce needles to the pine because they felt much friendlier compared with the sharp aggression of the former.

Nathaniel was three times as quick as I was in removing each decoration and putting it in its box, which itself was waiting to be placed in a stuffy storage container for another eleven months. I could not help but feel sorry for the ornaments. I knew full well that they were inanimate objects—but I could not help but doubt that they were not sentient. If there was the tiniest chance that they could be conscious, I dreaded the indifferent way we were treating them. How I would loathe being handled in such a manner.

Nate began humming the tune for *O Come all ye Faithful*, probably sensing my discomfort and trying to cheer me up. Could he tell that I was stalling? Trying to savor the last few moments with our loyal friend the tree who gave us so much joy and beauty over the last few weeks? We were going to repay the poor thing with our ingratitude by carelessly tossing it at our front curb to be dragged away to some garbage dump. Of course, I knew that if we kept the tree too long it would become decrepit and ugly over time. Good thing that we humans don't treat each other that way when we grow old.

Mom and Dad went out for the day and left the destroying of any residue holiday cheer (aka putting away the decorations) to Nate and me. Though I loved putting up the decorations, which reminded me greatly of the arrival of my favorite time of year, I could hardly stand doing the opposite, which only made me dwell on the fact that Christmas was over and so was one more year of our dreary temporal lives. People seemed to behave kinder at Christmas time from the prodigious sense of magic in the air that every kid could feel, but it was unfortunately time for everyone to return to being their normal selves.

Nate continued making me look extremely lazy by the fast way he was working. I pretended not to seem too disturbed at how often he looked at me with his concerned beady puppy dog eyes. I noticed him doing so ever since our parents reminded us that we had to expel our beloved evergreen from the family and send it into exile. It was starting to become really annoying. Nate probably did not want to ask me how I was doing for fear of making what he clearly wished to prevent, worse. I could not blame him for being so worried, considering what happened a few days ago. But however irritating and unsettling it was to be constantly watched, it did mean a lot to me to know that my little brother cared so much about me.

The dreaded moment finally arrived. It was time to take the tree out to the front yard. I gave it an embarrassingly long hug, but a careful one to make sure that such rare sentiment would not cover me with sap. One thing I could not stand was sticky fingers—or worse, gum from the tree in my hair, on my feet, or really any part of me. Whenever I got honey, syrup, cotton candy, or anything sticky on my hands or face, I would keep all my fingers spread out as widely as possible to make sure they did not get stuck together, until I could wash it off. There were a lot of things I would not even eat unless I knew for certain that I would have quick access to a sink if I needed it, so as not to risk that horrendous feeling of glueyness for too long. Merely the thought of it drove me insane, so I tried not to dwell on it.

Putting on my coat, scarf, boots, and brown winter toque, I found a pair of winter work gloves to protect my hands from the tree's sappiest part. I waited for Nate to finish getting dressed for the winter weather then grabbed the bottom trunk while he seized the top. Nate tried to hold his half with one hand, attempting to open the door with the other, both of us regretting not having done so sooner. I could not help but laugh at him as he fumbled with the door to get it open.

A swift gust of wind rushed through the entrance way, desperately trying to restrain us from the unfortunate deed that we were about to perform. Unable to keep up its force it waned for a moment. Picking up again it hummed eerily as if in solidarity with the forlorn tree. The frigid atmosphere gnawed at my conscience, reminding my heart how much colder it was for destroying this great Xmas symbol.

As soon as we were outside and walked down the steps of our porch, distress hit me—in small amounts at first, then all at once like an all-out attack. I began to quiver as my mind fell into the pit of anxiety and unbearable sorrow. My muscles suddenly weakened. I began to feel pins and needles all over my body, starting from my feet upwards. I wondered if it might happen to me again, or if last time was a one-time mental episode. Whenever time to take down the decorations, I was never capable of handing it well. Sometimes I was good at hiding my distress until alone; at others, it became uncontrollable without any way to prevent visible manifestations.

Every possible negative thought rushed into my head together, especially the thought of losing my brother. My lips tensed in an effort to hold it all in, at least until we could get the tree to its destination. My upper back and hands initiated the process by sweating profusely. Once we got the tree safely down by the curb, I turned away from Nate so that he would not see my eyes watering. "I've got to go for a walk," I told him. "I'll be back in a few minutes."

My breathing became shallow and my every exhalation turned into a sigh. Without even looking at Nate to see if he heard me, I began to walk towards the end of the street, hoping that a brisk walk might clear my troubled mind and relieve my crippling anxiety.

Despite this my brother ran quickly to my side and gently yet firmly took my arm, walking with me. "Not a chance," he asserted. "Not without me anyway."

My entire body turned rigid. I appreciated Nate's concern for me, but I did not want him to see me like this again or cause him more worry than he had already experienced for me. "Thank you, Nate, but please let me be alone for a few minutes if you don't mind."

"I'm sorry," Nate assured me, "I do mind."

The muscles under my right eye and upper lip began to twitch randomly, while the upper right side of my back emitted spasms. "But . . .," I tried to protest before being interrupted by him.

"Do you remember the promise you made to me two days ago?"

"Yes," I acknowledged, crushing any remaining hope that he had forgotten that whole ordeal. "I remember of course. But I really don't want you to see me like this. Just let me go off by myself, okay? I will keep my promise and head over there right now on my own."

Nate gave me a stern look, which though not uncommon, always made me feel guilty. "What kind of little brother would I be, if I didn't do my very best to look after you when you needed it? It's not that I don't trust you, but I would feel better if I stayed by you to make sure that you get there safely."

My vision narrowed as I began to experience nausea. Getting sudden vertigo, I stumbled as we continued to walk.

Nate went on, "And if I can't know for sure that you will keep to your commitment, I will have no choice but to fulfill my end of the bargain. I would hate to do that to you. Besides, look at you. You can't even walk straight. Let me help you."

What a pest! No, I didn't mean that. It's just something I can't help but think when he does not get off my back. Nathaniel however was not the kind of brother to tell on me to get me in trouble. So, I knew his threat of ratting me out to my parents was caused by his sincere concern for my well-being. And he knew it would work because I dreaded the thought of being sent away to the nearest mental institution. "Alright you've got me," I quavered. "We had a deal after all."

Nate's usual smile returned in gratitude for my giving into his demands. "Lead the way my loyal steed," I joked, hoping that the bad jest might lighten any remaining burden that Nate felt in looking after me. He laughed but kept hold of my arm.

After about a ten-minute walk, Nate and I arrived at our parish church, 'St. Nick's'. He led me up the steps towards the large wooden double doors. Before he could open them, I resisted his pull and leaned my back against the right-hand door with my arms crossed. My lungs became filled with icy air as I took in another breath of fresh winter atmosphere.

"What's the matter?" Nate asked me. "Let's go in."

"I can't let the priest see my face, Nate. Or he'll know who I am. It kind of defeats the purpose of confidentiality if he sees me."

"No," Nate corrected me. "The vow of secrecy holds good, even if he does see you, I think."

"That may be true. But I can't let him see me. What if he breaks his vow? It's impossible for him to do so if he does not know who I am."

Nate looked frustrated, probably thinking I was acting in a paranoid way or trying extra hard to be difficult. But he was not the type to give up so easily. "Alright then. You stay here. I will go and explain the situation, and get the priest to enter the confessional booth to wait for you. Then I'll come and get you. But you have to promise that you are not going to bail out on me. Sound fair?"

"That's fair. And thank you."

Nate began to open the door, but I grabbed his arm quickly to stop him. "Wait," I demanded. "I forgot something."

"What is it?" asked Nate. "Hurry up. I'm letting the cold in."

"Then close the door for a second."

Nate sighed and closed it.

"Listen! Don't tell the priest that you are my brother. Only say that you are a friend if you have to."

Nate rolled his eyes at me. "Okay, but why not?"

"Because they have a list of the families who attend here and you only have one brother. It would not take much effort to find out that I'm it."

"I understand, but I can't lie to a priest, can I?"

"No of course you can't. You should not lie to anyone, but certainly not to a priest. You don't have to say that you are not my brother. Simply don't say that you are. It's called being covert—very different from lying. Don't worry. You are my friend anyway, so it's not really a lie."

Nate smiled again and entered the church. It was true. I did consider him a friend as well as a brother. The only reason I told him this was to prevent him from being upset at me for the taxing demands which I just placed on him. I slid my back down the door until I was sitting on the step, trying my best to restrain my crying, laughter, and a whole lot of other expressions that were bubbling together at the surface of my mouth.

It was not that I did not trust priests. In fact, I admired them because of their complete devotion to God in setting apart their entire lives for him. I would even consider becoming a priest myself, if I were not so crippled by doubts of the afterlife. It was the promise of confidentiality that I was not sure about.

. . .

Several years ago, as a consequence of my strange mannerisms—mainly my constant need to touch things—my school set up an appointment with a 'specialist'. During the session I kept fairly silent, not wanting to tell a total stranger my inner workings, feeling sure that the woman in question was going to call up my parents and tell them everything I said. If I was afraid to tell my parents something, I certainly did not want a total stranger interpreting it for them. The specialist broke the deadly silence by assuring me that anything I told her would be kept between us. I don't know why I was so naive as to believe such a tale, but I bought it hook line and sinker. In my young mind, I became excited at having someone, even if a stranger, to tell everything to without having to worry that anyone else would find out.

I blurted out everything—my recurring nightmares, my crippling anx-ieties and fears, all my intrusive thoughts and obsessions. I felt such relief in letting out all that built-up accumulation that I had been unable to tell to a single soul for years. I had barely finished my story before the appointment was over. I wanted so badly to come back, perhaps even weekly to let off more steam.

But the specialist betrayed me. She told me to leave the room and to sit on the bench in the waiting room for a moment. I did so, but I could hear her pick up the phone once she closed the door. And whom did she call? My parents! I'm not sure whether it was Mom or Dad she talked to, but she told them everything—even the worst parts. What a rotten traitor and liar she was. What would my parents think of me now? They would strap me in a straight-jacket for sure and lock me in a room with padded walls.

When the woman called me back in, I crossed my arms and would not even look at her. She was not going to get another word out of me. She let me know that she had talked to my parents, apparently not even remembering her promise not to. I felt like trashing the room, but instead shut down and went into my own internal world for a while, imagining what life might be like in the nuthouse.

. . .

Continuing to sit against the right wooden door of the church, I placed my arms around my legs and rested my head on them. My heart changed from beating really fast, to very slowly, then would skip a beat or two. My heart acting weird always made me feel ill. Was I dying? Could someone die from too much stress?

My family did not attend church weekly. I was not against the idea but I was always afraid to ask my parents if we could attend more often. I guess that I should have been grateful for the few times a year that we did participate in public worship.

The other side of the door opened and my brother popped out, lending me his hand. "Come on," he said as I looked up at him. "Don't worry. I set it all up for you. He's in the confessional booth waiting."

I took Nate's hand and he led me into the nave of the church. We both signed ourselves with Holy Water from the font while genuflecting as we entered. Taking me over to the Confessional, Nate said, "Go on in. I'll wait out here for you. Take your time."

I nodded and hesitantly entered the booth. I really did not want to go through with this and had only agreed to it to ease my brother's worry and keep him from telling on me. I knelt down on the kneeler in front of the screen.

"Go ahead," said a peaceful but firm voice.

I gulped and tried not to stutter. Unsuccessfully. "Listen Father, I am sorry for having wasted your time. I'm only in here as a favor to my friend who brought me, to ease his concern about me. So, if you want to merely preach to me for a few minutes, I will listen and then leave."

"Son," said the alluring and mysterious voice, "are you asking me, someone who has vowed to uphold the teachings of the Catholic Church, to help you deceive your little friend?"

Yikes! He had me there. I couldn't believe I had actually tried to manipulate a man of the cloth. Perhaps I was even more wicked than I thought. "No sir . . . I mean, Father," I stuttered. "Of course not. I'm so sorry. I wasn't thinking clearly. Please forgive me."

"How long has it been since your last Confession?"

"I've never been before, Father."

"Have you been confirmed?"

"No, Father. But I have been baptized."

"Do you attend a Catholic school?"

"No, Father." I was beginning to wonder if I was in trouble.

"Hmm. But you are Catholic?"

"Yes, Father."

"Are you taking classes to prepare for confirmation?"

"No, Father. I'm sorry."

"I'm sorry if this feels like an interrogation, my son. I needed to inquire a little to find out how best to help you. It's good that you've come to confession. I cannot absolve you at the moment, but I can hear your confession still and give you a blessing. And I encourage you to talk to me afterwards about signing up for classes, with the permission of your parents. Once you are ready to be confirmed, then come back for your first confession and I or another priest can absolve you. Okay? Now tell me your sins."

"Thank you. Well Father, to be honest, I do not know where to begin."

"Why don't you start for now with why your friend is worried about you."

"It's based on a promise I made to him several days ago to prevent some previous circumstances from repeating themselves if I felt overwhelmed again."

"And what were the circumstances, my son?"

PART 2

January 2/1998/The Episode (a few days ago).

Christmas was over and the wind was not happy. It made a desperate fuss, hitting itself loudly against every object that it could. It would stop suddenly after tiring itself out, only to begin again once it got a second life. The trees were so distraught that they picked futile fights with the wind, flailing their branches every time they made contact.

Nate was trying to keep up with me as I walked as quickly as possible, wishing as I did that he would give up and go back home. But he was persistent and my legs were starting to feel the strain. Soon I would have no choice but to slow down. All I could do was hope Nate would not clue in to my increasing fatigue and leave me alone for a while.

Mom and Dad had told us, right before going out for the day, that we would need to take down the Christmas decorations and remove the tree to the curb soon. Ever since I could remember, I would get this overwhelming sense of grief near the end of the holidays, often triggered by taking down our seasonal ornaments. Christmas gave me hope. Getting rid of all traces of it felt as though we were giving up the promise it offered.

Yet this was not like the other times. I could not explain why, but this year felt more despairing. Perhaps it was the fact that childhood comes with distractions that more easily take the mind off fears. The older I got, the less easily distracted I was by childish things. And the closer I got to adulthood, the less I could ignore my impending death and particularly the demise of my childhood. Or maybe I felt devastated by the overpowering concern of perhaps being lied to about my Xmas hero.

Whatever it was, I was so overwhelmed with dread by simply the mention of removing the holiday reminders that I felt the need to get away from everyone. To avoid the embarrassment by which this terrifying sorrow would inevitably express itself. Perhaps it is similar to how a dog wishes to leave all company once it realizes how short its remaining time is. Whatever the reason, I needed to be by myself.

Finally, I had no choice but to curb my pace. My brother, likely imagining that I slowed down for virtuous reasons—mainly his benefit—was relieved to slack off as well, and his usual consoling smile returned as he tried to catch his breath. His daily running did not seem to be helping him become a faster walker considering how out of breath he was.

"Good thing I've been jogging every morning," Nate said, congratulating himself. "Now I can keep up with you more easily." He grabbed his stomach with one hand, probably from a cramp, something he would frequently get after running.

Nate had sensed my otherwise incomprehensible affliction and with his kind and loyal nature wished to keep me company. It could not be helped. Even if I told him that I wanted to be by myself, he would likely not be persuaded. At times he could be stubbornly clinging.

But I did not desire to have Nate witness my losing it. It was not something that I could explain to him or to anyone. Nor did I want him to worry about me, which seeing me overwhelmed by distress would certainly bring about.

Not only could I not prevent him from agonizing over me but I was unable to help myself as well. I was getting nauseous and dizzy, and tunnel vision had started to come on. Such things I had experienced before, but I could explain it then as the flu or some other recognized cause. Not knowing the reason for these symptoms only made my fretting about them worse. I slouched over and slowed my pace again in desperate hope of being closer to the ground if I ended up fainting.

There was another nerve-racking warning sign that something was deeply wrong with me. One I had not experienced before. I saw in my mind's eye a pin being stuck into my big toe and could feel the pain as though it were actually happening. It was similar to a phantom stab I'd heard about experienced by those who have lost limbs. Yet I still had all my limbs, so why was it happening to me?

I tried to ignore it, but it only became more vivid. I attempted to overwhelm my mind with all sorts of other thoughts to get rid of it, but to no avail. Every once in a while, I would think it had stopped, then it would surprise me by returning with even more vigor. Each time it happened I felt as if my face were what I can only call cringing, likely an automatic attempt to distract myself from the pain. I could not understand why this was happening to me. Would it ever stop or would it become even worse? Perhaps I could not postpone my being institutionalized much longer.

"Where are we going, Tommy?" Nate inquired of me.

"To the lake," my voice quavered in reply. There was a moderately nice beach on the shore of Lake Ontario about forty-five minutes from our house. I found it a relaxing place. At least when hardly anyone else was there. The sound of the waves crashing against the rocks and sand soothed me. I was hoping that if I walked along the beach for a little, my mind would return to normal.

"But it's winter," he observed.

"The lake is still there during the winter."

"Yes, but won't it be freezing cold?"

"Yeah, but we're not going swimming. I merely want the view. You know the way back home, right? You should probably head there. I'll be back shortly."

"No, I'll stay." He didn't fall for it. Not that I really expected him to

We finally made it to the lake. The wind was heavier than I expected. I had forgotten that it is always windier at the lakeside. Like two animals arguing to prove who is louder and more intimidating it howled and whistled simultaneously and separately. We walked along the boardwalk for a while. Regardless of the bitterly cold wind repeatedly buffeting our faces, the lake itself looked gorgeous. I expected it to be frozen, but it had remained liquid. As we passed by the playground, I said, "Why don't you have fun on the playground for a bit?"

Nate gave me a look, as if to ask me whether I was serious. And he was right to do so. I'm not sure why I suggested it. The metal bars would be far too cold for anyone to have fun on, not to mention that the playground was covered in snow. I wasn't thinking straight.

"You're right," I told Nate, "I'm s . . . I'm . . ." I couldn't finish the sentence. For some reason I was having trouble thinking of the word. I bent down and placed my hands on my knees, feeling very dizzy.

With no other souls around to bring her warm relief from a lonely winter, the beach begged for our company. Though there was plenty of litter there, it was not the same as a human coming to admire her beauty. I wish I could have been better company to her.

Nate guided me to a nearby bench so I could sit down. He cleared the snow off with his glove and then helped me be seated. "Are you okay?"

I was having trouble answering him. My mind was not working properly. "I'm no . . . I'm not sure," I finally managed to say to him. I started to laugh uncontrollably and tears ran down my face.

Nate put his arms around me as he sat down next to me. "It's okay. Everything's fine. It's okay to be sad sometimes."

He looked over at the year-round Fry truck which stood in the parking lot a few minutes away. "You know what makes me feel better when I'm upset? French fries. Are you hungry?"

"No," I sobbed.

"I'll only get one, and we can share it. It doesn't seem as if there's a line up, so I'll be five minutes tops. Just wait right here." He ran off as quickly as he could.

I had no appetite at that moment, but was glad that he left so that I could have a second to myself—not that I did not appreciate his trying to help. "God, I don't know what's wrong with me. Please help me."

An overbearing thought abruptly came into my mind—a dreadful inaudible voice. "I'm going to kill him," it said.

That was strange. It was like another person speaking to me in my own mind. What did it mean about killing someone? And who was it threatening? Trying my best to ignore it, I found it too overbearing for me to pretend that it was not there. Immediately I was reminded of that terrifying shadowy figure from my nightmare, the dark being who brought about my family's demise with a single touch.

"Kill him and your whole family!" the abhorrent inner voice commanded.

A voice didn't have the power to hurt someone, did it? Or had my prior nightmare been foretelling some tragedy? Regardless—hating, the fact that someone was threatening my family, and using my own mind to do so, I began to argue with the voice. "I would never let you do that! Who do you think you are?"

"You're going to kill your family, starting with your little brother. He's a parasite after all, always clinging to you."

Clearly this ugly voice did not know how much I cared for my family to suggest such an horrendous thing. "He is not!" I exclaimed. "I love him and would never hurt him or any of my family. Get out of my head!"

"You think this is bad? I'm just getting started. I'm only going to get stronger, and soon I will take over your body."

"Are you a demon?" I asked, chilled at the possibility that I was possessed.

"You wish. I'm you. Actually, I'm the real you. You know that I'm stronger than your docile weak little self. You don't have the strength to fight me."

A terrifying despair came over me when I realized that he was right. How could I fight him if I couldn't even handle the thought of taking down decorations? "What do you want with me?"

"If you do what I tell you, then I will leave your family alone."

"Do what then?" I demanded.

"Go for a swim."

I cringed, terrorized by the thought. "No way! It's too cold. Go away, you crazy dimwit."

"Do it now, or I will kill your brother," the malevolent voice threatened.

"But I'll freeze to death," I cried. "God help me!"

"Oh please, God hates you. How could God love someone who is going to kill his own family one day? Don't be a wuss. You've got thirty seconds to get in there. Or else."

Arguing back and forth with the unpleasant voice, I eventually caved into his demands. What if he really could hurt my family? "Fine," I agreed out of desperation. "Just leave my innocent little brother out of this."

I took off my jacket, socks and boots, and laid them on the bench. Then I stepped slowly off the boardwalk and onto the beach. I crossed my arms against my chest and began to shiver as I reluctantly got closer and closer to the cold waterfront. I stopped right at the edge of the beach, while an icy wave came up to meet me and stopped just at my toe. My foot immediately felt the freezing cold. I hesitated. *There's no way. I can't do this.*

The voice continued. "Don't hesitate. You know the consequences. Do it right now."

"Please don't hurt my brother," I cried as I began walking into the lake as quickly as my fears would allow—which was fairly slow.

A sharp pain shot up my leg as the first wave hit me in the knees. It made me jump, but I could not stop. I had to protect my family. I speeded up, knowing I would not go through with it if I hesitated much longer.

Feeling completely hopeless, I prayed earnestly the prayer that I often said when desperate. "Hail Mary, full of grace, the Lord is with thee. Blessed art though amongst women. and blessed is the fruit of thy womb, Jesus," it went. "Holy Mary, Mother of God, pray for us sinners now and at the hour of our death. Amen." I prayed the words repetitively, seeking again and again consolation in my anguish and desperately hoping for Heaven's assistance.

Shivering violently, I tried my best to keep on praying. I cried out fiercely with the pain as I crouched down quickly and the water went up to my chest. I gasped and shuddered uncontrollably. If I went quickly into the water, I had hoped that the suffering would be less, but I was not sure that was how it worked. One benefit of the freezing cold water robbing my body of its heat was that my internal woes vanished entirely for a moment. Perhaps my body, when it had to deal with immediate physical pain and the danger of hypothermia, did not have energy enough left to worry about the future or the past.

I crawled forward on my knees. A large deadly cold wave came and went over my head, leaving me gasping for air once my mouth was above the water again.

Suddenly I felt a hand grab my arm and try and pull me back but it did not seem to have a very strong force. I turned my head to see who it was. It was Nate. He had been calling out to me and had plunged into the water to recue me.

"Tommy," Nate said, shivering vehemently, "Let's go home. You said it was too cold to go swimming, remember?" He tugged my arm repeatedly but without much force. He must have been too cold to use his full strength.

How did I not hear him calling me? I had been completely in my own world. And how selfish of me. In trying to save my brother from some intangible danger, I completely neglected his immediate safety. I never even considered him when I gave into my mad impulse. My body was getting numb preventing me from moving swiftly. But I turned around as fast as I could and led my little brother out of the water, seconds before the next big wave would have put us under again.

Nate picked up my coat and gave it to me and I put it on quickly. I struggled to get my socks and boots on my feet which had lost a lot of feeling in them and Nate seemed to have as much trouble doing the same. Could we make it back home before getting severe hypothermia? I didn't want to chance it—at least not with my brother there. What could I do? All of a sudden it came to me. Brendan's house was only fifteen minutes away from the lake compared to the forty-five-minute walk to our house. He might not be home to help us, but I thought risking that was better than taking the long walk home.

"Let's go Nate," I asserted. "We have to try and walk as quickly as possible, okay?"

"I didn't do all that training for nothing," Nate reassured me with chattering teeth.

Our hands clenched to our chest, both of us shivered uncontrollably while walking. I kept a close eye on Nate to make sure that he was okay as we made our way to Brendan's house. I really hoped he could help us out. Otherwise we might be in big trouble. Since we were not able to walk very fast with our numb feet it took longer than normal to get there.

Finally, we reached the house safely and I tried in vain to knock on the door. Unfortunately, my hands were so numb that I could not make a proper fist and hardly any noise came from my attempted whack. Nate, clearly smarter than I was, rang the doorbell, but was far too cold to be smug about it.

A few moments later, the door opened slightly. Brendan slipped through the tiny opening and closed the door behind him. "Whoa!" he said, obviously shocked at our soaking-wet appearance. "What happened to you guys?"

"Can you help us?" I begged my voice quivering. "It's an emergency. We need to get warm or we're going to freeze to death."

Brendan looked concerned. "Okay, come in. But be as quiet as possible. I don't want to wake up my Mom." He opened the door and we sneaked in slowly. "Brendan!" I spoke as loudly as I could without letting my voice get beyond a whisper. "Please move faster."

He picked up the pace and let us in, closing the door behind us. The house looked neglected. It was cluttered, and not in a homely way. Dishes were everywhere, even occupying the floor. And thick layers of dust utilized many of the visible surfaces, which looked as if they had not been cleaned in years. I wasn't going to insult his house though. I was simply glad to be getting warm.

Brendan led Nate and me to the basement and opened the door to his room and let us enter. "Hold on a second," he said. "I'll be right back with some towels for you."

"Thank you," I said gratefully as he left the room. I felt bad for thinking so, but considering the condition of the house I hoped to God that the towels would be clean. A consoling heat began to surge through my body, which was slightly painful (like sharp cold needles), but I knew I had to endure it in order for my body temperature to return to normal.

Nate looked around the room, still shivering but pretending not to be scared. I was actually a little startled myself. It did not really look like a bedroom, but more like a dungeon or a prison cell. The lighting was dim. Half of the wallpaper was either missing or partially torn off the wall. And several places on the walls had varying size holes in them.

I started to wiggle my fingers and toes to test my returning dexterity for I was finally getting some feeling back in my hands and feet.

There was a certain stench in the air which I had been trying to identify ever since I first entered the house. I think it may have been stale yeast. The only furniture was a dresser with a Bible on top of it, a mattress with no sheets which was resting on the floor, and a homemade bookshelf made out of bricks and wooden planks. There was only one indication that confirmed it was Brendan's room—the book shelf was covered in *Frightful Sight* books

"I wonder what kind of dog he has," Nate said to me staring at the big cage in the middle of the room.

"I'm not sure," I said while I examined it. Noticing its unusually large size and how enormous the food bowl was, I added, "It must be a big dog though."

"I hope it's a golden retriever," Nate said. "That's my favorite breed."

Brendan returned after a short while, and closed the door behind him. He handed us some clean towels, extra clothes, and a really old looking plaid winter coat. "I hope these fit."

"I'm sure they'll be fine," I said, so grateful that the towels were clean. "Thank you so much."

"I'll let you guys dry off and change in here. Make sure that you only pat yourself dry. Don't rub the towel against your skin in case you have frost bite. And don't put any of the wet clothes back on until they're completely dry, or you might get pneumonia. Only use the dry clothes, even if they don't quite fit properly. I'll be just outside the door if you guys need anything. Just open the door when you're finished, okay?"

"Alright. Thanks again," I said. "How did you learn so much about this sort of thing anyway?" I asked as Brendan exited the room.

"From a survival book," Brendan whispered as he closed the door.

I let Brendan back into the room once Nate and I were done drying off and changing.

After giving us some plastic bags to put our wet clothes in, Brendan said, "So if you guys are okay now, you have some explaining to do. What on earth happened to you? And is this your brother?"

I laughed. "Yes, this is Nate. I guess I forgot to introduce him to you."

Brendan shook Nate's hand, "Nice to meet you, Nate. Your hand is still really cold though."

"Great to meet you too. Tommy told me so much about you."

"Only the good stuff I hope," Brendan joked.

"Please," I reassured him. "There was nothing bad to tell."

"So, are you guys going to fill me in or not?"

Brendan was one person whom I had come to trust absolutely, so I had no reason to keep anything from him. As swiftly as I could, I told him the whole story.

Both Brendan and Nate were speechless, looking surprised and deeply concerned. I realized right then after telling Brendan the story, that Nate did not know about the internal voice and the other things that were going on. That would explain the worried expression he had while staring at me. For some reason I had it in my mind that since he was there when it happened, he had known all the details. Maybe my mind was still not working right. But what could I do? It's not as if I could take back what I said.

"Wow!" I said to try and ease the tension. "You guys are looking at me as if I'm crazy. And you're right."

"Na," Brendan said while Nate ran up to give me a hug. "My brain was overwhelmed by the thought of it, that's all; so, my face looked weirder than usual. You're not crazy. You're merely overcome with worry. It could happen to anyone."

"I don't think you're insane either," Nate assured me. "Maybe just a little peculiar. But that's not a bad thing."

"Thanks, you guys," I said, happy to have their compassion. "But let's be honest. I'm going to end up institutionalized. It's only a matter of time."

"Listen," Brendan asserted calmly. "After we find what we're looking for on the trip, it will solve everything. You won't need to worry anymore."

Oh no! I forgot to tell Brendan to not mention the trip to Nate.

"What trip?" Nate asked, looking back and forth between the two of us.

I put my index finger up to my mouth while looking at Brendan to indicate secrecy. "Don't worry about that, Nate. He's only being silly."

With Nate not looking convinced by my poor attempt at covering up my negligence, I tried to change the subject as soon as I could think of something else. I put my hand on Nate's shoulder. "Thank you for coming to get me out of the water. You have no idea how much it means to me. I feel dreadful for putting you through all that."

Nate looked up at me with worried eyes, "I wasn't strong enough though."

"What do you mean?" I asked, curious as to what he could be talking about.

"You couldn't hear me calling out to you. You were completely in your own world. It was up to me to pull you out of the water, but I couldn't even get you to budge. You could have died because I was too weak. I still have to get stronger."

Surprised that Nate was blaming himself for what was completely my fault, I said sternly, "Look, it was not your fault in any way. It was all mine. And I'm so sorry that you had to see me like that. I'm very grateful to you for risking your own safety to save me, but you never should have had to. And besides, you *were* strong enough. How many people do you think would go into freezing cold water to retrieve a dumb brother? It was you who brought me back to reality—your voice. Do you understand?"

"Yes," Nate said, still not looking entirely persuaded.

"I need to ask you a favor though, okay?"

Nate nodded.

"Please don't tell Mom and Dad what happened. I beg you."

Nate started to cry. "But they can help you. They'd know what to do."

I bent down a little and gave him a big hug to comfort him. "Please don't tell them. They'll send me away for sure. I'd hardly ever see you then. I'd be institutionalized. Do you get it?"

"Alright," Nate agreed crying his tears with his sleeve, "I won't say anything."

I breathed a sigh of relief. "Thank you. You don't know how much that means to me."

"On one condition, though," he continued.

"Anything," I said. "I'll get you ice cream. I'll let you stay up late when Mom and Dad are away. Whatever you want, just don't say a word about what happened."

"Maybe I should have asked for more than one condition," Nate joked, "since all of that sounds good as well. But that's not what I had in mind."

"What is it then?" I asked as Brendan handed Nate a tissue.

Nate blew his nose then continued. "I need you to promise me something."

"What?" I asked.

"If you ever feel that badly again, you have to promise to go and talk to an adult. A grown up will understand and be able to help you. I don't want to see you in that kind of danger again. I'm worried about you. That's the only condition on which I agree not to tell. So I know that you'll be okay."

"But Nate, they'll have me locked up in an asylum. That's how the adult world deals with mental cases."

"Then at least agree to talk to a priest. They take vows so that everything you say would be confidential."

I really didn't want to agree. But I also didn't want my brother to worry and definitely not to tell our parents on me. "Okay, fine. I will go to a priest if I ever feel that overburdened again."

Nate smiled and I hugged him once more in gratitude for agreeing not to rat me out. When I let go of him, I could not help notice that he was eating something.

"Did you just pull a box of French fries out of Tommy's coat pocket?" asked Brendan.

"Yes I did," Nate confessed. "I'm really hungry. And there's no point in letting these go to waste. You guys want some?"

"Do they still taste okay?" I asked. "I didn't even know that you put them there."

"Yeah, they're fine," Nate responded. "I wouldn't be eating them if they weren't."

"I can't believe that I'm saying this," I answered, "but yes I would like some pocket fries." I was just as hungry as my brother.

Brendan hesitantly took a fry yet became less reluctant after finding that they were still okay. The three of us finished them off quickly.

The moment we did, we heard a sudden loud crash from upstairs, a noise like the sound of breaking glass. Brendan jumped up in fear and ran to the window. Placing a trash can upside down to step on, he unlocked the basement window and opened it.

"What's wrong?" I asked, getting uneasy from the anxious look on his face. There was another crash, then footsteps. Clouds of dust fell towards us from the ceiling.

"I'm sorry," Brendan explained, "but you guys have to go. Mom doesn't know that I have company over, so we can't use the front door."

"Brendan!!!" yelled a dismal and nasally female voice, coming from upstairs.

I had tons of questions, but nervously followed Brendan's lead in helping Nate out through the window, not wanting to have the terrifying experience of meeting the frightful sounding lady who just called out to my friend. After crawling out, Nate turned back around and put his arms out to take hold of mine, while Brendan helped lift my feet up. I made it through and Brendan handed us our bags. He picked up his own coat and then let us take him by the hand and pull him through. We closed the window and ran as quickly as we could down the driveway.

"Sorry about that, guys," said Brendan, as the three of us kept up a constant pace to put distance between ourselves and the house. "She gets a little cranky when she wakes up. I'll walk you both home, alright?"

"Okay, thanks," I agreed, getting more and more curious about Brendan's household. None of us spoke a word the entire journey. I wanted to ask Brendan about what it was that just happened, but did not want to pry, at least not in front of my brother. I hoped that he would tell me everything when he felt ready.

TOM'S JOURNAL:

January 2/1998.

I am so disappointed in myself. Today was a tough one for me. I felt overwhelmed after we were told that it was soon time to imprison our Christmas decorations, but in a different way than normal. And I did not know how to handle it.

I went for a walk to the lake to clear my head. I figured that the walk would either help me feel better or at least prevent my little brother from seeing me have an episode. Unfortunately, Nate insisted on tagging along and would not take no for an answer.

I'm not exactly sure what happened. I remember that I couldn't get this image of needles pricking me out of my head. Then a petrifying internal voice, which seemed stronger to me than my own, started taunting me and asking me to do stuff so that my family would not get hurt. I wasn't thinking straight, and I became convinced somehow that the threat was real.

The voice told me to go into the freezing cold lake. I argued with it but eventually succumbed to its demand, thinking it would be the only way to get it to shut up and make sure that my family was okay. It was so cold! I have heard there are groups of people who go swimming in icy winter water just for fun. I can't imagine how it could be fun for anyone.

I don't remember where my brother had gone off to, but he must have seen me in the lake and have run over to help me. He was apparently calling me, but I couldn't hear him. I was completely zoned out. He risked his own safety to come in to rescue me. When Nate grabbed my arm, my mind came back to the real world, and I could hear him saying my name.

Perhaps the cold got rid of the weird voice, but anyhow I got it out of my own head and then led Nate to a warm place to get dry as quickly as possible. He could have contracted severe hypothermia. And so could I. I had been so worried about some obscure threat to my family, that I was not even thinking about the immediate danger to Nate. I didn't think of the possibility that he would come after me. I was only thinking of myself.

I am grateful that he is okay though, and he agreed to not tell Mom and Dad about what happened. He probably should. I deserve to be punished for putting Nate's life in danger like that, but all I could think about was our parents sending me away if they found out. Nate is much more selfless than I am. I'm so thankful to have him as a little brother.

Goodnight journal.

PART 1 CONTINUED

January 4/1998.

". . . And I endangered my brother's life, and then asked him to keep it a secret, solely because of my own selfish fears. Is there any chance that God could forgive someone like me, Father?"

I had told the priest everything about the attack I had a couple of days ago in which I risked my little brother's life. I never intended opening up but anytime I get the chance it seems as if it all simply comes out—except with my parents. I think that is the reason I fear therapy so much. It is not that I do not want someone to talk to on a regular basis, a recourse which would likely be very healthy for me, but I know that I would not be able to hold back once I got going. And once it is said there is no taking it back. The benefit of having someone to talk to would cost me my freedom. I know that I will be locked up one day, but I hope to put it off as long as possible to enjoy whatever time I have left with those whom I love.

"It's good that you came to confession, my son. Of course, God is willing to forgive any sin, even sins much worse than what you have done. He only asks us to make right our wrongs, to be charitable to God and neighbor, and to try and do better in the future. Understand?"

"Yes, thank you Father."

"Now even though as I said I cannot absolve you yet, I can still give you some optional penance. Say three Hail Marys, one Our Father, and make sure to tell your brother that you love him. Does that suffice?"

"Yes, Father. Thank you."

"Then I bless you in the name of the Father, and of the Son, and of the Holy Spirit. Go in peace."

I made the sign of the Cross and was about to get up from my knees when I was interrupted.

"Wait! One more thing before you go. Don't forget to talk to your parents about signing you up for classes so that you can be confirmed in the faith. And also, I gave my card to your friend there which he will give to you. I have a degree in psychology. With permission from your parents and with your consent of course, I would like to set up a weekly meeting with you to help you sort out some of these escalating internal issues that you are experiencing."

I cringed a little. "I appreciate the offer, Father. But I can't do therapy."

"Don't think of it as therapy. Merely think of it as having a kind ear to listen to your problems for an hour each week. At least promise me that you will think about it, and talk it over with your parents. We can discuss St. Nick, your doubts about God, and anything else that you want."

Oh man. I'd love to be able to talk to him about my doubts. But I don't think I could risk it. If I tell him that I will think about it, he will likely leave it at that. "Okay Father. I'll take the card from my friend and consider it."

"Thank you. Now go in peace."

"Father, if I could ask you one more favor."

"Sure."

"Please wait three minutes after I exit, to give me time to leave. That way there's no chance of your accidentally seeing my face."

The priest laughed in a mild manner, "Sorry, I've never been asked to do that before. Of course, my son, I will make sure to wait the allotted time before exiting the booth. Now go in peace."

"Thank you, Father. Have a good day."

I left the confessional and met my brother at the front door. We both genuflected and crossed ourselves as we took Holy Water from the stoup before leaving.

"So how did it go?" Nate asked me in high hope.

Now that he mentioned it, I did feel much better after getting all that off my chest. "It actually went really well, Nate. Thank you for making me go. I appreciate it. Also, as part of my penance, I am supposed to tell you that I love you. But actually, I do love you. I'm not merely saying it for that reason."

Nate laughed. "I love you too, Tommy. I'm glad you are feeling better. I was worried about you, you know?"

"Yeah, I know. You're a good little brother. And I'm the worst elder one."

Nate gave me a stern look. "Don't say that. You're a Saint."

"Well it's nice of you to think so." Nate seemed to regard me as a Saint for praying more often than others do. He did not realize that Saints are also good people and don't have crippling doubts about God's existence and the afterlife. Nor do they put their younger brothers' lives in grave danger.

Chapter 5

Friends and Enemies

TOM'S JOURNAL:

January 6/1998/1:30 a.m.

I am so excited about the trip that I could not sleep at all. I feel bad for leaving my family because I know that it will make them worry about me. But it can't be helped. I can't cancel the trip now. Brendan would be so disappointed. I'm especially worried about how Nate will feel. He will probably hate me for keeping the expedition a secret from him. Yet I could not risk his finding out or else he would want to come along too. And as certain as it is that Mom and Dad are going to kill me already, I am sure they would make it much more painful for me if I got Nate involved. I hope he will understand.

I will be leaving my journal at home because I am packing light for the trip. So, I hope I will have a lot to write about when I get back. Anyway, I have to get ready for the journey now. I don't want to be late picking up Brendan, or else he might think I had bailed out on him.

Goodbye for now journal.

2:00 a.m.

One of the few street lights closest to me was still dark but flickered now and again, uncertain if it wanted to join me in the cold or stay asleep for the night. I had been sitting on the curb in front of Brendan's house, waiting for him to come out. I wished he were not so late. I felt like a creep sitting in front of someone's home in the middle of the night. I was worried that he might have deserted me to go on this trip alone. That would not be like him but he could have got cold feet about the whole thing.

I would not have blamed him if he had. But I hoped he would at least come out to let me know instead of leaving me outside in the dark—literally! Perhaps he had fallen asleep and did not wake up in time. I could not just knock on the door of the house. The hour was too late for that, and in addition it would have defeated the entire purpose of keeping our plans a secret from our parents.

I wondered if I should sneak over and throw a stone at the bedroom window. I didn't really feel like getting arrested—but then again whoever does?

O thank God someone was coming out of the house at last. I hoped it was Brendan and not a parent, but it was impossible to tell from that distance away.

There were not too many street lights to illuminate the houses on that tiny side street in the small city of Awahso, Ontario, Canada. Brendan's house in particular was positioned on a corner, from which the road took a curve, making it even less bright compared to the rest of the dark avenue. Lack of visibility caused me to be especially nervous when a dark figure walked toward the curb on which I sat and I tried to make out who it was. Was it Brendan, a parent or someone else entirely?

My heart beat incredibly fast as the person moved forward and I considered possible excuses to explain my being there in case it was not my friend. Or could it be that Brendan's family were monsters and he was trying to lure me into a trap. Clearly, I'd been reading too many *Frightful Sight* novels.

Finally, the guy—I could see now it was male—was getting close enough that I could start to make out what he was wearing, and suspiciously enough the clothes were black. The crunching of snow became louder and louder with each step that he took.

"Hi there, Tommy," the voice said. Being so dark I could still hardly see him, but I would recognize that agreeably toned voice anywhere. It was definitely Brendan, unless he and a sibling of his sounded exactly alike. But how would a sibling know my name? No, it was Brendan for sure.

"Why are you dressed all in black?" I asked, never yet having seen him dress that way before. "It's ominous."

"I thought it would be easier to sneak around like this," Brendan insisted as I got up from the curb and gave him a pat on the shoulder.

"Are you kidding?" I laughed. "It looks extremely suspicious. I guess it's too late to change now though."

"Sorry for being late," he whispered as we began to walk towards the end of the street. "Something unexpected came up and I lost track of time."

"I understand," I said, "and you're here now. I hope you packed more than merely books though." Brendan laughed, but I am not sure if that meant he did bring more than only books or not. *At least if we don't freeze to death, we'll have plenty to read.*

The streets were completely silent. Not even the bad kids would be dumb enough to be outside at that time of night and season of the year. Setting off together, once we reached the main street we headed towards the north part of the city where the houses start to turn into farms which lead into the country. Neither of us spoke much; each, in his own little world was likely pondering what the next few days would bring.

Close to the edge of the city there was a dimly lit park, darker even than Brendan's street—the kind of darkness that could not just be seen but felt too. It is a place that always gave me the creeps. I tensed up a bit as we approached it and the two of us quickened our steps in unison, wanting to get past that abyss of darkness as soon as possible. Out of pure instinct I glanced over at it to see if my life was in immediate danger or if the space was empty.

But it was not empty. A figure was sitting on the hill which led into the park. Or was it my imagination? No, it was real, and seemed to sense my fixed look. It got up and without a sound darted towards me. I couldn't move. Brendan threw his arms around me. I couldn't tell if it was to protect himself or me. Either way we were both defenseless. In unison or perhaps following my cue we fell over backwards into the snow as the stranger made it to where we had stood seconds before.

Covering my face for protection as the short—extremely short considering I was lying down—presence put out his hand towards me, I felt very stupid when I realized that he was merely giving me a hand up off the ground. I took the pudgy hand and slowly began to recognize who he was as he pulled me up.

Revulsion came with recognition. I immediately let go of his hand and fell right back down again. I am gullible and whenever I trusted the classmate, whom I now recognized as Paul Revell, I always found my confidence misplaced. But not this time. Not a chance of it. Not after the nasty trick he played on me. That was the last straw.

"Hey there, Spazsky!" said Paul. "Who's your friend? And why are you guys out so late?"

Brendan looked at me for a cue to see if this guy could be told any secrets. Seeing I kept silent, he did likewise. I hated being called Spazsky but this guy seemed to have a nickname for everybody. Then again who was I to talk, considering how often I called my brother by his hated nickname 'Yobro'?

"Oh! A secret, eh?" exclaimed Paul obnoxiously, crossing his arms as if trying to figure a way of finding out what the mission was. "Well, you can at least tell me who your little friend is, can't you?"

"I'm Brendan," my naïve new chum answered as his smile returned and he attempted to shake Paul's hand. So much for taking my cue. Brendan's positivity made him incapable of remaining suspicious or upset for any prolonged period.

"Ah! A gentleman, I see! Nothing wrong with that," Paul said in a condescending voice.

Don't fall for it, Brendan. This guy is a snake. Oh no! Paul is going to exaggerate some out-of-context school stories and make me seem like a friendless freak. He's going to turn my best friend against me. Well, it was good while it lasted, I suppose, even if only for a short while.

"I'm sure you'll find Tom here to be a really good friend," Paul claimed patronizingly through his yellow-stained and unevenly spaced teeth (he really needed braces). "He's a good guy."

Well, that was surprisingly nice. *No, don't fall for his kindness again. It's always a trick. He's likely trying to lure me into a trap to get the story out of us. If I'm mindful, perhaps I can see the snare before falling into it.*

Paul glared at my backpack and then at Brendon's. "Going on a trip, eh? . . .. In the middle of the night? Hmmm. Interesting."

Great, he was onto us. Brendan looked excited, as if he wanted to share our plans so badly. He had to rock back and forth on his boots a little, just to keep himself from blurting them out.

Paul smiled. "Well, you don't have to tell me, I guess, but I'm coming with you either way." Before I could protest at this, he went on. "I'm sure, Tom that your parents would not appreciate a knock on the door in the middle of the night by a sincerely concerned classmate asking them where you two could possibly be going at this ungodly hour."

I looked down at the ground accepting my defeat. Paul put his hand on my shoulder and went on. "If you think differently you are of course welcome to try me. You two guys both wait here. I'll only be ten minutes tops getting my stuff. If you don't wait for me, I will have no choice but to do the responsible thing."

I nodded and Paul ran swiftly off through the park towards his house. There was no helping it. I did not know whether I should tell Brendan more about this classmate or if it would be better to leave him in the dark for now.

The two of us went over to sit on the hill that Paul had previously occupied while we waited for his return.

Brendan flailed his arms for a bit while we sat. It was a habit he had and often resorted to when excited. Since he seemed oblivious to the situation and far more optimistic about the trip than I was, I did not wish to dampen his high spirits.

Chapter 6

Tom's Poetry Recital

MAY 13/1997.

I still remembered the last straw. Why I had promised myself never to trust Paul Revell again.

During lunch hour at school that day, I was sitting on the pavement leaning back against the outer brick wall. My poetry notebook was open and resting on my crossed legs waiting for me to finish my latest verse.

Pen in hand, I let my mind wander, grateful for the fact that my class now used pens as opposed to pencils. The switch could not have made me happier. Even though I was no longer able to erase my mistakes as easily from the permanent nature of writing with a pen, I preferred the feel of it, not to mention the look of ink on the page compared to lead graphite. The noise of the pencil scraping against the paper used to drive me crazy too. It was like a subtle form of nails scraping a chalk board. And let's not forget the constant need to sharpen them. But enough zoning out. I needed to figure out the last line.

Noise from every square inch of the playground surrounded me. Crying, laughing, spouts of anger and rage, as well as unpredictable and unexpectedly random sounds were funneled through my ears. Though complete chaos, they came across in their way as harmonic, perhaps because I was used to them or maybe from a misguided feeling of nostalgia.

A gentle breeze every now and then brushed my face and filled my nose with all the scents it carried with it. This time in particular I enjoyed the alluring aroma of dandelion which reminded me that spring had taken up residence in the city.

Trying my best not to let so many externals un-focus me again, I fiddled with my pen thinking of the next line for my poem. What I did find unbearably distracting though was not the noise but the aftertaste of peanut butter from lunch just moments earlier. Finally, the line I was searching for came to me and I wrote it down before I could forget it. Though I could now sense a presence in front of me, whoever it was would have to wait. Finishing the last line of the poem, I placed the notebook in my bag next to me before looking up to see whose shadow hovered over me.

Even though I was sitting down, Paul—for it was Paul—still looked short to me and his tiny stature exaggerated his pudginess in an unflattering way. What could he want? Usually he only sought me out if he was bored or required something.

"I'm bored!" he assured me as if reading my mind and blaming me for the condition.

As I began to stand up, Paul pushed me down against the cold pavement. I could feel my spine hit the brick wall behind me right between my shoulders. It took a few moments to realize what had happened. But now fully awake, I was shocked. Was he trying to bully me?

I looked up at him (not far because of his lack of growth spurts) and shouted, "Don't you know this school has adopted a policy of zero tolerance towards bullying?"

It was true, it had. I had experienced problems with bullying before. With the stricter stance the facility was taking against peer-harassment, however, I had high hopes of being left alone. Had I been misled?

Paul smiled as I got back up from the dirty ground. "You're right. I forgot," he sneered, only to push me roughly back down to the ground a moment later.

I was sure I got a bruise that time. My face heated up and I could feel it turn red with frustration. How was I going to get out of this predicament? And where was the playground supervisor? If she knew this was going on, I'm sure she would put an immediate stop to it. Anyway, I thought I had better stay down for now. It seemed safer.

Yet with a surprisingly genuine looking smile, Paul offered his hand and for some reason I grabbed it without hesitation. Pulling me back up from the ground he asked me, "What's that number you're always obsessed with? Is it three?"

I knew what was coming next and immediately regretted taking Paul's hand, asking myself why I had done so. This time he pushed me much harder, causing me to stiffen up like a board and making the back of my head hit the hard brick wall. I blacked out for a moment and tears began to build up pressure behind my eyes. As I came to, I ignored the throbbing pain in the back of my skull and put all my effort into preventing myself from bursting into tears. This only caused me to dwell on it more, making it more difficult to postpone sobbing.

Paul sat down beside me and pretended to console me while he looked around to see if his cowardly actions had been caught. "Sorry. I got a little carried away," he reassured me. "What are you doing over here by yourself anyway?" he enquired. "And what are you writing?" Noticing my hesitation, he ventured, "You know writing is cool, right? I write myself sometimes."

Thinking Paul might be trying to make peace with me, I did not see any threat in honesty. "I was writing a poem—just finishing it, actually," I told him.

"Really?" Paul exclaimed. "That's amazing. You know, I'd love to read it."

I was not going to fall for that one. He must have simply wanted to take my book and read it to the class or something similar.

"Can you read it to me?" he asked abruptly.

But maybe he was being kind for once. I supposed it could not hurt to read it aloud since I would be holding the book. I took the notebook out of the bag and recited the poem, but did so as if I had no audience.

"That was beautifully read," Paul stated. "Wow! Well done! I think you may have some raw talent there!"

Was he being sarcastic? Often, I could not tell when people were. "Thank you," I said with slight reservation.

"You know what would raise your cool level to at least seven, not solely in my eyes but for the whole class?"

I looked at him with keen interest and prudent suspicion. I always was wanting to know how to make others like me more, but Paul did not seem to be the kind of person who would normally wish to help with that.

"If you read that poem in front of the class," Paul said with glee, "you would be seen as so cool by all your peers."

Now I could see the trap. Could he possibly think I was stupid enough to be caught in so obvious a snare? But before I could object, Paul quickly interjected, "I'll recite one first . . . one of my own, and then you do yours after it."

"You write poems too?" I asked, surprised and happy to have found a fellow poet. Perhaps he would be kinder to me now that we had found solidarity in something. There was no way it could be a deception to try and humiliate me if he himself were going to be part of the public embarrass-ment. If he was willing to go first, then he must be telling the truth.

"That's a great idea!" I cheered, matching his enthusiasm. "Are you sure you're not messing with me?" I asked, just to double check.

"No. I'm serious," Paul insisted.

"Alright, it's settled then. We will recite our poems after lunch. I can hardly wait to hear yours."

. . .. Lunch had ended and everyone was back in their seats in class, still noisy and rambunctious from being outside only moments ago. Most at least were sitting down. There were always the one or two students standing around their friends' desks, chatting away, trying to get in that last conversa-tion before the period began. Mr. Stamper, the teacher, often waited a few minutes before starting the class. I preferred it to start right on time to keep to the schedule but he was the teacher after all. A nauseating smell of sweaty socks permeated the room. The only way I could stand the odor was by reminding myself that after five minutes or so I would be used to it again.

Paul, sitting to my left, pulled out a notebook with his hands shaking. It must have been his book of poetry. Suddenly looking straight at me, he assured me, "I can't do it. I'm sorry. Just too nervous."

Waiting a moment to test his sincerity, I decided I could not doubt him. I had never seen him act so vulnerable before, and I doubted that he was faking it. "I'll go first," I reassured him. "Then you may feel more up to it. Okay?"

Paul shook his head no, "That simply wouldn't be fair to you. I prom-ised I would go first. What if you do yours and I still chicken out in the end?"

This was my moment to show Paul that I was not a wimp and help him gain more confidence. I needed to show him how it was done. What the class would think no longer worried me. I needed to inspire my new fellow poet not to be afraid of expressing his feelings through the art of writing.

"Don't worry about it," I told him. "With or without you, I'm going for it."

Before I could think twice or hear Paul's response, I got off my chair and walked towards the teacher's desk. Mr. Stamper was reading a book and continued reading it as I whispered to him, "Mr. Stamper, if you don't mind, I would like to read a poem to the class that I have written." He nodded his consent without even looking at me. He must really have been engrossed in that book.

I stepped in front of the class and the noise immediately ceased, per-haps out of curiosity about why I was up there. My newly found confidence sank lower and lower and I started to doubt my decision. But there was no turning back now. Not at least without humiliating myself. Whether it went well or badly, I risked being embarrassed if I recited the poem or abandoned the task completely. If I am going to risk erring, I might as well err on the side of trying.

"Everyone!" Though there was no noise to compete with, I shouted much louder than I had intended. I don't know how it was possible but at the sound of my voice the dead silence became even quieter. "I have a poem to recite which I wrote earlier today, called, "Death Finds Us All." I hope you like it. Here it goes."

Such a tight knot was forming in my stomach and so great a feeling of nausea came over me that I could have fainted. I coughed into my fist to clear my throat and then began in a soft yet somber tone to read:

DEATH FINDS US ALL

Death awaits me. Death awaits you.
Just as each ingredient in a stew
Is taken up and eaten one by one
Without anywhere to hide or run.
In its due time, he comes for us all,
Whether scrawny, big, small, or tall.
Resistance is futile when we take our last breath.
There is no arguing with the Angel of Death.
But what awaits us? Is it dark or grim?
Or perhaps everlasting peace with him?
Is my crippling doubt an insufferable fate?
Or can God save me from this wretched state?
Please God my friend, look upon me with pity.
And bring my soul to your eternal city.
Stamp out my doubts, and all the darkness within.
I beg you, don't leave me in this swamp that I'm in.

Looking up from my notebook, which I had not done in the entire recitation, I said, "Thank you." My heart continued to pound as it had done non-stop since the beginning of my reading. Surprisingly, there was still silence. It was as if no one wanted to make the first response. Everyone was staring. Some with blank faces, others with shock, and even a few in anger. *Should I sit back down or wait for applause? Surely, I could not begin clapping for myself, for my own performance, could I?*

Reality finally hit me. A laugh steadily increasing in loudness came from one student. It caused a chain reaction of scoffing and distasteful mockery. And who started it? It was Paul. That slime-ball! How did I fall for his trick again? How could I be that stupid and gullible? I put my head down as I walked towards the teacher's desk, beating myself up mentally and assuring myself that I would refuse ever to trust Paul again. How could all my friends laugh without even one coming to my defense?

Perhaps sensing my aura of frustration, Mr. Stamper finally put his book down while I stared at him as resentfully as my kind-hearted nature would allow. "Mr. Stamper, you can start the class now. I've finished my poem."

"Thank you, Tom," he answered as I walked back to my desk with still bowed head. "And thank you for sharing your poem. It was quite lovely."

I doubted that he had even listened to it, knowing how hard it is to read a book and listen at the same time. Served me right for being so gullible, I suppose.

TOM'S JOURNAL:

May 13/1997.

I was humiliated in class today. And it was my own fault for trusting Paul. He slammed me into the wall three times in the playground and I still have a headache from it. And then he pretended to be my friend to make me feel better.

Professing to be a poet himself, he showed interest in my writing and misled me into reading my latest poem in front of the class. Then he led the class in laughing at me. I tried not to look at him for the rest of the day. I have never felt so mortified in my life. How could he be so mean? I guess he was sick of merely hurting me physically and wanted to beat up my soul as well.

And it worked. I felt resentment towards Mr. Stamper for letting me recite my poem even though it was not his fault in the slightest. May God forgive me for such hateful feelings, and especially those I have towards Paul.

He's not going to win though. I am still going to write. And one day I may find an audience that appreciates my poetry.

Goodbye journal.

Chapter 7

Nicknames and Snow Angels

JANUARY 6 /1998/3:15 A.M.

Once Paul showed up again with his backpack, the three of us began our journey. We were heading north when we located a main street. My hope was to make as much ground as possible and be far away from the city by the time day broke. There was barely any talk among us for the longest while. Not surprisingly, perhaps, because each of us were in our own little world.

Brendan marched casually along with his usual—though unusual to the rest of the world—smile. He seemed so positive that I might even have sworn that he was skipping if I did not double check his feet every once in a while, just to be sure that he was only walking. I had no idea how anyone could stay so upbeat, but I certainly did not want to take that characteristic away from him. It was very inspiring. Even in my saddest state I could not help but smile when seeing his countenance. Its good humor was contagious.

So far Paul had not been causing problems for us. Perhaps it was only because if he had there would have been no one to back him up without his peers around. To be honest though I think he could take the two of us on at the same time with very little if any injury to himself. He may be short but he makes up for it in strength—at least compared to the strength of my frail looking body. But I wonder if all that pudginess is pure muscle.

Why would Paul want to join us on this trip anyway? Especially without knowing yet what it was? Perhaps he was looking for an hilarious story to tell when school started again, new material to use against me. Or maybe he was really just bored. Either way I did not wish to take any chance. I must keep him in the dark as much as possible, though I didn't see how. If our mission was a success, Paul would then realize everything. In that case though, I wondered if it would even matter.

An hour must have passed since we began walking from the park. It had been a while since the last street light was seen, and the stars above were no longer hidden from us. Though I doubted that I would last long living in the countryside, being more of a city boy, there was a longing I often had for the rural atmosphere every time I experienced it. There is something pure about the air in a way that I cannot only smell but somehow feel. Though it was winter. I might feel differently when the odor of manure was in the air. I would choose city smells over manure any day. And if I ever began to doubt my convictions it would only take one whiff of the foul stench to convince me again.

A large snow flake somehow found its way directly into my eye, causing me temporary blindness as well as a sharp pain. "Looks like it's starting to snow!" I exclaimed with glee as I rubbed the eye. Snow always got me excited since it was the most beautiful part of winter (at least in nature), even right now when it was only snowing a little. It was the darkest season's greatest earthly consolation.

Following Brendan's lead, we all tried to catch a snowflake on our tongue which must have looked extremely silly. I had never done such a thing and it was actually kind of fun—not the taste, which is simply like cold and fluffy ice, but the pursuit itself.

"Casper!" Paul called out unexpectedly while pointing at Brendan. "That's it! The perfect nick name for you. I was wondering for a while what I should call you. And it's perfect because you're pale as a ghost!"

Oh no. I was wondering how long it would take for Paul to start picking on Brendan. Not that I wanted him to pick on me instead—though I would imprudently take on such a burden if it meant keeping my friend free from being bullied. But Brendan did not seem the least phased by the comment. He continued spinning around like an airplane trying to catch snow on his tongue, completely oblivious to the outside world. I'm not even sure he heard Paul.

"Did you hear me?" Paul asked, seemingly irritated for being ignored.

"Yeah," Brendan said cheerfully as he dropped to the ground to attempt a snow angel. "It's actually Brendan though. Don't worry. I forget names all the time too. It's no big deal."

Could it be that Brendan was such an innocent that he was not even familiar with nick names? Or was he just kidding around? Either way Paul, looking agitated, did not seem to be giving him the benefit of the doubt.

The best way to deal with people like Paul is just to go along with their badgering and pretend it didn't bother you. But Brendan could not possibly be aware of that since he hardly knew Paul. Squatting down in front of Brendan, who sat up from the angel image recently imprinted in the snow, I tried to explain it to him to avoid what seemed to be an escalating misunderstanding between two extremely different personality types.

"No," I laughed, hoping to ease Paul's tension, "It's a nick name. It's like a code name used among friends, different from your real name."

"Like Spazky," Paul said as he placed his hand on my shoulder. "That's what I call Tom here."

I sighed much louder than I intended, not really liking Paul to touch my shoulder or the irritating nick name. When one is the quiet type who hardly contradicts, argues, or even shows any signs of hostility, lashing out becomes even more embarrassing. Since it can seem so unexpected and out of character, it is far more noticeable than it is when louder people have an angry outburst.

. . .

I think it was about a little more than a year ago when it happened to me for the first time. I suppose having all that anger build up for years without finding a healthy way to release it, everything came out at once. In grade six, Paul convinced me to let him read my letter to St. Nicholas which I had written during lunch hour. I don't even remember how he made me think I could trust him, but it served me right for being so gullible. He read the letter out loud to the whole class. I had never been so embarrassed in all my life.

I should simply have taken the humiliation normally, but that day was different. No mortal ears should ever hear the kind of words that came out of my mouth at that moment. I think it was just from the shock or fear of what I said; or my peers may have wondered what else I was capable of doing and been unwilling to take the risk at the time—but whatever the reason, I got my letter back quite quickly. Of course, a teacher had heard me lash out, though teachers were nowhere to be found when my letter was read out loud, and I was sent to the principal's office. That is when I started being called 'Spazky'. For spazzing out at Paul. I am not sure who came up with the nick name. I am guessing it was Paul however.

The main reason I hate the name so much is not because of being made fun of for lashing out last year, but because it is a constant reminder of the terrible things I said, some of which I did not even realize were in my mind.

I would likely regret saying them for the rest of my life. I don't like to say anything that God would find offensive and I am certain that I offended God that day.

I needed to make sure that I found a healthy way to deal with any built-up anger so that such a loss of self-control never happened again. I don't care whether the person deserved my lashing out at him or not. I never wanted to behave in such a manner again.

. . .

Brendan thought for a second after being taught about nick names by me. "Ah I see!" Brendan cheered as he leaped up from the ground. "Then what's yours?" he asked Paul.

"I don't have one yet," said Paul, looking ashamed of trapping himself.

"Well we all need a code name for the mission, don't we?" Brendan explained. "Otherwise it would be pointless."

"He's right," I said smiling and happy to see Paul outwitted for once even if it was not likely by design. "What should we call you?"

Paul thought for a moment. But before he could say anything, Brendan blurted out, "I know. How about 'Big Tall Paul'?"

I couldn't help but laugh. Paul did not look impressed. He shoved me aside and with one hand grabbed Brendan by the collar, getting ready to hit him with the other. What a jerk Paul was. I guess that is like the saying, that some people enjoy dealing out to others what they cannot take themselves. He should learn to take a joke.

I scrambled to get back up while Brendan tried to explain himself. "It was meant to be an ironic code name. You know because you are so short. Though I guess the 'big' part is kind of true."

Yikes! What was Brendan thinking? Was he trying to get Paul more irritated? Leave it to Mr. Positive to dig himself into a deeper hole, though I don't think he meant to. I ran over to attempt a bear hug on Paul and try and separate the two of them, but naturally I tripped and fell on the way, accidentally pushing them both and myself to the ground. How could I be so clumsy in my friend's time of need? I had no idea though that I could be so strong when it was not on purpose.

"Apologize to me!" Paul demanded as he grabbed Brendan by the shoulders and shook him violently.

Brendan for a split second looked so terrified that it sent shivers down my spine. "I didn't mean it, Mom!"

That was odd. Why would he say that? He must be so scared that he can't even think straight. I don't blame him. Paul can be alarming when he gets upset.

"Now you're calling me a girl?" Paul asked accusingly, infuriated and shaking Brendan even harder than before. "Are you serious? You are really asking for it."

I managed to get up and bear hug Paul this time and out of desperation said the first thing that came to mind. "He meant that you're protective like a Mom. He's like your kid because you look out for him! You wouldn't hurt your own kid, would you?" Paul did not seem to be buying my weak attempt at mediation. It was a really awful idea, but was the only thing I could think of at the time.

Paul let go of Brendan suddenly and darted backwards a few steps, taking me with him as we stumbled to the ground. "What's wrong with our friend?" Paul asked, suddenly looking worried.

What did Paul mean by 'our' friend? Does he really think Brendan would want to be friends with someone who was about to beat him up after knowing him for only a few hours? He really needed to work on his social skills. Then again, who was I to talk about social skills when I couldn't even get any of my friends from school to hang out with me? They can't always have plans, so perhaps I could use some social lessons myself. I can't believe I could actually worry about such silly things at a time like this. My parents were right after all about how distracted I get.

Paul crawled towards Brendan again, examining him closely. "I think I broke him." Looking over at me, he inquired, "Is he okay? Has he ever done anything like this before?"

What could he mean? I had not even noticed with all the commotion, but Brendan was reciting words nonstop while staring aloofly into space. Moving in a little nearer and listening closely for a moment I realized that he was saying verses from the Psalter in the Bible. Seemingly from memory.

Was this some sort of a trick? Or maybe he was in shock or something? Unfortunately, I did not even know what shock symptoms looked like. I hoped he was okay. But how did he memorize so much Scripture, and why? It seemed as if there was far more to my friend than met the eye. Could he be a secret alien? If he was one, I hoped he remained friendly, especially after having been shown so much hostility by Paul. I tried to stop myself from imagining Brendan taking vengeance on Paul with super advanced Martian laser weaponry, but it crept back into my mind now and again. Anyway, I couldn't really ask Brendan about it if he didn't come back to us.

I needed to try and wake him up without making his condition worse. I approached Brendan and shook him gently by the shoulders. "Pst . . . Brendan, are you okay? It's safe now." No response. It was as if none of us were even there. He didn't seem to be faking it. What could be the matter with him? And how could we help? I had never felt so useless and helpless. My friend needed me, and there was nothing I could do for him.

"You know what?" I reassured Paul, who looked like a nervous wreck and ashamed of what he had done. "I think all he needs is just a few minutes. He'll be fine."

At least I hoped he'd be. I was really worried but wanted to console Paul who seemed overwhelmed because he was the main cause of whatever was wrong. That's right, it was entirely his fault. He hurt my best friend. So why did I feel the need to show him compassion?

I gave Brendan a hug, hoping that if he felt consoled by someone it might help him recover, then stepped over to Paul. "We'll just take a break for a few minutes," I said to him calmly, holding back all the bitterness I felt towards him at that moment. "Then he'll be better and we'll continue, okay?"

Paul nodded silently. I was so glad that he did not apologize. He did seem sorry but he must have understood that an apology would be meaningless at that moment since it would only have come across as justification of his actions. He sat down on the spot and watched Brendan like a hawk, perhaps trying to redeem himself by protecting him from further harm.

I walked a few meters towards the farm and sat down by the cedar fence, leaning against it, trying to think what to do. How long would Brendan take to recover? And what if he never did? I'd hadn't had such a close friend before, even with what little time we'd had to get to know each other. I couldn't bear losing him already.

My eyes turned rapidly at a sudden noise which came from the direction from which we arrived. The hairs on the back of my head stood up. The sound was just like a quiet foot step crunching the snow but the atmosphere was so silent that even the smallest pin dropping could be heard. Someone was approaching, which at that time of night was concerning in itself. What had me more frightened was that I only heard one step. Whoever it was either was moving very slowly or trying not to be heard. The mysterious person seemed still too far off to be seen in the dark—but I did not want to take my eyes away, just in case.

I rubbed my index finger and thumb together repetitively in sequences of three, to try and stay focused and to take my mind off the fears rushing into my mind. It was a habit my parents often complained to me about. I also began quietly to recite a prayer repetitively, not only for the feeling of consolation it gave me but also in case we needed assistance.

Was what approached an animal, a person, or some kind of monster? Was it dangerous? If not, then why was it trying not to be heard? There was no point in hiding since we had likely already been seen (why else would it be sneaking around?). It would be difficult to make a run for it if we had to with Brendan still not having returned to our planet. The options for escape were few and I had trouble thinking of even one.

As quietly as possible, I rose from where I sat into a squatting position in case I had to run quickly. I wanted to be ready to protect Brendan and Paul if it was some predatory animal. With no solution springing to mind, all I could do was watch desperately, hoping to God that we were not in any great danger.

Paul did not seem to hear the first noise, but the second crunching of snow caught his attention and his eyes flashed over in the same direction mine were looking. Knowing now that I was not imagining the sound, an icy shiver ran through my body as I waited helplessly to find out what it could possibly be.

Chapter 8

Miscalculated Guesses

The snowflakes dancing in front of my face gradually multiplied themselves. I loved watching snow fall to the ground and feeling the frigid crystals landing on my face. There is even a kind of smell to a snow fall. It is not something that I can put my finger on and say what it can be compared with, but it is distinguishable nonetheless.

This was not the time however to be distracted, considering the danger we might be in. I could listen even more intently for the footsteps now since Brendan had at last stopped reciting the sacred words. I wanted to check and see if he was better, but without putting him in more danger by doing so—in case my moving roused whatever creature was lurking in the shadows to immediately attack us. If Brendan was now okay though, I hoped we could get moving again as soon as possible. Yet obviously I had to make sure it was safe first. But how?

The falling snow slanted towards us from the opposite direction to where our eyes were fixed, the wind pushing the snowflakes away from whatever danger was lurking in the shadows.

"Hey there!" Brendan said, looking in the same direction in which both Paul and I were gazing.

Was Brendan able to see something we could not, or was he still in his own world?

"Oh man, you can see me?" said a disappointed voice which sounded a lot like my brother's.

"No," said Brendan. "I could sense someone was there. I didn't know it was you until you answered. I had no idea you were coming with us."

From the direction of the imagined danger Nate walked up to Brendan until he was fully visible.

"He wasn't supposed to come," I said, surprised to see that Nate had found us so easily. "What are you doing here, Nate?"

"Well," Nate admitted, "I've been following you from a distance the whole time. I was doing a good job not being caught too, up until now—staying far enough behind that you couldn't see me, yet close enough not to lose you. But I was getting so cold because you guys were taking such a long break that I had to move a little to keep warm. I'm guessing that's what gave me away."

"Okay hold on a sec," Paul said standing up. "First of all, are you okay?" he asked Brendan.

"Positively," answered Brendan, looking puzzled by the question. "Don't I look satisfactory?"

Brendan must not even have remembered anything about, well, whatever it was that happened. I put my index finger against my lip as a sign to Paul not to mention anything for now. I did not want to alarm Brendan by telling him he had been acting wacko while unconscious. Such a notion would certainly scare me if I was in the same situation and had that fact thrust onto me.

"Alright," Paul continued. "And second of all, who is this guy?" Paul pointed at Nate.

"I'm Tommy's brother, Nate," answered my brother. "Who are you?"

"Paul."

"Wait! You're the one that was picking on everyone a few moments ago, aren't you?" Nate asked. "Can't wait to see you try that stuff on me. I'm athletic."

Shocked at what Nate just said, I let a nervous laugh escape me, in hope that Paul might think he was joking. My brother can be a bit direct at times, which is probably more often a virtue than a vice. I actually found it refreshingly admirable much of the time, since most people are too needlessly indirect—which I often found confusing. Unfortunately, Nate did not always use prudence in figuring out when to be more diplomatic. In this situation he certainly could have shown greater discernment. I understood his wish to protect the dignity of his elder brother and his friends and show his loyalty, but when it came to dealing with someone who could probably kill all three of us with one punch it was much wiser to be tactful.

"I wouldn't dream of it," said Paul. "You're straight forward. I like that."

Wow! That was good of Paul. I did not know he could be so docile when threatened. Then again, I suppose he would have nothing to prove. In fact, it could give evidence to the opposite effect when it came to teaching a violent lesson to someone two years his junior.

To be honest, I was glad Nate had tagged along. But I hated myself for letting him do so. Not only would I get in triple the amount of trouble for bringing my brother into this, I also would not be able to cope if anything happened to him on my account. Still, perhaps that would be the case if something happened to him by his own fault as well.

"How did you find out about the trip?" I asked, curious to know.

"Well," Nate responded looking rather pleased with himself, "I heard you and Brendan mention an adventure. Keeping me in the dark about it made me all the more suspicious that you were planning something crazy. I kept a close eye on you, hoping to find out as much as I could.

"None of that helped at all. Finding out ended up being pure luck. I happened to wake up in need of using the facilities at the exact same time you sneaked out of our room and down the stairs. And I heard you slip out of the house. I crept down the stairs myself, as quickly as I could without alerting Mom and Dad, and saw the note you left for us. After reading the letter I was so upset that you didn't invite me that I decided to invite myself out of spite, to show you how much you needed me to come. I certainly did not want to hear that you were able to meet St. Nick and I missed out on such an opportunity due to your selfishness.

"I knew you would be going with Brendan, so I headed in that direction myself. Once I saw you sitting on the curb, I knew I had to stay hidden for the first stage of the way. Otherwise you would have sent me back home. I wanted to make sure that I did not join the group until it would be too late to make me go back. I tried my best to step in your footprints to stay warm, until now."

"Okay, whoa!" Paul interjected. "So many questions. First off, what on earth are you talking about with the footprints?"

"Yeah, that's a good place to start," I added.

"Don't you guys get it?" asked Brendan. "It's like the verse from the carol."

Paul and I both stared at Brendan, wondering what he could mean.

Brendan began to hum the tune of *Good King Wenceslaus* then laughed since we still did not get it. "The page in the carol is warmed by his saintly King's footsteps in the midst of a very bitter winter. You must know that one?"

Paul still gazed at Brendan, confused. But I finally got it. "No Nate," I said, "that only works with Saints."

"Yeah, I know," explained Nate, "but you are one."

"Definitely not," I argued. "Saints don't lure their younger brothers into death traps and don't have doubts about the afterlife."

"So you say," Nate responded smugly. "Yet I stayed warm up until we stopped moving."

Not knowing where to go with this argument, I was happy that Paul intervened—at least until I realized what it was about.

"So hold on a second," Paul said. "Never mind all that stuff. What did you mean when you said this trip was about finding St. Nick?"

Oh no. It had slipped my mind to tell Nate about keeping the purpose of the trip from Paul. And before I could intervene, Nate said, "Precisely that. We are heading north to the pole."

My heart skipped a beat. I was not ashamed of the trip but something about Paul always made me feel abashed about everything in his presence, even if he were the only one among us to think of it as silly. How would he respond to this news?

Paul smirked as if trying to hold back his displeasure. "Wait. Wait. Wait. Are you telling me, that we have come all this way to try and find St. Nicholas?"

"Naturally," Nate responded unabashed. "What did you think this trip was about? Any other reason to risk getting into so much trouble would seem silly after all."

I was getting more and more happy that Nate ended up coming along. His lack of embarrassment about most things, apart from his athletic failures, seemed to counteract the humiliation I felt. I would be able to lean on his strength instead of being torn down by Paul's patronizing gestures. I only wished that I had my brother's self-confidence. And as the younger of us, it made my shame over my timidity even greater.

Paul started to look enraged again. "Do you guys have any idea how far away the North Pole is from here?"

"Three days?" asked Nate.

"I presumed it was twelve," said Brendan.

"Two weeks," I stated, not wanting to be left out.

"You mean you merely guessed?" Paul asked furiously.

I was trying very hard to contain my laughter. Brendan and Nate were tag teaming against Paul. I wasn't even sure they were doing it on purpose but they seemed to work really well together against his condescending attitude. I was enjoying every second of it. This was not at all how I expected the conversation to go. It also made me happy that the two of them had connected so easily over a common enemy—if they even saw it that way. Though part of me was worried that if Nate and Brendan became close friends, I would be abandoned as obsolete by both of them, I tried to repress those insecurities, reminding myself to be happy that the three of us could hang out together.

"Do you know how far it is to the North Pole?" I asked Paul, trying to get in on the action.

"Were our calculations off a little?" asked Brendan.

"How many days does it take to get to the North Pole?" inquired Nate.

"You guys are overwhelming me with all these questions," Paul responded, frustrated. "I would need a map and a compass to figure it out. Secondly, it is not a miscalculation if it was only a guess. But the point is that we'll never make it. I will stick around for the ride though. I have nothing better to do anyway."

I was really worried that Paul was going to mortify me in front of the whole class over this once we got back to school. But I was not going to let that destroy the thrill of taking the trip, and spending time with my two best friends. Even Paul's company I thought was not so bad once you got used to it, but perhaps that's only because it is now three against one.

Not that I ever wanted to take the role of leader. But since no one else was suggesting it, I would not avoid doing so out of an ambiguous fear of being a terrible one. "Listen," I insisted reluctantly, "We can talk more on the way, but we should get moving again. We need to make more distance before dawn.

Chapter 9

Dueling Trees and Scouts in the Snow Storm

5:30 A.M.

After we walked for some time along the edge of the road, the wind picked up. It would stop for a few moments then hit us again without warning. Opening my mouth at the wrong time, I took a large amount of snow into it at the next gust. The sudden cold on my tongue and throat was to be expected. What surprised me was how sharp snow could feel with enough speed behind it. I learned my lesson quickly and tied my scarf around my face.

Each tree we passed looked as though it were challenging us to a duel with all its frosty branches swinging violently around in a taunting way. I wondered if anyone had ever been killed by tree branches before except by a falling one. I imagined sword fighting with a tree but could not figure out how to win against so large and sturdy an opponent.

"Ca-a-a-a-a-ar!" Nate hollered loudly, as though we were playing street hockey. Paul and I both sighed, each in his own way. The four of us ran quickly into the forest on the right and went prone, waiting for the vehicle to pass. Though it was unlikely that our parents already knew we were missing, none of us wanted to take a chance. As soon as the car was safely by and enough distance ahead, we stood up and went back to the road, dusting off the snow we had picked up from the ground.

The vehicles were becoming more frequent which meant that morning was soon to arrive. If we wished to continue traveling in daylight, we would have to get off the road for good. People would be looking for us by that point. Perhaps it would be better to find a shelter to sleep in during the day and start our travels again by nightfall to decrease the chance of being seen. But where would we ever find lodging? We should really have planned this trip better.

A large grave yard approaching on our right warned us to pick up the pace. Or it did so for me anyway, but the others followed suit to keep up. A terrifying electricity ran through my body, telling me that I was being watched by a ghastly presence—or many. I knew it was likely all in my head, but I could not bear to take even the slightest glance in that direction—making sure that my eyes were pointed slightly left for extra reassurance that I would not accidentally catch a glimpse of the horrifying cemetery.

Regardless of my efforts at veering my eyes away from the perceived danger, I could see in the corner of my vision a shadowy cluster of smoky fog. It was that cringe worthy presence from my nightmares and the voice in my head, a frightful personification of death. I knew of course that it was only a delusion. My eyes often played distasteful pranks on me in the dark when I was most vulnerable.

If it were real, I knew that the others would be reacting to it in some way—which gratefully they were not. Yet knowing it was fake did not keep it from petrifying me, since trying to explain it away failed to change the fact that I perceived it. Perhaps it was real, a paranormal being that only I could perceive for some reason.

As we kept pace, I crossed my arms tightly to my chest to cover up how tense my body was getting, hoping that the delusion would go away as soon as we passed the chilling burial ground. Good thing I was skilled at hiding my fears from the others. Fear I knew could be contagious and I did not want to spread it.

"Why do you fear death so much?" Paul asked me out of the blue. "Aren't you a little young for that?"

Perhaps I was not hiding it as well as I thought. I don't know what started my crippling fear of death, but I do remember an early memory of one of my first real encounters with it.

. . .

With taunting demeanor, a thousand gravestones jeered at me from every nook of the cemetery, telling me of the coming time for me to call one of the solemn markers my own. I stood there that day in front of my Grandmother's grave with Dad and Nate. When she died, I was about six and it was a few weeks after the funeral. I hardly remembered her at all, yet somehow, I recall staring at her gravestone so short a while after her passing.

After her death Dad visited his Mom's grave often at first, and Nate and I sometimes went with him if he was looking after us at the time.

"Is Grandma down there, Daddy?" I asked, wondering how that could be.

"Yes, Tommy," Dad responded.

"Why?" I asked, worrying about the possibility of it happening to me or anyone else I knew.

"She's dead," Dad said, with a subtle crack in his voice. "People are buried when they die. But her soul lives on."

Yikes! What did that mean? Were we still conscious once we were dead? Did we just stay in the grave, still perceiving everything yet not able to move?

The sun was bright that day but slowly became covered by clouds, leaving us in the dismally grey graveyard. Images of being buried alive in the earth flooded my mind, large patches of sandy muck slowly dimmed my vision as it scratched and covered my eyes until there was only darkness left. The gritty mineral-like taste of dirt and clay filled my mouth with disgust as I panicked from being unable to move out of the way—with nothing to look forward to but an eternity of feeling the weight of heavy soil.

"So, after we die and can no longer move," I asked gulping, petrified by the idea of being perpetually conscious without the ability to shift around, "is our soul still aware?"

"Yes, that's right," Dad answered.

"So, she can still hear us and everything?" I asked, thinking that maybe he meant that she was asleep instead.

"Yes, Tom," Dad replied. "She can hear us but is unable to answer."

. . .

The startling belief haunted me for months after that cemetery visit. Eventually of course, I realized that Dad did not mean that our soul stayed in the body after death. But for some reason that is what I thought he meant at the time. I took it too literally. I have no idea how I could have misunderstood him so completely. Perhaps that was what started my dread of death. Or maybe I was just naturally messed up. Who knew? But what I did know was that I could not trust Paul with any of this information, so I had to be covert in answering him—making sure not to give him any fuel for future torture.

"I'm not really sure," I said to Paul, grateful that we were finally stepping beyond the desert of death's remains. "I have been for as long as I can remember."

"Well don't worry so much about it," Paul advised with certainty. "You have a long life ahead of you."

"Do you know how many children die?" I asked him.

"No," he answered.

Realizing that I did not know either, I changed course a little: "Well the point is that kids do die. No one knows how long he has. And even if I lived a thousand years, it's not really that long when you think about it."

"You think too much," Paul assured me.

I did not disagree with that. But admitting it would not stop me from doing so.

Another half hour of walking through the unpredictable gusts of wind and the worst suddenly hit us—a great deluge of snow. It was a complete white-out. Rather than falling down to the ground, it seemed to come horizontally towards us. We tried to keep walking, but were not making a lot of progress. The wind was too strong and powerful to let us travel at a robust gait.

I continued on for a few minutes but was getting too cold from the bitter wind. We needed to find refuge fast. I looked behind me to tell the others but could not see them. They were right behind me only a few minutes ago. Where could they be? My mind rushed to the worst possible scenarios. Had they been blown away by the wind?

"Hey guys!" I called out. "Brendan! Nate! Paul! Where are you?"

There was no answer. What a fool I was to agree to this trip. Sure, it was not my idea, but I could have said no. I had selfishly put everyone in danger for a small chance to quench my doubts. What would my parents do? But who cared about punishment when all my friends could be dead, or worse? And it was entirely my fault.

Shivering frantically, I fell to my knees to pray. "God please don't let them die or get hurt because of me. If someone needs to be punished for our mistakes, let it be me—which I say in fear and trembling, but you know my heart better than I do." Unable to think of further words, I started to recite continually the first prayer that I learned from Mom, "Hail Mary, full of grace, the Lord is with thee. Blessed art though amongst women, and blessed is the fruit of thy womb, Jesus. Holy Mary, Mother of God, pray for us sinners now and at the hour of our death. Amen."

After praying a few minutes, I felt a hand gently placed on my shoulder. It was Nate. The other three were with him as well. Wait, who was the fourth guy?

"Glad we finally found you," said Brendan.

"We all got separated and couldn't find each other in this crazy blizzard," Nate added.

"And suspiciously, this fellow here," Paul explained, "showed up—to help apparently."

Nate continued, "He found me first; then led me to Brendan; and then the two of us to Paul; then all of us to you."

I stood up and examined our new guest. He was an older youth dressed in a long grey military style overcoat and carrying a lantern. His face was pure and innocent-looking. There was a slightly aloof gaze in his abnormally large eyes, yet not a condescending one. "Well thank you, sir," I said to the helpful stranger. "I don't know what we would have done without you."

The singular looking stripling bowed his head slightly to show gratitude for the thank you, and then said with a stern but friendly voice, "Follow me!" He turned right and headed in the direction of the woods.

I wanted to ask more questions before following him, but since he had the lantern and we could see nothing without it in this snow storm, I saw no other option but to trust him. Paul was more reluctant than I was. He stood there for the longest time before deciding to come with us. Yet Brendan and Nate obeyed the unusual stranger's command immediately with no noticeable hesitancy. I wondered if that was lack of prudence or a virtue.

While we followed him, I decided to question our curious helper to see if I could get some information. "So, what is your name, sir?" I asked. "I really appreciate your help."

"What does it matter what my name is, my friend?" the withdrawn stranger said, politely dismissing my question. "I am here to help. Is that not all that matters?"

Paul looked at me and whispered, "That's extremely suspicious don't you think? I've heard of stories like this before. I'll bet his Dad's a serial killer who uses his son to lure new victims. He's going to get us killed."

"Nah, he's probably just shy," I whispered back, pretending that I was not going to be frightened of a person only because he did not want to give us his name.

I was grateful that the heavy snow storm was less noticeable in the forest. The trees blocked the wind a bit and provided an umbrella to lessen the amount of snow falling on us. The atypical stranger did not seem at all bothered by the weather, but I am sure he noticed the difference.

"How did you find us?" I asked.

With his free hand the distant guide silently took something out of his pocket and handed it to me. It was a Search and Rescue Scouts merit badge.

"Ah, I see," I said relieved. "So, you know these woods quite well then I suppose."

After studying the badge himself, something Paul mentioned brought back my discomfort: he whispered into my ear, "That merit badge does not even exist."

"What are you talking about, Paul?" I asked. "It's right here in my hand."

"No," Paul corrected me. "I mean that particular badge of merit is not a real badge."

I looked at Paul, still trying to figure out what he meant.

"The Scouts don't have this sort of badge. It doesn't exist. It's a fake. I'm telling you, he's a phony—and probably a cannibal."

"You're not a Scout. How would you know?"

"None of your business. Just trust me, okay?"

Feeling uneasy, I handed the badge back to the stranger.

"Where are you taking us?" Brendan asked our alleged benefactor.

"To find shelter," replied our apparent patron, adding, "my friend."

"You guys don't have to worry," explained Brendan. "This comrade has helped me before. He's completely trustworthy."

Apparently, our whispering was louder than we thought if Brendan could hear us. But what on earth was he talking about?

"You see," Paul whispered as quietly as he possibly could. "Casper . . . I mean Brendan, has seen him before. That means this guy has been stalking him. That's a bad sign. We're all going to die."

"Nah," I reassured him in hope also of consoling myself, "you're jumping to conclusions."

"What do you mean, Brendan?" asked Nate. "When did you see him before?"

"He saved me from a head injury," answered Brendan. "A while back, I fell out of a tree house in some woods near my home. This Scout happened to be around and saw me falling. He couldn't get there in time to catch me, but he was able to stop my head from hitting the ground."

"That's wonderful," said Nate. "I knew we could trust him."

Paul whispered into my ear again, "Tom, that story does not make any sense. Clearly this guy has been drugging Brendan and causing him to see things."

Though I did find Brendan's story questionable, Paul's alternative seemed more bizarre. It is not that I did not trust Brendan, but I wondered if he might have hit his head after all when he fell and then had a confused memory of what happened. Before I could respond to Paul, he decided to assert himself without warning.

"Okay enough of this," said Paul.

Oh no, what was he going to do? I knew this unusual stranger seemed a bit off somehow, but he was still probably trying to help us. I hoped that Paul would do nothing to insult him, and in the process get us stuck out here lost in the woods.

"Brendan," said Paul, "You might want to make sure that you don't still have a concussion from falling out of that tree house. And I'm not letting this guy take us another step without giving us some solid answers." With that statement Paul ran past us all to get in front of the stranger to confront him, but the careless stranger walked right by him without flinching. Embarrassed, Paul tried the same thing again, but this time reached up a little too roughly and put his hand on the stranger's shoulder.

The eccentric stranger halted so quickly that those of us behind him not being able to stop in time all fell down.

"I want some answers," Paul demanded.

Without showing the slightest concern, the odd stranger bent down a little and whispered something into Paul's ear. Paul turned paler than a ghost and his eyes widened more than I even thought possible.

What could our guide possibly have said to Paul to frighten him so much? Did he confirm Paul's suspicions by threatening to cook and eat him? Or was it something else entirely? I considered asking Paul directly, but was afraid to—for fear of learning what might have been said to him and what hostility he might show me for asking.

"We are there," the stranger declared, interrupting my thoughts. "Enjoy your stay," he said, pointing at a small wooden cabin. "I wish you peace and happiness in this life and the next. And may God shine the face of his countenance upon you."

With that, the stranger turned back and began to walk away from us. I ran a little to catch him up, wanting to thank him for saving us and finding us the lodge. I placed my hand gently on his shoulder as I tried to keep pace with him and he turned to me and glared into my soul. A mesmerizing light shot from his astonishing orb-like eyes and temporarily blinded me. A few seconds and I was able to see again. And my eyes revealed that I was now in another place entirely.

Chapter 10

A Scout's Honor

Where did everybody go? I was still in the woodlands but all my companions were gone, and so was the mysterious stranger who now blindsided me. I took a step forward and a dry fallen branch snapped beneath my feet. The snow was no longer there. Where had it all disappeared? It was not even cold anymore but seemed to be summer temperature. Should I take off my winter layers so as not to overheat? Or would the cold come back again as quickly as it left? I had better keep it on for now, just in case. The harsh wind from where I used to be had given up too. Now only a slow breeze toiled by me, barely moving the tree branches, and lifting up debris from all over the ground. The light filtering through the trees dimmed to a bare minimum, no longer wishing to share itself with those below.

How did I get here? Or was I dreaming? Perhaps that unknown stranger hypnotized me or knocked me out. What if this was all some sort of intensely vivid hallucination? I wondered why he would do such a thing to me—and how? All I wanted was to say 'thank you' to him. Would I ever see my friends again, or was I trapped in this unknown place? Whatever the case, I needed to try and figure a way out of here.

From above me a sorrowful echo alerted my ears and I tried to make out exactly what it could be. Was it crying? It seemed so. Noticing that a rope ladder on a deciduous tree beside me led to a tree house above about two stories high, I began to climb it to see if I could help whoever was up there. Maybe he could help me out as well.

I reached the top of the ladder and entered the tiny tree house through a hatch opening in the floor. I noticed several books lying around the floorboards—*Frightful Sight* books. Was it Brendan then? Sure enough, it was. There he was sitting among the books looking out the open window and weeping unceasingly. Thank God I was not alone after all. Somehow, we both must have been transported here.

"Brendan!" I exclaimed. "I'm so happy to see you. Do you have any idea where we are or how we got here?"

Brendan continued to sob and paid no attention to my plea.

"It's okay," I said. "You must have been scared. So was I, but I'm here now. We can figure out how to get out of here together."

He still paid me no heed. I went over to put my hand on his shoulder to see if he was alright, but my hand slipped through him as though he wasn't there at all. What was this? *How could this happen? I must be dreaming after all. Or was I dead?* I began to shout as loudly as I could into Brendan's ear, hoping desperately that he might hear me. There was no reaction from him. What was I to do?

"He's never coming back and it's all my fault," Brendan lamented.

I listened closely to try and figure out what was wrong; wanting desperately to help my friend, yet knowing that in my current state I could do nothing to console him.

As Brendan continued to grieve, I heard a kind voice say, "It's not your fault."

"But it is my fault," Brendan responded. "If I wasn't such a troublemaker he would never have left. I miss him so much."

Where did that voice come from? I couldn't see anyone, but it seemed as though Brendan could hear it too.

"It is your fault," said a second voice, sounding much more ominous. "How could anyone love you? All you do is seek attention. There's only one thing you can do to get your Dad to come back—parents never miss their kids' funeral, even if they hate them. Everyone will come to your memorial service and feel sorry for you, giving you the attention you've always wanted."

I tried, to no avail, to figure out where the voices were coming from, so that I could get the second voice to shut up as Brendan continued to wail bitterly. I recognized that evil voice. It haunted my nightmares constantly. It was the shadowy figure of death that had threatened all whom I loved. It could not be the same voice since that was only a dream, but it sounded exactly identical to me.

"Ending your life early is a serious wrong," said the kinder voice.

Brendan wiped his red eyes with his hand and said, "Cutting my life short is ingratitude towards God who gave it to me as a precious gift."

I was so happy to see that he had listened to the good voice.

"So what if it is a depravity?" pleaded the menacing voice. "So is self-harm, and it never stopped you. Look at the soles of your feet after all!"

What on earth did the strange voice mean by that?

"God gives us the grace necessary to overcome," said the gentle voice.

Brendan planted his face into his knees in shame and then raised his head again. "But one sin does not justify another act of wickedness. Every idle word and deed matters."

Good for you, Brendan. You tell that degenerate!

"Alright," the creepy voice said, "maybe suicide is too far. Not everyone is brave enough for so noble a deed. But a serious injury would certainly merit a visit from your Dad in the hospital, wouldn't it? He'd feel so sorry for you that he would have no choice but to come and see you. Maybe he would even stay."

Not liking where this was going, considering Brendan's hesitation in responding, and not knowing what else to do, in desperation I got on my knees and began to pray for my friend, hoping that Heaven might assist him and rid him of that wretched voice which seemed only to wish his ruin. I recited and repeated the Hail Mary on his behalf after making the sign of the Cross.

Brendan moaned in anguish, uttering what seemed to be an inexpressible sorrow churning up inside him. Then he began to rock back and forth hugging his knees.

"That's still the same sin, only lesser," pointed out the nice voice.

"Evil is evil," said Brendan, "and I don't wish to displease God by being selfish."

I tried not to let my happiness for what Brendan now said distract me from my prayers, but to some extent it could not be helped.

"Sure. Sure. Of course. But why not just sit on the edge of the window sill?" the dreadful voice suggested, "You don't have to worry. If you happen to fall by accident then it's not really your fault, now is it? As long as you don't do it on purpose, right?"

No Brendan, don't listen to that reprobate! God, please help my friend.

"That's true," Brendan said as he stood up. "There's nothing wrong with sitting on a window sill."

"You're playing with fire," warned the compassionate voice as Brendan proceeded to get his legs over the edge of the window and sit down on it "Don't test God."

"What a beautiful view," Brendan tried to convince himself. "That's why I'm up here. The view justifies it."

I cringed as I tried my best not to stop praying, knowing that it was the one thing I could do for my friend in my current condition. The considerate voice whispered into my ear, "Are you willing to suffer for your friend, in union with Christ's sacrifice?"

"Yes." I accepted without a second thought then continued, "If I can bear it."

I became more and more worried about what I had just agreed to. I felt an invisible force take me by the collar, then hit me in the face several times, leaving me with an agonizing burning throb. "Stop praying for him, you fiend! Or you'll get even worse." The unseen force gave me a final painful blow in the stomach and then let me go as my back fell onto the floor.

What was that? Was it the voice of a demon? Or perhaps a ghost? No matter. Whatever this enemy was, the threat to Brendan was the same. My face was in too much pain for me to continue praying audibly, and I was now afraid to, so I continued to intercede mentally instead.

The bad voice began to target Brendan again. "Now what if you were to fall asleep while up here or to zone out? What a terrible accident that would be. You wouldn't be jumping. You merely would not stop yourself from falling—a big difference, don't you think? Just let all your muscles relax at the same time."

"He's lying," said the soothing voice. "Don't listen to him."

Brendan took a few deep breaths, as if trying to prepare himself for something.

Please, Brendan, don't listen to that stupid voice. God, I beg of you not to let me lose my friend so soon.

Brendan started to cry again in despair. Then he slid off the window.

"No!" I yelled, as I got up to climb back down the ladder as swiftly as possible. When I reached the bottom, I ran over to see if Brendan was okay.

Brendan lay stretched out on his back and was gasping noisily for breath. He had a shocked look in his eyes. But there was someone with him. It was a Boy Scout with his hands resting under Brendan's head.

"It's okay," said the kind Scout. "You've got the wind knocked out of you. Don't panic. Your breathing will return to normal in a few moments."

Where did this helpful Scout come from? Wait a minute. Taking a closer look at his face, I recognized him as the same secretive stranger who had helped us find the cabin. That's right, I remember now. Brendan did mention that he met the kind Scout before. He was telling the truth. But how peculiar.

"I wasn't able to stop you from falling," said the nameless Scout. "But I got here in time to lessen your impact and protect your head. You must have some good friends praying for you."

Brendan's eyes filled with water, and the Scout assured him, "It's okay to get sad and cry. You don't have to hold back your tears."

He looked at me for a moment and then back at Brendan. Was he able to see me?

"I'll stay with you a while," the Scout assured Brendan. "Until you're ready to get up. You've got to be more careful next time, buddy."

Although unable to speak, Brendan looked at him with deep gratitude and regret in his eyes.

"Thank you," I said to the charitable rescuer. Looking at my changed surroundings, I noticed that I was back by the cabin again.

"And thank you," replied the generous stranger, "for all your help." He continued walking back into the woods until we could see him no more.

Awestruck by what had just happened, and still not quite sure even what did happen, I made my way towards the cabin.

"Your eye!" said Nate. "How'd you get a black eye? And you've got a cut on your face."

Brendan ran up to me to see if I was okay. And Paul walked over as well, looking as though he had still not completely lost the pale frightened complexion from earlier.

"I'm honestly not sure," I replied, not knowing how or if I should even bother trying to explain what just took place. And what did just happen? Was it a vision? Was I teleported through time? Did all that actually occur, or did I imagine it? And who was that caring but odd youth? How did he get there to help Brendan so fast? I hope he shows up again so that I can ask a ton of questions. Though he does not seem like the type to answer to an inquisition.

"Let's go into the cabin," Nate suggested, "and see if they have a first aid kit."

Chapter 11

Fallen Beads and Barriers

The cottage, which felt strangely alluring, greeted us with a warm welcome when we entered through the unlocked front door. And we ran all around the place in excitement to check it out. Well, some of us ran, mainly Nate, while the rest made the inspection at a more prudent pace. The homely inner walls were covered in thin cedar. I could feel a draft but the atmosphere on the whole was not a cold one. There was a definite cabin smell in the air—the good kind, not the bad musty smell that haunts so many holiday dwellings. I could never tell what caused pleasant cabin odors. Maybe it was the wood.

There were two bedrooms, and a cozy kitchen with heavy cast iron pots hanging from a rack. A crackling and radiant warmth called us to the living room where a cozy fireplace offered refuge from our long cold journey. I loved the sound of a roaring fire and was so happy that one of the others was thoughtful enough to start it so that we could all get warm. For a moment I stood as close as I could to the flames to warm my hands. But soon the overwhelming radiance forced me to take a few steps back.

Over the fireplace hung a beautiful picture of St. Nicholas. The patron Saint of children was dressed in green holding a staff and wearing a large pointed hat. Everyone joined me around the fireplace for a few minutes to thaw their freezing digits, and then we all began to divest ourselves of our winter gear.

When Paul removed his winter coat, Nate noticed that he was wearing a brown Hawaiian bead necklace—as he did every day without fail. Running up to him, Nate reached out for the necklace and lifted it up to examine it closer. But Paul, still I think a little shook up from whatever it was the stranger had said to him, flinched and pushed Nate away and down to the floor, "Don't touch that!" he shouted.

Not expecting so intense a reaction, Nate did not think to let go of the necklace as he fell backwards. It broke in half and beads from it flew in every direction, with a large string of them remaining in Nate's hand.

Shocked, Nate sat on the floor looking as if he was barely holding back his tears. He was always much better at that than I was. "I'm really sorry," Nate muttered. "I only wanted to see it. I should have asked first and now I've broken it."

"No," Paul lamented, "I'm the one that's sorry. I just struck a little kid over a dumb necklace." Paul put out his hand to help Nate up off the ground.

As Nate cautiously took Paul's hand, he replied, "No harm done. I'm not simply some little kid anyway. You caught me off guard, that's all. Usually, I'm more prepared from all the training I am used to doing, you know?"

"I don't doubt it," Paul answered soberly.

"What's the matter with you?" I asked Paul, furious that he had hurt my brother.

Paul looked at me, then walked by me towards the door, saying, "What's the matter with me indeed?" Then he walked out the door without saying another word.

"You're sure that you're alright?" I asked Nate as Brendan started picking up the beads on the floor.

"Yeah, I'm fine," Nate responded, "But is Paul? He looked pretty upset about what I did, even if he didn't say so. And he left without his coat."

"I'll go check on him," I said, putting on my own coat and grabbing Paul's. "And you guys try and do what you can to fix his necklace, if possible."

"Alright," Brendan and Nate responded in unison.

"I'll be back," I said as I headed out the door to find Paul.

Paul did not walk very far. He was sitting down in front of the cabin with his back leaning against it. "Thank you," he said as I handed him his coat and he started to put it on. "I'll give you a free punch if you want on behalf of your brother."

"No thanks," I said, although I wanted to accept the offer. "He seems fine. And a strike from me would not do much damage to you anyway."

Paul laughed. "Well you said it, not me." After a long pause, he resumed. "You know I'm not very good at this sort of thing, but here it goes

I think I've been terrible to you. Why don't you retaliate or defend yourself more often?"

"I don't know," I said, startled that he actually acknowledged his crimes against me. "I guess I am saddened when people treat others poorly more than I'm angry about it. Sometimes I want to lash out, but I hate the idea of hurting anyone. Unfortunately, all of that builds up until I freak out and risk hurting people ten times worse than otherwise. I have not quite mastered the whole pacifism thing yet."

"You are too hard on yourself. I think you would hesitate to swat a mosquito."

I laughed. "Since we're on the subject, why do you act so terribly towards me most of the time at school? Did I do something to offend you? If I did, I can't remember what it was."

"Because I'm a coward."

Shocked, I inquired, "What do you mean?"

"I see you always by yourself, and I feel sorry for you. Not in a mean way. But I see you and me as the same. So, I feel sorry for myself."

"But we're nothing alike," I laughed.

"Not our personalities or temperaments. I mean more in the way that we don't fit in at school."

"I don't understand."

"Nobody likes you at school because they think you're weird, since you're always by yourself writing or in your own little world. I know that sounds insulting, but I mean it as a compliment. Being like everyone else is weird itself."

"I don't know what you're talking about. I'm different, but everyone likes me fine. And that still doesn't explain why you are so mean to me."

"Alright, forget I said all that. The point is that I don't fit in. Everyone assumes that I am mean and unapproachable so they don't approach me. I see you by yourself, and think of you as a companion—since we are both alone in the school yard. Every time I come up to you to hang out, I get nauseous."

"But why?"

"Because if the weird . . . I mean solitary kid told me to go away, then I would lose my only chance to have a real friend. Instead of being honest about my fears, I end up picking on you to cover it up—so that you don't see my weakness. That's a petty excuse though, right? It doesn't excuse the terrible way I've treated you in the slightest. But anyway, now you know the reason for it."

I could hardly believe that Paul was saying all this and finally opening up to me. "And why tell me all this now? Are you merely messing with me again, or what?"

"That's a good question. I think hurting your brother was the last straw. I realized that I'm so used to thinking people hate me that I automatically assume the worst when they approach me—likely causing the very thing I wish to prevent—rejection. Your brother merely wanted to admire and compliment my jewelry. I presumed that he was making fun of it before even giving him a chance to explain."

Wow. I hardly knew what to say.

"It's not solely that though," Paul continued. "It's something about this place. I can't explain it, but it's not normal. You can probably sense it better than I can since you have a natural piety about you."

He was right. There was something strangely odd about the old cottage that I could not quite put my finger on. And there was that weird vision that I had, but I was not sure whether I should mention that to him or not.

"Remember that fake Scout?" Paul asked.

"Yes of course." There was no way I could forget such an extraordinary person.

"Well, he said something to me. When I asked him for answers, he took it literally. That's what I mean about the strangeness of this place and the locals who live here."

"What did he say to you?" I asked, very curious to know what could possibly have got him to think so much and to turn so pale.

"Well he said, 'The answer you seek has already been given to you. Listen to your Angel and ignore the devil.'"

"What an odd thing to say," I blurted out, expecting something completely different. Actually, I'm not sure what I was expecting, but whatever it was it had to make more sense.

"You're telling me. But it's not peculiar for the reasons you may think."

My interest was piqued again, "What do you mean?"

"Well, 'Listen to your Angel and ignore the devil,' was something that my Grandmother used to say to me before she passed away. She was a very wise and pious woman."

"Really? That is bizarre. How would the Scout know what your Grandma said to you?"

"Yes exactly. And it really freaked me out. But it also got me thinking a lot. I thought about how, even though it was bizarre for him to say that to me, he was right nonetheless. I recognized that I was not following my Grandmother's advice very well. When I get the urge to bully you, I should ignore it and listen to my good nature instead."

"Well, I'm glad that you are trying to behave better."

"It's not going to be easy, because I'm so used to acting like a jerk. But I'm going to try to be better. I don't expect you to forgive me. I've treated you like garbage and don't deserve your kindness. But I promise to behave better to you at school from now on. I will take my Grandma's advice."

"I'm really glad to hear you say all this. To be honest though, I am worried that you are just messing with me again. I won't know if you are telling me the truth until we get back to school. I know I should give you the benefit of the doubt, but I'm not sure if I can anymore. You've fooled me so many times, you know?"

Even though I told Paul that I was not sure whether I could give him the benefit of the doubt, I actually did believe him. I merely did not want him to know that in case he was hoaxing me once more.

"I get it. Actions speak louder than words. I'll prove it to you at school. Regardless, though, thanks for your kindness, Tommy."

As I nodded, Nate and Brendan ran out the door and stood in front of us, Nate with his hands behind his back.

"Hey guys," Brendan said, "Nate has a gift for you, Paul."

Paul nodded, looking half concerned and half curious.

Nate showed Paul his hands which held the fixed necklace. It did not look exactly the same. A few beads were out of place and it was a little smaller, as a result of the knots added to the string needed to hold it back together.

"Wow!" Paul said in gratitude. "You guys did all this for me?"

Nate nodded.

"That's wonderful," Paul added. "Thank you truly. I think it looks even better than it did before." Then he continued, "You really like this necklace, don't you?"

"Yes," Nate agreed. "I've never seen anything like it before."

Paul explained. "This necklace is very important to me. It was a gift from my Grandmother. She got it for me when she went to Hawaii. It's not like one of those fake ones. Anyway, would you like to hold onto it for me? I think it's safer with you since I'm so clumsy."

Nate's smile increased substantially more than normal. "Really? Are you sure?"

"I'm sure," Paul said. "I've got something much better to remember her by now."

"Thank you so much," Nate said gleefully as he put it on. "But can we go back inside? It's super cold out here and I didn't bring my coat."

"Sure," I said. "Let's all go back inside."

Chapter 12

Healing Scars

"Thanks for starting the fire," Paul said to me, grateful for the warmth of the cabin as we re-entered it.

"No, it wasn't me," I said, correcting Paul. "It must have been one of the others."

After I took off my winter gear, I stood in front of the fireplace again to get warm. I stared at the St. Nicholas painting. It was a striking picture. The kind that compelled you to look at it. Eyes in pictures always make me feel as if they are staring at me and this was no exception. St Nick's expression looked so gentle that I found it consoling rather than creepy. I could see why he is supposed to be always watching us, knowing if we are good or bad.

We each took an old wooden chair from the kitchen and brought it to the living room so that we could sit and enjoy the fire. The flames dancing around the logs were mesmerizing. Yawning is contagious, so one by one we all succumbed to it, beginning with Nate. Everyone was tired from staying up the whole night, and not wanting any of us to faint the next day I figured that we should try and sleep for a bit, at least a few hours, and then after we woke up decide what to do.

No suggestion however was needed that we should slumber. My three companions dozed off quickly in their chairs, and I was not going to wake them to tell them to go back to sleep. Such a notion would be pointlessly redundant. My eyes felt heavy. As I gazed drowsily at the fire they opened and shut, staying closed longer and longer each time, until they no longer had the strength to open again.

A sudden noise woke me, but my eyelids felt so heavy that I had to focus a lot to force them open. I blocked the sunlight from my eyes for a moment with my arms, until my pupils got used to it. Finally, when they had adapted to the light, I scrutinized the room to see what the noise could have been. Nate and Paul were sound asleep, but Brendan's chair was empty. Where did he go? Probably to use the restroom.

I must have slept through the breaking of dawn. The daylight exposed many of the flaws in the living room that had been hidden during the night. Cracks in the woodwork, loose nails, and missing pieces of wood suggested that this cabin had been through a lot over the years, but was still standing strong even with its defects.

I was about to fall back into a deep sleep, but the sound of a chair being moved across the floor prevented me. The noise seemed to come from the kitchen. Wondering what Brendan was doing, I got up and headed over towards the door, wobbling a little from fatigue.

"Hey Brendan," I said yawning, as I sat down beside him facing away from the table in the remaining chair. "What are you up to? Aren't you still tired?"

Brendan froze for a second and then said, "I'm sorry I didn't mean to wake you. There's no first aid kit in this place so I was trying to be innovative in order to get this sliver out."

I was still half asleep when I walked into the kitchen so I had only seen that Brendan was sitting there. Now that I was more focused, I noticed why he froze. His facial expression was fidgety and his usual care free smile absent. His bare right foot was resting on top of his left knee. He was holding a small pocket knife in both hands and looking as though about to open it.

"How did you get a sliver on your foot?" I asked, not fully buying his story. "Can I see it? Maybe I can help?"

"Actually, you know what?" Brendan said. "It seems to have fallen out on its own."

Now what the evil voice had said during the peculiar vision I had had was beginning to make sense. "That seems unlike a sliver," I said, hoping that Brendan would confess his fib without my having to call him out on it directly."

"I'm sorry that I lied to you," he lamented, realizing that I did not believe his tale, as he placed the knife down on the table. "I panicked when I saw you come in and didn't know what to say."

"You can say the truth. It's me. You can trust me."

"It's not that," Brendan corrected me. "I don't want to burden you. You have so much on your mind already. Plus, I don't want you to think I'm crazy."

"Well maybe we can be roommates in the asylum together," I joked. "Look. I promise not to think that you are a nutcase. And don't worry about troubling me. It's not a burden to help a friend."

Brendan smiled again for a second, then almost at once returned to looking upset. "I appreciate it. But I don't think I can say. It's too difficult to put into words."

"Then show me."

"What do you mean?"

"Let me see your foot."

Brendan looked down in shame and said, "Okay, I guess. But you won't like what you see . . . Are you sure you want to see it? We've been walking for a long time. My foot's probably really gross right now."

"Stop stalling. You can either show me or tell me. It's up to you."

"Well you asked for it," Brendan said, lifting up his leg with his hands to show me the sole of his foot.

I cringed in dismay at the awful sight, hoping that Brendan did not notice. It was much worse than I feared. The bottom of his foot was covered in tiny white lines or scars. I expected a few, but it seemed that he had been doing this for quite a while. Out of concern for him I tried to hold back my tears which were building up so he would not think that he had overburdened me.

Knowing how sensitive my own feet were, I could not stand even the thought of experiencing the kind of excruciating pain the scars testified to, let alone actually inflicting it on oneself. The torment of walking on the soles of my feet with paper cuts all over them plagued my mind relentlessly. I tried to think of anything I could to distract myself from it. But how could I when my friend needed my help? I had no choice but to focus on it. I'd have to pretend not to be bothered by it to keep Brendan from regretting coming clean about his struggles.

As he put his foot down, Brendan to break the silence explained. "You don't have to worry about me though, okay? I only do this for attention. I've always been an attention-seeker. I hurt myself so that people will feel sorry for me. But you don't have to pity me because you're my friend. You know the real me."

I knew that he didn't want me to worry, but I could not help it. How could I not grieve after finding out that my best friend deliberately cut himself? "You keep saying that you are an attention-seeker, but I don't think it's true. If I were trying to get attention from people, I would not likely cut myself on the bottom of my feet where no one could see what I had done. I would make sure that it was where people could easily find it."

"But why else would I do it, if not for attention?"

"I honestly can't pretend to know the answer to that. How long have you been doing it?"

"Since a little after my Dad left, I think. It helped me to weep less. He left because I'm an attention-seeking cry-baby. So, if I changed all that he might come back, right?"

"But I don't understand. You are the most positive person I know."

"That's purely because I love people so much. I always have a smile on my face when around others. But I'm also too sensitive, so it takes very little to get me to cry. It's one extreme or the other. I'm either really happy or horribly depressed. It's when I'm by myself that I get sad and lonely the most. I miss him so much."

"Listen, you are the best friend I have ever had. And I'm really worried about you. This is unhealthy. You've got to figure out a way to cope with your emotions without resorting to this sort of thing. You have to stop it. Alright?"

"I know. You're right. It's a terrible sin. And I want to quit doing it so badly. But I just can't seem to shake off the grave habit."

"Have you tried to quit before?"

"Yes. The first few times I cut myself, it was a relief and I had complete control over it. Yet when I tried to stop, I couldn't. I've come to depend on it. It feels like a need, the same as food and water."

"That doesn't sound good. I think you might be addicted to the practice. How could it be a relief? Doesn't it hurt a lot? I honestly did not even know that it was possible to get badly hooked on self-harm."

"It hurts very much. That's why it's a relief. It distracts me from how much worse I sometimes feel inside."

I had no idea that he was in so much pain. I often wondered about his family life, but he always seemed to handle it well with his positive attitude. "I'm sorry," I told him, not being able to think of any better words of comfort.

"I'm afraid I lured you into this friendship under false pretenses. You thought that I was good. I'm actually a bad kid—terrible in fact."

I snorted like a pig from trying to hold in my laughter.

"It's true though," Brendan insisted, seeing that I was not convinced. "I didn't think you'd want to be my friend if you knew how wicked I was, so I misled you. I'm sorry."

"Well I don't feel misled at all. Even if you think that you are evil, to me you seem better than most kids. You need to get out more. We all make terrible mistakes, even daily, and I am sure you are no exception. But you're good willed, not some insolently defiant rebel. Maybe you go to a really well-behaved school but if you attended my school, you'd quickly see how ungodly everyone can be. What school do you attend anyway?"

Brendan looked confused by my question, probably because he was still as exhausted as I was.

"Anyway," I asserted, "I think we need to get you some help when we get back. You may not be able to get over this problem on your own."

"But I have you."

"And I will be there for you as much as I can. But I'm saying that you may need extra professional help too, from those who know how to deal with addiction and its causes."

"You don't think they'd send me away? You always seem so worried about that sort of thing yourself."

He was right. I was worried about it. But I had no idea how to help him. This sort of problem seemed beyond what a kid could handle. "I won't let them lock you up. Don't worry," I tried to encourage him.

"Well I can't promise, but only that I'll consider it if you come with me."

"Sure!" I accepted. Reluctant though I was to go near the people who had the power to put me in a straight-jacket, what else could I do? My friend's wellbeing was more important than preventing my own fears from coming to pass. Not wanting Brendan to be able to cut himself so easily at the next opportunity, I snatched the pocket knife off the table and slipped it into my trousers' pocket. "I'll hold on to this for you for a bit, okay?"

Brendan fidgeted a little, then responded, "That's okay, Tommy. You don't need to do that. You don't have to worry. I'll never do it again, I swear. Now give it back to me. That knife was a gift."

His reaction made me even more concerned that he had a greater addiction to cutting himself than I thought. "It's alright. I won't lose it on you. Who gave it to you?"

"Um. My Dad. I need it because it reminds me of him, you know?"

"Well I'm sorry, but you will have to find another way to remember him by for now. I don't feel comfortable with you having this at the moment. It's for your own good."

Brendan stood up from his chair and began pacing back and forth with his hands on his head. "You don't understand. I need it. I'll lose my mind without it. It's not so much that I need it to use, but only to know that I can use it. Does that make sense?"

"It makes perfect sense. And that's exactly why I have to hold onto it."

"Listen. I'm sorry that I freaked you out earlier with all that stuff. I'm completely calm now and in the right state of mind . . . I'll give you my whole *Frightful Sight* book collection . . ."

Ah, man. That was tempting, but I had to be unselfish and put his needs first. "Nope. Sorry."

We argued back and forth for a while, until Brendan finally gave up.

"Let's go back to sleep," Brendan suggested, yawning. "And thank you for being such a good friend. Sorry if I scared you."

"What are friends for if not to scare each other," I laughed.

We got up to head back to the living room fireplace for a few more hours of sleep. Though still tired, I had trouble dropping off again because of my concern for Brendan. Growing sick of trying to make myself go to sleep I went back into the kitchen and looked through all the drawers as soundlessly as possible, removing every knife I could find and hiding them all in my bag as a temporary solution. I was grateful that doing so helped take my mind off the issue and so I returned to my seat. Eventually I succumbed to exhaustion and in a while was sound asleep again in the chair.

Chapter 13

Missing Utensils

Hearing whispers and laughs, I wondered if I was awake or still dreaming. I opened my eyes to see what appeared to be Nate's face two inches away from mine.

"Hallo!" he declared cheerfully, confirming that it was really Nate.

"Whoa!" I shouted, startled, while I fell backwards with my chair onto the floor. "Alright, you got me," I admitted, as the four of us laughed.

"Are you alright though?" asked Nate while giving me a hand to help me up. "I didn't mean you to fall back like that."

"No worries," I said, double checking my pocket to make sure that the knife had not been snatched away during my sleep. "No harm done."

A piece of wood snapped in the fireplace which still had a bright burning fire.

"What time is it?" I asked.

"It's about two in the afternoon," replied Brendan.

"Oh no," I admitted. "I really slept in."

"We all did," said Nate. "We didn't get up much before you."

"We've been trying to figure out this fire and the kitchen," explained Paul, who was staring at the fireplace fretfully.

"What do you mean?" I asked.

"First of all," Paul replied. "The kitchen is bizarre. There's food in the cupboards and silverware in the drawers, but all the knives are missing."

I was the one who had hidden the knives in my bag until we needed them, but I could not think of how to explain that to everyone. I could not betray Brendan's trust and tell them what had happened. At least not without his say-so. Neither could I admit that I stole the knives without giving some sort of justifiable explanation. None came to mind.

Brendan was looking at the floor, as though he were worried that I might say something. But I would not do that to him. I would just have to keep quiet about stealing the knives for now until I could think of a worthwhile explanation to give for my actions.

"That certainly is odd," I said. "Whoever took all those knives, must have been wacko," I added, hoping to ease Brendan's tension.

"Secondly," said Paul, "none of us has added any fuel to this fire and it's been going the same the whole time. And thirdly, we can't figure out which one of us started the fire to begin with."

"So, it was burning when we got here?" I asked.

"It seems that way," said Paul. "This whole place gives me the creeps."

"I thought it was abandoned," Brendan said.

"So did I," said Paul. "But if the fire was on when we got here, someone must have been in the cottage shortly before us to start it."

"And," Nate said, looking terrified, "someone must have come in while we were sleeping and added logs to the fire."

"So some person knows we are here," I said, getting a little alarmed myself. "Yet whoever it is has not confronted us about why we are crashing his abode."

"Are you guys saying," Brendan inquired, "that someone is out there in the woods and is waiting for us to go to sleep before coming into the house? That's super creepy."

"It's probably that Scout guy," Paul suggested. "He seemed to know so much about us. That's a red flag in itself. He's the one who led us here. I think we're done for."

"Don't worry Nate," I said. "Paul's jumping to conclusions. There's no need to worry."

"No need to worry?" Paul asked, frantically. "Are you serious?"

"There's no need to scare my brother," I whispered to Paul. "It won't help."

"What are you guys whispering about?" asked Nate.

"It can't be the Scout," insisted Brendan. "I'm sure he's got our backs. He wouldn't mess with us like that."

Remembering that I was so tired that I had forgotten to say my night prayers before falling asleep, I told everyone, "I want to make sure to say my morning prayers, and then after that I think we should take a second look around the house to see if we can find out anything we might have missed in the dark."

"But it's the afternoon," Nate pointed out.

"Thank you, Nate," I laughed. "Afternoon prayers then. You guys can start looking without me if you want, and I'll catch up, okay? I'll only be five minutes or so."

I went into the kitchen and knelt down to pray.

Nate followed me and asked, "Can I join you?"

"Of course," I said, happy to see Nate wanting to intercede along with me.

Brendan also entered the kitchen, inquiring, "Mind if I join too?"

"Sure," I answered and they both knelt beside me.

Lastly, Paul came in, and said, "Well I don't want to be the only one left out."

As he knelt down beside us, I led everyone in prayer for a few minutes, so grateful to have others join me in something I was so used to doing on my own.

We then proceeded to check the house, hoping to find a clue to those who lived in it. An eerie feeling came over me as I began to search the living room, and wondered why the resident did not want to be seen by us.

"I found something!" yelled Nate, who was searching one of the bedrooms.

We all went rushing over to him to see what he had discovered.

"What is it?" asked Brendan.

"Yes," I inquired, "what did you find?"

"It looks like a letter," replied Nate, who was standing over a desk by the wall, staring at a piece of paper. "Do you want me to read it?"

"Go for it," said Paul.

We hovered around Nate with deep anticipation. After about a minute of silence, I couldn't take it anymore, and said, "He meant out loud. Read it aloud, please."

"Oh," Nate laughed, "Okay, here goes:

DECEMBER 25TH, 1997.

To weary travelers,

May God bless and keep whoever finds this letter. My name is Francis Dominic. I have been living alone in these woods, dedicating my life to prayer and penance for the past fifty years. And they have been the most fulfilling years of my life. However, it has been made known to me, mystically, that my earthly life is about to end. I will be taken home to Heaven, God willing, on this most joyful day of the year—Christmas day. I could not have asked for a better day to meet our Lord, and I could not be happier.

It has been shown to me that some weary travelers coming this way will be in need of a temporary dwelling. I could think of no greater final deed, than to show hospitality and charity to strangers in need.

So, whoever finds this letter, please make good use of my abode for as long as you need it. And pray for the repose of my soul, which will, by the time you read this letter, no longer be in the land of the living.

I am leaving the fridge and cupboards fully stocked, and have enough dry wood stored for an entire winter. I pray you to eat your fill, with good Christian temperance of course. Please enjoy your stay. And may God grant you peace and happiness in this life and the next.

Your friend in Jesus, Mary, and Joseph,
Francis Dominic

"That's it," said Nate. "That's the end of it."

"Hold on a second," said Paul. "That means that there's a dead body somewhere in this place. No wonder it feels so creepy."

"I don't think so," explained Brendan. "If this guy knew that he was going to die somehow and would have guests coming over, the last thing he would want is to freak out those he wished to help by leaving his corpse lying around the house."

Nate said, "That means we no longer have to worry. The owner wants us here, so we are not stealing or trespassing after all. Let's go eat something from the kitchen."

"It doesn't explain the fire though," Paul objected. "That still seems pretty strange and concerning to me. Perhaps the guests this hermit is referring to are people other than us. Plus, this guy seems neurotic and that's reason enough to be insecure about all of this."

I wondered how he knew when he was going to die? I pondered. And he sounded so at peace, even though he knew death was imminent. I wish I could have had the chance to ask him about it. But I guess it was too late now.

As we were all talking, Nate slipped out of the chair and headed towards the kitchen.

"I'm hungry too," Brendan said, following my brother's lead.

"Well he did say we were to help ourselves, didn't he?" I asked rhetorically.

"Fine, let's go," Paul said, as we followed the others to the kitchen.

Not having eaten for so long, we did not heed the hermit's advice about temperance, but hoped he would understand. I was soon so full that I had a little trouble breathing, my stomach and chest being so tight.

I felt a strong urge to head back to the other room and examine the document that we had just read a little more closely, in case there was something that Nate had missed. Or perhaps I only wanted to touch the letter, and was simply telling myself that story to excuse the lack of self-control over my bizarre and inexplicable need to make contact with things all the time.

Whatever the reason, I was being drawn to the room nonetheless, and decided to go and take another look.

Chapter 14

Snow Place in the Inn

Leaving my friends at the table, I went to take a second look at the note Nate had read earlier. I examined the hermit's room when I entered it. There was a perfectly made single size bed facing away from the wall, and near it two fairly full bookshelves. Walking through the chamber, I found the squeak in the plank floor that all cottage bedrooms have. And I stepped on that same spot to hear the sound twice more before heading over to the desk.

An aura of peace unique to this room made me feel most welcome. Every square inch of the cell seemed to watch and smile at me warmly; causing me to regret that I would have to leave such a comfortable atmosphere at some point.

An old-fashioned quill pen, a wad of slightly yellow tinted paper, stick of red sealing wax, candle lantern, St. Michael paper weight and a letter opener were all placed neatly on the maple-wood desk. I took the letter opener and put it in my pocket, not wanting to take any risks now that I was aware of Brendan's severe addiction. I hoped I would remember that there was something sharp in my pocket and not accidentally stab myself if I put my hand in when hiding the letter opener in my bag later. I laughed a little as I remembered all of us trying to use forks as knives when eating earlier. Desperation is the Mother of invention.

I sat down in the homely chair, picked up the letter and brought it close to my eyes, wondering if I should stop trying to get out of that eye exam I was supposed to have. I hated eye doctors. Whenever I have been asked to follow the light, I've had to try very hard not to laugh—either because I felt so uncomfortable or because doing so actually seemed funny to me.

All of a sudden, the paper in my hand became transparent. Through it I could see a second letter back on the desk from where I had picked the first up. Was it possible to hallucinate from eating too much? I saw two hands on the paper—one holding it down, the other writing on it with a quill pen. The arms were coming from me yet were not my arms.

Freaked out entirely by the sensation, I leaped out of the chair and took a few steps back from it. A joyful-looking old man was sitting in the chair writing. The hands must have been his. But how did he not notice that I was sitting on top of him? And how did I fail to see him before?

"Excuse me, sir," I said. The peaceful old-timer did not appear to hear. Perhaps he was deaf. He was wearing a raggedy grey robe with the hood down and he had a beard that was so long it almost hit the paper on which his pen was placing ink.

I put my hand out hesitantly towards his shoulder to tap it, worried that I might scare him and give him a heart attack, but not sure how else to get his attention since he seemed unable to hear well. But to my amazement my fingers went through his shoulder as if he were not even there.

What on earth was happening? Hold on. This was what took place before when I had the vision of Brendan in the tree house. Had I been transported somewhere else again? It looked like the exact same cabin to me. Then perhaps it was not like before. Maybe this old man was a ghost. Could he be the hermit who wrote the letter?

A loud knock sounded on the door. The old man got up from the chair, walked past me and left the room. Well clearly, he couldn't see me or else he would have said something I'm sure. I followed him towards the door. With another shock I realized that none of my friends or my belongings were anywhere to be seen. Where had they run off to? And why did they take my gear? Maybe Brendan found the knives and stole my bag to get them. I'd have to remember to scold him. Oh no, was I starting to sound like a parent?

In response to the knock, the kind-looking ancient opened the door and revealed that the person outside was a gentle but sturdy young man with a short clean beard and black hair. The man's hands were rough, suggesting that he probably worked with them doing manual labor.

"Hello," said the old man to him in a raspy yet tender-sounding tone. "Can I help you?"

"I really hope so," replied the younger man, with a worried look but in a sweet and gentle voice. "My wife is about to give birth and we need a place to stay. So far, all the inns we have gone to have been full and no one will take us. Can you help?"

The old man smiled. "Well, I am expecting guests soon, so you cannot stay here. But what I do have I will give you. Come with me. I know the perfect place."

Following them out the door I realized, with a start, that it had become dark. When had night come? The old man closed the door behind him and put his key in to lock it, but then stopped and instead left the key in the door. Together the old and young man headed into the woods. I hesitated, scared to follow two strangers into the depth of the forest, but then having realized that I would be just as afraid if I stayed in the cabin alone since my friends did not seem to be there at the moment, I ran to catch up to the other two.

After a few minutes of walking, a beautiful young lady joined us. She must have been the pregnant wife. She had been waiting among the trees resting on a camel. The young man had now taken the reins after greeting her. *Well that is certainly an odd animal to see around here*, I mused. Then again, the whole situation of being invisible was extremely strange to say the least.

Walking for about five minutes more, we stopped in front of a small cave set in a hillside. The old man led his two guests up the hill and into the cave. I was reluctant to follow them for fear that there might be a bear inside. But before I could muster enough courage to reconsider going in, the old man returned. He knelt in front of the cave for a few minutes in prayer with his hands together.

I kneeled down as well, not really knowing why, but feeling strongly drawn to do so. Suddenly a splendid, bright light shone out from the cave. It was almost blinding, yet I could not look away. I had never seen anything like it. Without warning the most beautiful choir of voices that had ever been heard began singing the old Christmas Carol 'O Come all Ye Faithful.'

It started quietly but kept increasing in volume. So loud did it become that I could hear nothing else, yet it did not bother my ears. Some of the voices were singing in harmony, while many others broke into solos above the rest at intervals; however, not in a way that seemed chaotic—which was strange considering the number of voices there were. It was a heavenly motet. I smiled in awe. And a few tears rolled down my face, for I was unable to hide how much I loved that hymn and that this had now become my favorite rendition of it. So taken by it was I that I sang along, hoping no one would mind. They probably could not hear me anyway since I seemed to be invisible to them. The old man got slowly back to his feet and entered the cave a second time, but now even more reverently with his arms crossed against his chest.

I jumped up in fright as a small strangely dressed child hurried by me with a tiny lamb resting in his arms. He was about a foot shorter than Nate.

"Sorry," I said, still trying to recover my heart beat's normal speed. "I didn't see you there. You scared me."

Feeling stupid for forgetting again that I was invisible, I watched the little kid start to carry the lamb up the hill. Half way up, he turned to me and said, "Come on. Don't you want to see him?"

So, this kid could see me and the others couldn't? I was amazed. Or maybe I am no longer invisible. "Who are we going to see?" I asked as I followed him up the hill.

"The newborn King of course," the child answered as we got closer and closer to the light emanating from the cave.

Wondering what a King would be doing in a cave, I finally started to put two and two together. In awe and very nervous about what I might see, I entered into the brightness of the cavern. Unable to make out anything thing but pure light, I went down on my knees again in unison with the shepherd boy beside me. I did not know what else to do, so I joined again in the song and sang at the top of my lungs.

The light abruptly vanished, disappearing as swiftly as it had come. But I still continued to sing, so entranced by what I had just experienced. Reality hit me as my eyes veered left and right, and I now saw Nate, Brendan, and Paul standing in the cave, watching me intently with concern and wonder written on their faces. And it had somehow mysteriously become daytime again.

I finished the verse I was on, thinking how awkward it would be to stop singing in the middle of it. Would such awkwardness matter in a situation like this though? Feeling self-conscious with everyone gawking at me, I decided to break the silence. The first thing that came to mind was the obvious question, "How long have you all been standing there?"

"For as long as you have," Brendan responded.

Nate added, "We followed you here because you were acting weird and we were worried about you."

"I see," I said, clearing my throat. "Could you explain to me how I was acting?"

"Well," said Paul, "You didn't answer any of us when we called to you. You walked out of the cabin without saying a word and you were staring into space."

"Yeah," Nate agreed, "and then we followed you here. You stopped at the hill where this cave is."

Brendan threw in, "And you started singing, which sounded really good by the way. Next you started talking to someone, but it did not seem as though it was to us."

"We kept saying your name," Nate continued, "but you ignored us. Don't you remember any of that?"

At that point it seemed the easiest explanation was to tell the truth. Not that I wanted to keep it from them, but I did not know whether they would believe me or not. "Well guys, I'm not sure if you will believe this, but here goes."

I told them everything. About the vision, or whatever it was. How it started, and every detail, not leaving anything out. The only thing I avoided mentioning was that something similar had happened to me before, because I did not wish to embarrass Brendan.

After I finished recounting the story, there was a mortifying silence which I hoped someone would break as soon as possible. Did they believe me? Did they think I had gone mad?

"Wow!" it was Nate who finally spoke. "That's incredible. The man you saw must have been the hermit."

"Yeah, I was thinking the same thing," I said, relieved that at least my brother believed me.

"You know what this means, guys?" Nate asked Brendan and Paul.

"Don't say it," I warned, having a good idea what he meant, and not wanting him to put me on a pedestal by perceiving me as a hallow.

"Alright then," Nate said, "I won't say it. But everyone knows it's true."

I rolled my eyes at Nate while Brendan started to investigate the cave. The rest of us joined him, figuring it was a good idea.

"I believe you too," Brendan told me as he strolled around a few mounds of snow almost as tall as himself.

"Thank you," I said, grateful that at least two of my three companions did not think I had lost my mind. Considering Paul's silence on the matter, at least until he told me otherwise, I could only conclude that he did not buy my story. I didn't really want to ask him in case he accused me of having gone mad.

The cave was almost knee deep in snow, which probably had blown in from the storm the other night. Brendan started to brush the snow off one of the knolls he had been investigating.

"What are you doing?" I asked, thinking it seemed like an odd thing to waste time on. Then I remembered that I was the one who was having massive hallucinations. So, who was I to say what was weird?

"I think there maybe something under these banks of snow," Brendan replied, as a face became visible under the snow while it was being removed.

Thinking now that it might be a person, we all pitched in to get all the snow off. It ended up being a statue of the Blessed Virgin Mary.

"I think," Brendan said, "that the hermit might have set these statues up in here as a Nativity set."

"How did you know?" I asked him as I kissed Mary on the forehead.

Brendan, Nate, and then Paul, following my lead did the same.

"Well," Brendan answered. "Based on the vision you had, it seemed as if the Holy Family was here. I figured that maybe there would be some kind of representation of it in real life. Blessed statues and pictures are windows into Heaven. So, I considered what your vision was trying to show us."

"Really?" asked Nate. "That's amazing. I never thought of that."

"Neither did I," I admitted.

"Where did you learn all that stuff?" asked Paul, as he began to brush off the snow from the next hill of snow.

"From a book about sacred statues," Brendan responded without even a hint of superiority complex in his voice.

The Blessed Virgin Mary, St. Joseph, the three Kings, the baby Jesus in a trough, and three shepherds had all been unveiled and reverently kissed. One of the shepherd statues looked remarkably similar to the child I saw carrying the lamb in my vision. But I found that consoling rather than creepy.

Only one heap of snow remained uncovered. We couldn't figure out who it might be. As we had been working, we had each guessed the identity of every single next statue to be revealed and none of us got even one right. Other than the baby Jesus, that is. But what was left? Was there someone belonging to the Nativity scene I could not remember? Well, only one way to find out.

Carefully each of us helped brush off the snow until the statue of a contented-looking old man in a kneeling position was revealed. It looked strangely similar to the old man in my vision. Oddly enough, this statue also seemed much more life-like compared to the others. It was not that the other statues were not masterpieces, but you could tell they were made of resin. This one seemed out of place and I still couldn't figure out which character it was supposed to represent.

Then it was as if we all figured it out at the same time. The four of us fell backwards in shock. It was obvious now that though he was not a statue he did not seem to be what you would expect from a dead body. There was no stench, the face was smiling sincerely, and he was still kneeling with his hands crossed against his chest. Why did he not fall over when he died?

"Maybe he froze to death," suggested Nate in answer to the unspoken question.

Paul said, "You wouldn't think that he'd smile in his last moments if he froze though. That would likely be too painful a death for anybody to die looking happy."

Brendan crawled up to the deceased hermit. We cringed as he slowly moved his finger towards the dead man's hand until finally it made contact. "He's not cold," he exclaimed. Then Brendan put his finger against the neck. "His hand felt as if it was alive, but he has no pulse. Weird."

"That doesn't make any sense," said Paul. "He has to be cold. He was covered in snow."

"You are welcome to touch the stiff yourself if you want to prove him wrong," I taunted Paul.

"I wouldn't dream of it," Paul quickly assured me. "The man is dead. That's good enough for me. And Brendan, you should wash your hands as soon as possible after touching a dead person."

"I think this guy is a Saint," said Nate.

"What do you mean?" I asked.

"Well, though it does not happen with all Saints, there have been occasions where a miracle occurs with the dead body of one and it doesn't rot. They call it being incorruptible if I remember correctly."

"Wait a second," I said. "You're telling me that there are bodies out there that have never rotted and which can be seen by other people?"

"Absolutely," Nate confirmed. "There are even some on display in shrines for visiting pilgrims to revere. It points towards the future resurrection."

"Why did you never tell me? That's a miracle that people can actually see. That's what I've been looking for, to ease my doubts about the afterlife."

"I thought you knew," Nate answered. "There are tons of miracles out there that people can see, but even so still continue to doubt. I guess I thought you doubted for other reasons."

I wasn't going to question my brother's knowledge about Saints, since that was an obsession of his next only to athleticism. "That's amazing. Look, you've got to tell me all about this stuff sometime. I want to know everything." Who knew? The answers I was seeking on our journey might have been right in front of me the whole time.

"Anytime you want, Tommy," said Nate.

"There's no way that this is a miracle," said Paul. "I'm sure it can be explained somehow."

"See what I mean?" Nate whispered to me.

"What should we do?" asked Brendan. "The ground is too cold to bury him. We should report his death, but not until after the trip is over. I'm sure it'll be fine to leave him here for now."

"What if an animal comes along though?" I said. "We've got to do something, but I don't feel comfortable taking him back to the cabin with us."

"I know what," Brendan said, excited to have come up with an idea. "Let's build a thick wall of snow in front of the cave as a barrier so that no animal can come in. That should keep him safe for now as long as the snow doesn't melt."

"Good idea," Paul said.

"Might as well get started," Nate said as he walked out of the cave.

The rest of us followed him out and worked as fast as we could, building the wall, so that we could get back to the lodge.

Chapter 15

Pretending to Jog

Brendan, Nate, Paul, and I sat in front of the fireplace getting warm after having built the snow wall for the cave. Paul stared calmly at the fire in deep thought. Brendan in contrast was at the edge of his chair, tightly gripping the arms and looking as if he were going to bounce out of the seat at any moment. His usual smile was usual no longer but seemed forced. Though he gave me great concern, I did not want to single him out by asking how he was holding up. Nate alone seemed his usual happy self and was drinking something from a mug.

I wanted to discuss with everyone how to proceed with the rest of the trip but not without first hearing their suggestions. I was considering advising that we head home the next day since we did not have a very good plan of what to do. Keeping in mind how bad that snowstorm had been, I was concerned that we might be caught in another one if we tried to go on. Yet knowing how much Brendan had been looking forward to the journey, I hated to cause him grief by cutting it short. If I could only figure out how to put my advice tactfully, it might make the idea easier to accept.

Annoyingly my ponderings were interrupted. Nate was making the kind of strange noises and expressions that suggested he did not like the taste of what he was drinking. He hummed at times, perhaps to distract himself from thinking of his taste buds' discomfort. And then he made sounds similar to patients when doctors ask them to stick out their tongue and say 'ah'.

Curious about all the commotion, I looked over at him and saw a mug lifted to his face. As he lowered the cup, it was hard to restrain my laughter at the sight of the white powdery residue that remained all over the lower part of his face.

"What on earth are you drinking. . .or eating?" I laughed.

Nate tried to speak, but coughed at his first attempt and sent a tiny white cloud of dust into the air. Then he tried again, explaining, "It's protein powder mixed with water. This cottage has no blender, so I had to make do with what I had."

"Walk-er!" I said, hardly able to believe that he went to the trouble of packing protein powder for the trip.

"What did you call me?" asked Nate.

"I didn't call you anything. 'Walk-er!' is an old expression that means 'I can't believe what I am hearing'. It's from my favorite Xmas movie. 'A Christmas Carol'—the 1950's version."

"Oh, ok," Nate said. "But how else am I supposed to get enough protein?"

"I think there is a difference between enough protein and the surplus you're consuming."

"We'll just have to disagree to agree then."

"No, it's 'agree to disagree'."

"Good to know. Anyway, do any of you want to join me for a quick jog after I finish this protein shake? I didn't get a chance to do my run today. I want to do it before it gets dark, but I'm still scared to go out by myself. I don't know the area."

Brendan, who had been listening, leaped out of his chair and yelled, "That's a great idea! Let's get going."

"I want to finish my drink first," said Nate.

"Ok," Brendan said and sank back down into his chair.

"I'll come too," I put in, worrying that the two of them might get lost. "Not sure if I will be able to keep up though." I was only half joking. Nate was either a much slower jogger than he thought, or else was in denial.

"I'll keep it slow today," Nate reassured me.

"I'll look after the fire," Paul said. "Don't be too long though. I am not taking my eyes off this fire until I catch the prankster who keeps fueling it behind our backs."

The wind was beginning to die down a bit, exhausted from its long-suffering efforts earlier in the day. And the sun was making preparations to change shifts with the moon and stars, fatigued by a hard day's work.

For some reason it did not occur to me that winter jogging would be more difficult than in the summer. To begin with I did not enjoy the activity, but all the extra layers of clothes would make it a grievance. The one thing I did prefer was the cold air which felt refreshing compared to going for a run in other seasons.

Although he was short of breath, Brendan's sincere smile had returned. He kept a steady pace and showed no signs of wanting to quit, even though he was panting as much as I was.

My pace was less sturdy. For a few seconds I would slow down then speed up, trying my best to keep up with my brother. Nate's charade did not appear capable of long-sufferance. He was sprinting rather than trotting, perhaps to make his usual slow speed seem higher. He had no reason that I could tell to impress me, but apparently, he felt otherwise. I did not wish to see Nate embarrass himself but was glad when signs appeared that he was ready to slow down. One thing I hated worse than jogging was fast-paced running.

We had only been running for a few minutes when Nate's cut-off point for the length of time that he could sprint had been reached. He slowed down so quickly that I had to stop abruptly to avoid running into him. Now he was making the motions of jogging yet was moving slower than even his average walking speed. *Something must be wrong.*

Nate abruptly stopped pretending to jog and stood completely still, leaning over with his hands on his knees.

"What's wrong?" asked Brendan.

I squatted down in front of Nate and asked, "Is everything okay?"

Without warning Nate vomited all over me. My jacket was covered in the repulsive puke. The odor was so sickening I could almost taste it. Which made me extra grateful that it had not made its way into my mouth. My first reaction to seeing someone bring up was to gag myself until I spewed up the revolting contents of my own stomach. Already I could feel the gag reflexes starting, but this time worried as I was about my brother, I made a great effort and managed to control them. I needed to distract myself quickly to avoid the inevitable second heaving.

I deliberately fell backwards into the snow, hoping that if my head was no longer directly above the smell the odor would stop nauseating me. Frantically I began burying my body in snow until I had a thick layer coating me. Then I used it to brush off the disgusting upchuck from my coat. Nothing is more gross than being covered in filth.

Ghastly as I felt having been the target of horrifying stomach goo, I felt just as wretched because I realized that I should have been tending my brother. Though I knew I would be useless to help Nate if I did not clean myself up first, I still felt terrible and selfish for having neglected him.

I was grateful to find Brendan had been fulfilling my role while I was busy having a fit in the snow. He had placed his hand on Nate's back, telling him that everything was okay and to let it all come out.

That reminded me to roll over a few times so I would no longer be in the front lines if Nate had more ammo. As I began the process of covering my jacket with snow for the third time to try and remove any remains of Nate's toxic waste, other than the thin soaked-in layer which could only be destroyed by a wash cycle or incinerator, I tried to give words of comfort to my brother. "Please don't take any of that personally, Nate."

I stood up, not daring to look back at the horrendous filthy snow or the puke Angel I had likely made from getting clean in it. Could it pass for contemporary art? "That wasn't your fault, okay?" I added to Nate. "I'm not mad. I just can't stand vomit; you know what I mean? —so I freaked out a little . . . okay, a lot."

"I'm not offended," Nate Mumbled, kneeling on the ground with his head down. "I'm so sorry, Tommy."

"Don't worry," I reassured him, knowing that such words were likely futile when my actions only moments ago gave the opposite impression. "I can't blame you for getting sick, now can I?"

"No," Nate replied. "But I'm still sorry that I chucked my putrid bio-hazard all over you."

"Well, being ill has not affected your sense of humor," said Brendan. "Tell us what happened though."

"I was getting a cramp while running, but I kept on through the pain. I realized that it was not a normal cramp because my stomach had a heart-beat. It felt like a revolution was building up in there. Then I started to feel nauseous. I tried to run through that too, but my head felt heavy, the ground began spinning and I was losing my balance. I had to slow down to stop myself from falling. I felt that I needed to sit down for a second, but before I could, the captives broke out of their prison."

He was trying to be funny but I had a feeling that Nate was also using metaphors for my benefit so that I would be less grossed out by the description. Wondering if the protein was to blame, I insisted, "You've got to promise me something, Nate."

"What's that?"

"You've got to stop using the protein powder. Please!"

Nate looked at me without saying a word. It was as though he did not want to say no to me, yet also had no interest in agreeing.

"Look," I added. "When we get home, we'll talk to Mom and Dad and figure out a proper workout routine for you and a food plan—but one that's more appropriate to your age and weak complexion. Does that sound good?"

"Really?" Nate asked, excited for a moment until he remembered that he felt sick. "Yes, that would be awesome. Though I don't know what you mean about 'weak complexion.' But the rest of it sounds great. Thank you."

"Glad to help. I should have figured out something sooner anyway, instead of simply telling you not to eat protein powder. And if you want, I'll even jog with you in the mornings. Sometimes."

"Wow!" Nate responded. "That would be great. Thanks so much."

"Don't mention it," I said, cringing at the idea of running in the early morning, but glad at the same time to help my brother out. "Do you think you are able to walk back?"

Nate tried to stand up then put his hands on the ground and sat back down. "I'm too dizzy to stand."

Putting his hand on Nate's forehead, Brendan said, "I think he has a fever."

He took Nate's arm and placed it around his own shoulder, and I followed suit putting Nate's other arm around my shoulder—letting him lean on us while we headed back to the cabin.

We put Nate in bed in one of the bedrooms and told him to shout if he needed anything. Paul, Brendan, and I were sitting in front of the fireplace again, discussing what to do.

"So, we're all in agreement that we have to go back," said Paul, "since we can't risk Nate's health deteriorating any more, especially when it comes to chancing pneumonia."

"The problem," I explained, "is that if we do head back, it is almost a guarantee that Nate will get sicker while we're outside in the cold. And we can't leave him here by himself to go and get help, in case he needs us for something."

Paul scratched his chin for a moment then suggested, "I will head back and get help. You guys stay here with Nate to wait for assistance. Any objections?" No one said anything, and Paul continued, "Alright it's settled then. I'll head out first thing in the morning."

"Thanks, Paul," I said. "That is very good of you."

"You guys would likely get lost if you went out on your own," Paul scoffed, making me wonder if he was as uneasy as I was when it came to receiving compliments.

"That's true," I laughed scratching the back of my neck.

Brendan had not said much during the discussion, so I turned to him and said, "I'm sorry for cutting our trip short. I know how much it meant to you."

"It's alright," Brendan assured me. "I understand. It's unfortunate. But I would not want to risk Nate's health even if you suggested it. These things happen."

"Thank you for understanding," I said. "I'll make it up to you some-how, okay?"

Brendan nodded, but looked distant. He was always a little absent-minded, but this time he seemed deep in thought, making me wonder if the decision was bothering him more then he let on.

Chapter 16

Crying over Spilt Milk & Cereal

Feeling my shoulder gently nudged, I woke up all of a sudden then quickly realized that it must have been a dream. The daylight was beginning to come out but the night had not yet completed its cycle, so it was still a little dark. Where was I though? I did not recognize my surroundings. I was lying on a wooden floor in an improvised bed poorly made of a few sheets and comforters. An actual bed stood by my right side.

Finally, I remembered. I had set up camp for the night in Nate's temporary room in the cabin in case he needed anything during his illness, and so he would not be scared by finding himself alone. More likely it was so that I did not worry about him as much. At peace once more with my surroundings and feeling rather drowsy, I closed my heavy eyelids again and drifted back to sleep.

Another prod on the shoulder woke me up again. This time I did not bother opening my eyes, trusting that it was another dream. But did I ever have the same dream twice? The wind outside was howling loudly, making me worry about Paul heading off on his own. I wondered if he had left yet. I knew that I would probably spend the whole day concerned about everyone. I would annoy Nate by tending him like an overbearing Mother. I foresaw also distressing myself over whether Paul was safe in the bad weather. And most of the remaining time I expected to fuss over how disappointed Brendan must be in me for cancelling the remainder of the trip. I could not forget either to make room for one more thing to agonize about—how all our parents would react when we were taken home.

But I needed a lot of energy for all that anxiety and hoped a few more minutes of sleep would provide it. Nodding off again, I felt my shoulder poked a third time. My eyes jolted open and I realized that this time I could not be dreaming.

Immediately I was aware of a figure overshadowing me and I was about to scream—but I couldn't. I had become paralyzed with fear.

"Don't be afraid," the figure said quietly.

I recognized that voice. But from where? I saw it was a young man, covered by a charcoal shaded cape which was fastened around his neck by a cross-shaped pin. He had a glowing youthful face with a stern yet tender expression in his eyes. Then I remembered. It was the Eagle Scout who had helped us the other night. He was resting on his knees beside me to my left and holding a letter in his hand.

"Who are you?" I asked, already much less fretful about my safety. I was still a little frightened though that the Scout had come into the lodge without knocking, but I did not feel as if he meant me any harm. "And what are you doing here?" I added.

"I'm a friend," the Scout said as he handed me the envelope he was holding.

I clicked on my flashlight which I always kept beside me while sleeping, because I hated the idea of no longer being allowed to have a night-light by my parents. The note was sealed and addressed to me but without a stamp or return address. I stood up in the tangle of my sorry attempt at a bed and opened the memo, in which I found the following message:

BRENDAN'S LETTER TO TOMMY:

January 7th, 1998

Dear Tommy,

There is something I have wanted to tell you but was not able to do out fear that you would no longer wish to be friends with me. Though such a worry makes no difference now, I still feel I owe it to you to tell you the whole truth; yet from lack of courage on my part I do not find I can do it in person, so instead I have decided to write this letter for your eyes only.

First, I wanted to say that though we have not known each other long, you have been the best friend that I have ever had, and much more than I deserve. I've prayed my whole life for God to send me a friend, and I believe you are the answer to that prayer. Whatever happens, I would not trade that for the world. It has been a pleasure to know you and I am very grateful for the time we have spent together.

I have especially enjoyed this trip and getting to know the others, in particular your brother, Nate. I have no siblings, so I have come to see him in a short time as my younger brother as well. And though I am not sure if Paul likes me very much, I am glad to have come to know him a little too.

Now on to the hard part. I told you before that I am a bad kid and I know you don't believe me. If you did, a good kid like you would never have hung out with me in the first place. That is the main reason that I have kept so much of what I am now going to say from you; not because of lack of trust. I have also chafed about overburdening you when you have so many problems of your own. The truth is that I don't want to be bad, nor have ever wanted to be. It seems to be my nature however. For as long as I can remember. I hope though that your good influence has had a positive impact on my behavior.

One of my earliest memories—I don't remember how old I was—is of the first time that I was caught attention-seeking. Mom and Dad were sitting on the couch watching television. I was running around the room making airplane noises, trying to get them to look at me. I know now how selfish it was of me. If I wanted their attention, all I had to do was sit beside them and watch TV. Instead, I was jealous of the television and wanted their complete attention for myself.

Mom and Dad saw through my ploy and ignored me. At one point I tripped and fell face first into the corner of the room. I started crying. That got my parents very upset. Mom yelled at me. That was the first memory I have of her calling me a little attention-seeker. I didn't fall against the wall on purpose, but it was like the 'crying wolf' scenario. If I hadn't been seeking my parents' attention to begin with, they would not have had any reason to falsely accuse me of it over an innocent accident.

Dad used to tell me that if I wanted his attention, I should bring him a beer from the fridge. So, I brought him many beers and each time it would get me a smile from him. Mom's attention was not so easy to gain. I remember her telling me that I had been demanding attention from the moment I was born, when I cried my eyes out. I sometimes think that she secretly wishes I never had been born.

I also remember the first time Dad punished me. I was eating cheerios for dinner, one of my favorite and frequent meals, and knocked the bowl onto the floor. It was an accident, but I should have been more careful. It's not as if I could make cereal myself at that young age, so I should have shown myself more grateful for the effort he put into feeding me. I got let off easily though.

He only slapped me a few times across the face. For wasting all that food, I deserved far worse.

And Mom also hit me after Dad told her to clean up the mess I had made. I got off lightly with only a black eye. It started off with my getting punished only occasionally—maybe once a week at most. But I never learned my lesson and became clumsier. So out of necessity, the punishments became more frequent.

Eventually, I was being punished multiple times a day. After much experience, Mom and Dad stopped hitting my face to avoid misunderstandings that could occur from the reactions of those who saw the marks but did not know how much a problem child I was.

I became quite content with this arrangement. I even started to get into trouble on purpose sometimes, because it got me the attention I always wanted at home. Over time the feeling grew from one of contentment to actually being fond of the beatings, for they reminded me how much my parents must care about me. Sometimes Mom and Dad would be half-hearted in their punishments, at other times more severe. During the latter, I would often go off into my own little world to try and escape the pain.

Since I could not be trusted to behave, Dad came up with the brilliant idea of punishment and reward. If I behaved too poorly during the day, I would have to sleep in a cage with only Scripture to read. And if I made too much noise crying while I was locked up, he and Mom would take away my urine basin. And it worked. I sobbed a lot less. Unfortunately, the improvement in behavior was not enough to satisfy them. I have been told by that friendly Scout that it is okay to get sad and cry, and to not hold back my tears. I appreciated his advice. But my parents hate my crying and I need to try and please them so that they will want me around.

Because of my terrible conduct, Dad finally left us. I tried twice as hard to change then, so that he would come back, but to no avail. Mom punished me twice as hard to make up for his absence. I deserved it. If it were not for my deportment being so deplorable, he would still have been there for her.

I missed Dad so much. That's when I started hurting myself. I missed being beaten by Dad, so I attempted to beat myself to remind me of him. But it wasn't the same. Needing something more severe, I began to cut myself. And learning from my parents not to leave visible markings, I only injured the bottom of my foot so that no one would know the difference.

Though I know it is wrong to attention-seek, I find that I can't help myself. It is now so commonplace that Mom doesn't notice anymore. Remember when I told you that I ran away for three days, and you took me back home? Well Mom didn't notice that I was missing. Or else she was aware of it and did not care. I am such an awful child that Mom prefers it when I am gone.

She did not even open the note I left her. Perhaps this is a new strategy of hers. Maybe she thinks that if she does not pay heed to my nonsense, I will be less likely to behave in such a ridiculous way.

Anyway, now that you know the truth about what a disgraceful person I am, I doubt you will want to continue our friendship. But I couldn't keep it from you anymore because I felt as if I was not being honest with you. Either way, I am happy to have met you and to have spent what little time we had together.

Even though you are ending the trip early, I am happy you came this far with me. It would not have been the same without you. I am not resentful. I understand why you must go home but I am not ready to go back yet myself. I did not tell you before, but I have not been able to get Mom to wake up. So, unless, I can find St. Nicholas and ask him to bring my Dad back and to fix my Mom, I might not have a home left to go back to. So, I will continue this journey on my own in hope of finding St. Nick. And if he can't bring my Dad back or help Mom, perhaps he can take me to Heaven instead, God willing. I'll put in a good word for all of you.

I am leaving during the night because I do not think I could bear to say goodbye in person. I wish you guys all the best. Get home safely. And if I don't make it back from this trip, I hope you have a good life. Take good care of Nate. Remember not to worry so much about what you can't control, and to live every moment in gratitude and peace. God bless you.

Your true friend,
Brendan Mascent

P.S. I leave all my Frightful Sight books and any other novels I have to you.

In a terrible state of mind, I folded the letter up and replaced it in the envelope, holding it close to my chest for a moment while I thought about what to do. I had no idea that Brendan's home life was that bad. Sure, the sound of his Mom's voice calling to him scared me, but I figured that I had imagined it to be worse than it was. All Moms are scary when mad. I did know his Dad had left and that he missed him so terribly. I would never have guessed though that both Brendan's parents had been beating him all his life. He did not even seem to realize that it's wrong or abnormal for parents to treat their children that way. The poor guy thought it his own fault. I feel guilty that I failed to realize my friend was going through such troubles. But enough of beating myself up. I needed to figure out how I could fix the situation.

The Scout was no longer there. He must have left quietly while I read the letter. I had not even noticed him get up to leave. But how did he know about the letter that Brendan wrote me? He must've been the one coming in and adding fuel to the fireplace. Perhaps he saw the note then and thought it best to bring it to me. Yet the envelope was sealed. So how could he have known the urgency of the message? I would have to think about that later. For now, I needed to focus on what to do.

I got up from my makeshift bed to check if Paul had already left and found that he had. I wished the Scout had not gone because I could really have used his help. I did not even know his name to try and call out to him with in case he was still close by. With neither Paul nor the Scout at hand, I had no one to leave with Nate who was still in bed with the fever. Obviously, I could not take Nate with me without making his condition worse.

Yet could I bear to leave Brendan to his demise? I did not think he could survive out there in the cold on his own. *What should I do?* Even if I found him, would I be able to convince him to come back with us? No matter what I did it seemed that I would be causing someone I cared about dire harm.

Why had I not talked to Brendan last night and made sure he was okay? If I had I could have avoided this entire mess. I did ask him, but I should have been more straightforward in light of his misery of self-harm. No, I was distracting myself again. I needed to figure something out and quickly.

Feeling as if I had no choice, even though I would have preferred to let him rest longer, I woke Nate. After making sure that he was alright, I explained the situation to him the best I could, wondering if he had any ideas to suggest.

"It's okay, Tommy," Nate reassured me. "My guardian Angel will look after me. Go and find Brendan. I'll be fine."

Nate's sickness was worse than I thought. He was becoming delirious. Above Nate's head on the wall behind his bed was hanging a picture of an Angel. The illustration showed the Angel, a candle in one hand and the other covering his own heart, standing guard beside a small sleeping child. The Angel's eyes gazed upward towards Heaven and he had a sword and sheath strapped around his waist. Nate must have been confusing the painting with reality, and that was not a good sign.

I went to the kitchen to get him a cup of water, thinking that perhaps dehydration was causing his hysteria. On the way, I began to pray desperately, not knowing how to handle this dire situation—a predicament in which I risked both my brother and my friend's safety. "God, please help me. Show me what I should do. By the merits and prayers of the Saint who lived here and by the Passion and death of Christ, please aid me. Let Brendan and Nate be okay. And protect Paul on his way to get us help." Then I prayed the Hail Mary until I got back to Nate's room with the glass of water.

My hand trembled and I nearly dropped the glass in shock as I entered the room. An Angel with two wings, shaped like a heart when together, was standing at the right side of Nate, looking exactly the same as the one in the icon on the wall. Was I now seeing things as well, from too much stress? I had experienced delusions before but never this vivid.

Then I realized, did I not just pray and ask for assistance? Now, was I doubting what was right before my eyes? I knew I should not seek after signs or wonders but this was different. I needed to give what I was seeing the benefit of the doubt, at least in a situation where no other explanation was likely.

My heart failed for fear. I dared not approach the Angel who was twice my size, so I spoke to Nate from the doorway. "Listen, Nate. Thanks for your understanding earlier. I'm going to leave for a bit to go and help Brendan. I am entrusting your safety, while I'm gone, to the Angel of God you mentioned. I just have to write a note first in case Paul gets back before me, okay?"

"Don't worry about that," Nate assured me. "I'll take care of the note. I've got to do something to feel useful while I'm staying in bed and everyone else is helping. And I'll pray while you're gone that Heaven will help the three of you return safely."

"Thank you, Nate. That means a lot to me."

"Can you leave me the water though before you go? I'm quite thirsty."

"Sure," I said as I approached the bed very slowly, trying my best to hide the terror that made my flesh tremble, and not to look at the Angel.

Nate laughed. "You don't have to be afraid of him you know? He knows that you won't harm me."

That was not quite true unfortunately. It was my fault that Nate got sick in the first place through my accidentally enticing him to go on this journey in the middle of winter. So even if I did not do it intentionally, I felt guilty about it.

Nate seized the water from my hand and looked as if he was about to chug it. "Wait," I insisted. "I know that you are parched but it is important that you sip that slowly since you are still sick."

"Okay," Nate responded, "I promise I will."

"Thank you. Also, there is a flashlight and a crowbar beside your bed where I was sleeping if you need them for extra protection."

"Walk-er!" Nate tried to yell causing himself to cough.

I smiled, but was beginning to regret teaching Nate that expression, worrying that he would make me tired of it by overusing it.

"Now, get going," Nate urged me, sensing that I was stalling from not wanting to leave him there. "I'll be fine."

I felt a terrible older brother for doing so, but I took his advice and headed out, snatching my winter coat from where it was drying by the fireplace as I went. I had not noticed before, but the icon of St. Nicholas was no longer hanging above the fireplace. There was no time to think about that now however. Having wasted too much time already, I hastened out the door.

Chapter 17

Buried in Snow

The wind wailed throughout the woods like a frantic Mother searching for her lost children. Having combed the trees for about an hour, I began to wonder if Brendan would even be able to hear me calling over the volume of the gale. Likewise, would I be able to pick up his voice if he were calling to me? I was losing hope of finding him. He could be anywhere—even miles away from me. But I had to keep looking.

What a terrible friend I was for not keeping a closer eye on Brendan. This could all have been prevented had I been more careful about him in his time of need. Yet I could not back track. I could only try to do the best I could manage for him now if it were not too late.

I was grateful to be wearing a scarf but wondered whether it was doing me more harm than good. After breathing into it for so long, the water from my breath had frozen in it and I could now feel the icy scarf sharply against my face and neck. It felt like being wrapped in frozen cardboard. Yet I was afraid to take the scarf off in case the wind felt worse without it.

Not having any success on my own, I remembered how God had answered my prayer earlier, and wondered if he would help me find my friend. I prayed as I continued to walk. "God, Brendan needs my help. But I feel useless. I have no idea where he is or how to find him. I don't know what to do. Please don't let me lose my friend. By the merits of the hermit who lived in the cabin and by the Precious Blood of Christ, please help us." I then repeated the Hail Mary until I could figure out what to do.

The entire time I had been out in the woods I had not seen a single animal—perhaps they had given up finding food for the day. Whatever the reason, it caused the forest to feel far lonelier. The bleak grey tone of the sky did not help either. Praying however reminded me that there was someone watching over us, even though invisible. With that invisible companion I was never truly alone whatever my fluctuating moods.

Suddenly I felt like an idiot for not realizing where Brendan had likely gone. I headed towards the cave of the nativity set and the dead hermit. Brendan probably took the St. Nick picture there because of Nate's previous remark about religious images being a portal into Heaven. Perhaps he thought that by bringing the St. Nicholas icon to the site where the hermit had met St. Joseph and then died, it would increase his chances of having a vision. I hoped my supposition was correct, otherwise I didn't think I would ever be able to find him. *Please God, don't let me be too late.*

I finally arrived at the lifeless knoll. And I noticed a small void had been made through the snow wall which we built as a barrier in front of the desolate chamber. It seemed my hunch was right. Or perhaps an animal had dug through the barrier. There was only one way to find out. The hill was a lot harder to climb than I remembered. Maybe I was more exhausted than I thought from all the searching.

Finally reaching the top, I peeked through the narrow opening in nature's tomb, hoping that I would not see any signs of a dangerous animal. Gratefully I saw none. Mustering up all my bravery, I crawled through the opening of the catacomb in desperate hope that I would not be confronted by an unfriendly bear without any way to escape.

As I entered the abyss my mood became ecstatic. At least for a moment. My friend was okay. Or, he was there anyway. Brendan was sitting down, leaning against the wall on the right side of the cave. Was he okay? His jacket and other winter outer layers were sitting beside him. And his eyes were closed. He must've been freezing. Or, God forbid was he dead?

I ran over to him and picked up his jacket. "Hey Brendan," I said as I tried to hand him his coat, "Are you okay?"

He opened his eyes which were glazed over, and he needed to make a great effort to speak. "I feel hot . . . fever," he managed to get out.

"Stop kidding around," I chastised him. "This is serious. Put your coat back on. How long has it been off?"

Brendan shut his eyes again then reopened them with a jolt when I shook him. Slowly he explained, "Re-cent-ly . . . over-hea-ting. Nate?"

Was he delirious from the cold?

"No, it's me Tommy," I said putting my hand on Brendan's forehead to check his temperature.

"Right," Brendan laughed. "Tooth-fairy!"

He was speaking nonsense. That was not a good sign. "Brendan," I said fretfully, "your forehead isn't warm—it's like ice. Let's get this jacket back on you, okay? You're just going to have to trust me."

I helped Brendan away from the icy cavern wall and tried to assist him back into his jacket, but he cringed whenever I attempted to get his arms into the sleeves. Not knowing what else to do, I wrapped the coat around his body and arms and then zipped it up. I placed his toque and scarf back on as well. Worried about how badly the hypothermia seemed to affect him, I feared that his outer clothing would not be enough to get him warm. Removing my own jacket, I also wrapped it around Brendan temporarily, figuring that I could stand the cold for a few minutes or so. I hoped that five minutes with an extra layer would allow him to regain some body heat.

"Heat-stroke," Brendan complained with great strain in his voice.

"You'll be fine," I said as I crossed my arms and shivered. Would he be though? I was not so sure. His feeling that he was overheating in this bitter cold was alarming. I was grateful that thanks to the barrier there was no wind in the cave other than a light draft from the hole. It was much colder outside with the wind-chill.

What should I do? Because it was colder outside than in it would be difficult to take Brendan back to the cabin. Yet staying in the cave would not necessarily buy him much extra time. He likely would not be able to walk and I would have to carry him, which would slow me down tremendously. But what else could I do? We could either stay in the cave and slowly freeze to death or try to head back to the cabin—which would at least give us a fighting chance.

Unexpectedly, a thought flashed through my mind. Why had it not occurred to me sooner? My parents once told Nate and me that if you are ever stuck somewhere in the winter, bury yourself in snow because of the insulating effect it has. If I covered Brendan in snow for half an hour or so, his body temperature might become stable enough to make the journey. Then I could help him more when we got to the warm cabin.

"Brendan," I said, "lie down on your back. I'm going to bury you in snow, okay?"

"Game?" Brendan asked as he stretched out.

"Sure is," I pretended, hoping it would make him participate with less hassle. My arms were getting very numb, but I managed with a great effort to cover him in a thick layer of snow, leaving only his face visible.

Then I proceeded to try and bury myself in a mound of snow too, so that I could stay warm while giving Brendan more time with the extra coat. Every little bit might have made a difference. Yet I was not making much progress. Oh no. I was in trouble. My arms had lost all dexterity. I knew they were getting numb, but I did not realize how soon all feeling in them would be gone. This was bad. Even if I were able to get my coat back from Brendan, I could no longer put it on. *It's not very helpful to save a friend if by doing so you bring about your own destruction.* How careless of me. And if I died there, then Brendan's life would not really be saved anyway. What had I done? I'd killed us both. And likely my brother too, if I could never get back to him, for I was not sure how long that Angel would stay at his side. My only consolation I suppose was the thought that I would die beside my friend. But enough of giving up. I needed to come up with a plan quickly while my mind was still warm enough to work. But nothing at all was coming to me.

Using only my legs I crawled as close to Brendan as I could. Doing my best to recite the Hail Mary again with chattering teeth, I hoped it would offer comfort to Brendan as well as console me. I could use all the peace of mind I could get. How painful was freezing to death going to be? If getting dog-sick cold was awful, freezing had to be worse. Shivering quite violently now, I eventually began to feel exhausted and reluctantly shut my eyes. *It would only be for a moment,* I told myself.

The distinct crackling of fire awoke me. I was covered in many layers of woolen blanket and there was a small fire a few meters to my right which seemed to have warmed the cave quite nicely—or maybe it was the blankets. A surge of heat traveled through my arms and body and I was able to move my fingers a little when I tested them to see if my dexterity was returning.

Brendan was still beside me, but now covered in blankets instead of snow. Perhaps the snow burial worked, and he had become warm enough to start a fire. "Brendan," I whispered, checking to see if he was awake. He did not answer. He must've still been exhausted from hypothermia. Or at least I hoped that was why he did not answer. I could not bear to think of the alternative. I guessed it was not Brendan after all. But if he did not wake up to start the fire, then who did? And who gave us all these blankets?

"He's still resting," said a stern yet friendly voice.

Could it be? Yes, the Eagle Scout had found us. Thank God. He must have been the one who started the fire and brought us the blankets.

"Come and sit by the fire with me for a moment," said the Scout, offering me back my jacket which he was holding in his hand.

I took off the thick layer of blankets, got up, and went to retrieve my coat. Putting it back on, I said, "Thank you so much for saving us. We were goners for sure."

The Scout handed me a cup of hot cocoa as I sat beside him at the fire. "Thanks," I told him again, as I gladly accepted the much-needed hot beverage. I took a careful first sip to see if it would burn me. The temperature was perfect—hot enough to warm me up yet not so calid as to burn my lips.

"That was a very charitable thing you did," the Scout said.

"What do you mean?" I asked.

"You wanted to help your friend so badly that you put your own life in danger."

"Yes," I acknowledged, "but look what good it did. I was not able to help him or me. I nearly got us both killed by my imprudence."

"Charity never goes unnoticed by God or unrewarded, my friend. Even when it seems to do no good, every deed is accounted for—both good and bad."

"You really think so?" I asked, hoping that it was true for all my good deeds, but equally worrying if it was true for my many bad ones.

"I know that it is true. I am incapable of telling a lie."

I laughed. "The Scouts honor code, right? I don't suppose you're willing to give me your name, now that you have saved us several times?"

"I have a name," answered the Scout. "But I am not permitted to give it. My kind is currently bound by the keys of St. Peter to keep their names hidden from men, except for three of us."

The more he spoke the more mysterious this Scout seemed to get. Even when I tried to learn more about him, he seemed to become more enveloped in cloud. "There are three more of you around?" I asked.

"Yes," he responded. "Michael, Gabriel, and Raphael. Actually, there are plenty of us, but they are the only ones who can reveal their names."

I had no idea that Scouts had such strange rules. Perhaps it was so that they could remain anonymous and not gloat over their good deeds.

"Would you like to know your reward?"

"For what?" I asked, confused. "I thought you guys only gave out badges to your own people."

"You have earned the hermit's favor. And because of the merits and petitions of Francis Dominic the Hermit, Heaven has decided to reward your kind and charitable act by answering your prayers in a unique way. We are going to take you on an adventure."

I stared at the Scout to try and see if he was messing with me. What was he talking about? Perhaps he was not right in the head. "Well I can't leave my friend here all alone," I said, trying to refuse the offer politely. I did not feel comfortable going somewhere with a person who was not able even to give me his name.

"He will be safe with me until you return. I'm his guardian."

I laughed. "You're a little young to be someone's guardian, aren't you? Besides, Brendan has a Mom. What are you talking about?" Then I remembered what Brendan stated in the letter about his Mom not waking up, reminding me that he might no longer have one after all. But there was no way that this Scout could know that already.

"Angel of God, my guardian dear, to whom His love commits me here. Ever this day, be at my side to light and guard, to rule and guide."

I recognized that prayer. It was the one I said every night and morning. The Scout must be pious as well. "Are you Catholic?" I asked. "I say that same prayer every day and night."

"I know you do. Your Guardian Angel told me. I'm Brendan's Guardian Angel."

I stared at the Scout again, not seeing any sign that he was kidding. He must've been trying for dead pan humor. "Is that so?" I asked, playing along. Wait a second. Even though hard to believe, it would actually answer a lot of questions if he were telling the truth. He did keep showing up out of nowhere and seemed familiar with Brendan. He knew about Brendan's note. He helped him in that vision when Brendan fell out of the tree house. I wanted to believe him. But what if he was lying? What if he was even a fallen Angel and meant us harm—saving us as some sort of sick game to cause us ill by his own hand later on?

"Then why don't you look like an Angel?"

"Angels are here to serve and help mankind. Most of the time, we don't want anyone to know who we are, so we appear as ordinary trustworthy people. It is only on unique occasions that we appear as Angels."

"Okay. But if this is one of those unique occasions of revealing your true identity, why haven't you shown yourself yet to me in your angelic form?"

"Because I've been messing with you, friend. As you pointed out earlier. I've been trying to hint at who I was, to see if you would guess. Though Angels are not capable of sinning, having already passed the test and been sealed in grace, we still have a sense of humor you know? At least I do." Suddenly a bright glow shone from all around him and gorgeous gargantuan wings spread out from behind him.

I fell backwards in shock. "I'm sorry that I did not believe you," I stammered.

"It's alright," said the Angel putting out his hand to help me up. "It's my fault for messing with you." As suddenly as it first changed, his appearance returned to normal.

I could hardly believe what had happened. I had so many questions. But where to start?

Chapter 18

Globes Perceived by Two Dimensions

The radiant and alluring light caught my attention. A luminous beam seemed to be originating from the St. Nicholas portrait, which was leaning against the cave, directly to the right of where Brendan had been sitting prior to our moving him.

I fell over backwards when I heard Brendon's voice ask, "Can I come too?" I had not even noticed him sitting beside me at the fire until now, thinking that he was still resting. How long had he been there and how did he get up so quietly?

"Of course," said Brendan's Guardian Angel.

I smiled, glad to have my companion come with me wherever we were going. "And will you come with us?" I asked the Angel.

"No, I cannot. I must stay here and watch over you."

If he must watch over us, wouldn't that mean he should come with us?

A strange translucent silver cord seemed to be attached to Brendan's core, going through his clothing, which I had never noticed before. That was odd. I followed the cord with my eyes to see where it ended. To my amazement, it ended where Brendan was lying down underneath all the blankets. So, he was still lying down? How could there be two Brendans? Was one an imposter? But why were they attached together by a cord?

Wait. There was another body beside Brendan's. Who could that be? He was right where I used to be lying. Hold on, it looked like me. Why were there two of me? And how had I not noticed the cord that attached me to my imposter? Or was I the fake one? Did someone clone me while I was sleeping? What was going on here? Beginning to tremble I broke into a deep sweat.

"I see you've become aware," said the Angel. "Don't worry. Your bodies will be safe with me."

"Our bodies?" I asked, not wanting to know the answer and yet needing to know. "Are we dead?" I shuddered at the thought.

"No," replied the Angel. "But you are in dire straits."

I gulped. "Are we about to die?"

"Neither you nor I are privy to that knowledge yet," the Angel said.

"Isn't this great?" asked Brendan. "I've never been a ghost before."

I fell to my knees sobbing, not knowing if I was ready for death. Sure, I thought about it a lot, but I would rather have prepared better before its immediate occurrence. I would not be able to say goodbye to Nate or my parents. And would Nate be okay without me? And I would not want Paul to lose his first friend the moment he found one—or not see him try to make up to me for all his prior torments.

Realizing my distress, Brendan crouched down beside me and put his arm around me. "I'm sorry, Tommy. I'm the one who got you into this. You should not have to suffer for my carelessness."

"No," I said, drying my eyes and standing back up. "I made my own path. You are not to blame." I did feel as if it was at least half his fault but was not going to hold it against him. And if I did have to die, I was happy to at least die with my friend by my side.

At that instant a tall, lustrous, red haired figure came forth out of nothing. He stood a few inches in front of me and put his hand on my shoulder. "Hello Tommy," he said shyly.

I fell backwards again in fear.

"Don't be afraid," said the gleaming well decorated figure, a young man looking about twenty or so. He appeared to be quite reserved. "I'm your Guardian Angel."

"Would everyone stop sneaking up on me. Please!" I hollered, tired of being frightened so often today. Then realizing that I might have hurt my Guardian Angel's feelings, I got up and hugged him, his enormous wings folding around me to return the affection. "I'm very sorry. You scared me, that's all. It's nice to meet you. My name's Tommy—well that's what my friends call me."

"Yes," the Angel said bashfully. "I know who you are."

"Of course, you do," I acknowledged, feeling rather stupid. "You did say my name already, didn't you?"

"Normally," he continued, "I wouldn't appear so close in front of someone, taking him off guard like that. Brendan's guardian put me up to it. Messing with people is more his thing. I'm no good at it. I'm much more reserved."

Brendan's Guardian Angel laughed. "It's no fun if you tell him I put you up to it. Now he's going to think I'm the only Angel with a sense of humor."

"No," my Angel remarked, "I have one. It's more reserved that's all. Pranks are beneath the dignity of a Blessed Spirit."

"Wow!" I said to Brendan, "I had no idea Angels could be so different from one another. Did you?"

"No," he replied, "I thought they were pretty much all the same too."

My Angel laughed timidly, "That would be very boring, wouldn't it?"

"Yes," added Brendan's guardian. "Naturally we all have our own personalities, as unique from each other as humans are from one another."

"Indeed," agreed my Angel.

"Oh!" said Brendan's Angel as an orb of rotating blue energy appeared in his hand. "I almost forgot."

"Me too," my Angel said, as a similar object appeared in his hand.

Each Angel tossed his orb to the other, whispered into it, and then tossed it back.

Seeing our confused faces, my Angel explained, "These orbs of light are the prayers that we take to Heaven. Whenever we Angels greet each other, we add to each other's prayers—kind of like a game of catch."

"Wow!" I said, amazed at such a concept, "that is awesome." I thought for a moment while gawking at my Angel, recalling that I recognized him but could not remember from where. "Have I seen you somewhere before?"

My Angel looked firmly at me and said, "You are always loved and never truly alone."

. . .

Suddenly the memory of it hit me. I could never forget those words. I sat on a bench in the subway station, at eight years old, not knowing what to do. Thousands of people walked by in every direction, each lost in their own thoughts. A large chunk of muffin stood in front of me on the grimy floor, having been separated from the original baked goods. I knew just how it felt, not being able to find Mom, Dad, or Nate.

It was my own fault. Sometimes I would go off into my own little world, and before I realized it, wander off away from whoever was looking after me. But as soon as I came to, I had no reference point to where my family were or how long they had been gone.

Should I go and look for a security guard? If I did, then I might get even more lost. And what if one of my parents came back to get me and I wasn't here? Or what if a similar looking family came to take me and I didn't even realize it was not the same one until we got home?

Not knowing what else to do, I cried to God, "Please bring my family back to me. I'm sorry for wandering off." After signing myself with the Cross, I prayed the Hail Mary repetitiously both to help me feel better and to ask for her assistance.

A young red-haired security guard noticed me as he walked by and sat down beside me on the bench. "That's a nice prayer," he told me. "Where are your parents'?"

"I lost them," I admitted, hoping that I was not in trouble with the law for doing so. "What if I can never find them again? I'll be all alone."

"Come with me," the kind guard said. "We'll find your family together." He held my hand as we walked and then added, "Remember . . . you are loved, and never truly alone."

We found my family surprisingly quickly, and they were so happy to see me that I did not get in as much trouble as I thought I would for wandering off. The security guard left as quickly as he came, without even giving me a chance to thank him. But those words he said about never being alone always stuck with me.

. . .

The security guard at the subway!" I exclaimed. "Now I remember. That was you? Wow! Thank you for helping me then."

My Angel smiled, "Be careful how you treat a stranger. You never know when you might be entertaining Angels."

"That's right," Brendan's Angel agreed.

My Angel waited a moment and then said, "Anyway, we had best be going now. I will be your guide on this journey, Tommy."

Having only just met my own Guardian Angel, I looked over at Brendan's to make sure they both agreed. His nodded his head.

"Lead the way," I said as Brendan and I followed my guardian through the welcoming luminescent portal that had opened in the St. Nicholas picture.

Suddenly I was weightless, like an astronaut in space, yet without having any control over where I was heading. It was as if I was being pulled by an invisible string. In this pool of light, many souls were heading in all sorts of directions. The scene made me think of a slow folk dance of spirits. The untainted light pulled at my heart, urging me to let go of all earthly woes. However, Brendan was being drawn in another direction than I was; and so, my heart was torn between embracing the fullness of the light into my soul while also made anxious by my friend's leaving my side. By reaching for him I tried to protest but it did not seem as if he could see me anymore.

My spirit gloomed as I hypothesized that Brendan was being taken to Heaven and I led to the dark abyss. But not desiring to wish ill on my friend, I would not have wanted to trade places with him; I wanted him to be at peace. Only I wanted to be at peace as well, though it seemed I was going to end up in despair, alone forever as I always feared.

"Almost there," said my Angel, having noticed my distress.

All of a sudden, I could perceive a desert of endless sparkling snow before me and then I was there, no longer in the pool of light. Burying my face in the snow, I wept bitterly, not being able to bear the soon-to-be-announced judgement informing me that I was to be in darkness forever.

My guide put his hand on my shoulder, "Cheer up, Tommy. We are here now."

"Cheer up?" I asked, surprised at my Angel's statement. "There is no cheeriness in Hell is there?"

"Hell?" inquired my Angel, "This is the North Pole."

"Ah," I said, quickly standing up and wiping what snow there was off my pants. "Perhaps I should stop jumping to conclusions so fast to save myself embarrassment."

"There's no reason to be embarrassed on my account. I've been with you your whole life, even though you have not seen me. I know all your quirks, virtues, and weaknesses."

"I know you're trying to make me feel better, but it only enhances my mortification, making me feel as if I'm exposed—since you know everything about me and I know nothing about you."

"Of course," my guide said, blushing as he led me forward to start our walk through the snowy wasteland. "I'm sorry. I did not mean to make you feel uneasy. Just know that you can trust me. I have been and am a friend for life and into paradise. Feel free to ask me anything. I am your humble servant."

I thought for a moment, then asked, "What happened to Brendan? I thought he was coming with us."

"Well these sorts of journeys are very internal, and although they can be supported by your friends, they need to be undertaken independently. Therefore, he is going on his own journey and you on yours. But you can compare notes afterwards if you want."

I was relieved to hear that Brendan was okay, but disappointed that he would not be joining us. As we continued hiking, the light glistened off the endless plains of snow, bringing a welcoming and hopeful warmth to the dimmest season of the year. Yet the reflected glare did not hurt my eyes. The temperature was frigid and there was a moderate wind chill, but somehow, I was not bothered by it. Was it perhaps because I did not have my body with me that I did not feel physical pain? No, that could not be it considering that I was sweating and bawling earlier. The only sounds I could hear were the crunch of snow from the steps we took and the creaking noise of expanding and retreating ice, similar to the way in which an old house creaks at night time. And though I could not hear music audibly, inspiring Xmas Carols were being sung by the air in some way which I am at a loss to describe. How did I ever think this place could be Hell?

Not wanting to lose the opportunity to ask things I could not normally inquire about, I said, "I have another question if you don't mind. How am I able to sweat and cry as a soul without a body?"

"As I'm sure you are aware, internal pain can be much greater than physical suffering. You see the manifestations of these things in a way that you are used to, as a point of reference."

"I see. Can I ask another question?"

The Angel nodded.

"You said we are at the North Pole? So, St. Nick really does live there?"

"Sort of. We are not on earth or in Heaven at the moment. This is a temporary chamber to help you on your journey. We are outside space and time, so you're perceiving what you see based on what you need to see."

With that explanation I think I became more confused than enlightened. "Could you please repeat that, but in human terms?"

The Angel laughed. "Think of it as like drawing shapes on a paper. The paper can only have two dimensions while the drawer has three. If you took a three-dimensional object like a globe and placed it in a two-dimensional world, people there would perceive it differently because they could only see two dimensions at a time. Likewise, you are incapable of seeing the many dimensions that govern outside space and time. You are experiencing them with the limited dimensions that you are capable of. That's a simplified version of it anyway. Does that make more sense?"

I was starting to get it a little more, but some of it still went over my head. "Are you saying then that what I am seeing is not real?"

"Not quite. It is more that you are seeing the truth through the lens of your own limitations. Only God is capable of seeing all. As an Angel I can see more than you, but still not everything."

"Okay. I think I understand now," I said. "But if this is a temporary chamber for my own benefit, then St. Nick does not actually live here, right? Where does he live then?"

"All of the Saints dwell in Heaven, but they often come to earth to help mankind; especially those who ask for assistance. St. Nicholas is the patron of children. He often comes to their aid, in particular the most vulnerable among them. The Saints help to bring Heaven to earth, but they need the prayers, sacrifices, and merits of the visible and invisible church to do so—because God does not want to force his help on anyone."

"I see." I wanted to ask still another question yet was afraid of what the answer might be. But knowing that I would likely never get another opportunity, I decided to risk it. "What about the gifts? Does St. Nicholas bring all those gifts to kids, or is it the parents?"

"A bit of both. You see, charity is contagious, inspiring others to do the same. While he still lived on earth, St Nicholas, as a representative of Christ, gave many gifts to help the poor. For centuries, people have been led to be more charitable around Xmas time because of the Saint. But rather than say by whom the gift is given, sometimes they wish to be anonymous, and so they put St. Nicholas' name on it to make it in his honor. In a sense, all presents given and charity done in St. Nicholas' honor are his doing by the extension of those devoted to him. It is similar to how Christians act as an extension of Christ. However, there are occasions where St. Nicholas himself does directly give gifts to those in need even to this very day."

"Really?"

"Absolutely."

Still feeling a little resentful for having been misled by my parents, I asked, "But why didn't my parents tell me that when I asked? I understand the anonymous benefits, but why the direct lying once I was old enough to understand? It can't be Christian charity purposely to tell falsehoods."

My Angel sighed. "Unfortunately, many people are caught up in sentimentalism and forget the original meaning of customs and practices. They often can cause more harm than good—you are the perfect example since you have taken finding out the truth harder than some. I have seen all your woes and have been there for you always, even though you could not see me. I'm so sorry that this happened to you, Tommy. But don't let it cause you to lose faith in God. Use your sufferings to bring you closer to God. Who has suffered more than Christ after all?"

Being reminded that God had endowed me with an invisible companion to console me in my sorrows made me feel extremely grateful. I gave the Angel a hug and held on to him for a while as we walked on. "Thank you for being my invisible friend . . . that I can currently see."

"Thank you for having me," the Angel responded with a thankful smile.

In the far distance, there seemed a large pole, and someone kneeling in front of it all veiled in black.

Chapter 19

Our Lady of the Snow and Sorrows

The air became heavy and thick, trying to pull my heart down with it. But I attempted to keep my spirits up. I counted my steps in threes as we walked. Not really having a reason for doing so, yet feeling I had to just the same. It did not feel worthwhile arguing about it with myself. I wondered where exactly we were heading and how to ask my Guardian Angel without seeming rude. Staring again at the wooden pole which we had slowly been making ground towards, I decided instead to inquire about that first and hold off on the other question until afterwards. Pointing towards the pole I asked my guide, "Is that the actual North Pole?"

As if trying to sound mysterious on purpose, my Angel answered, "It is the North, South, East, and West Pole—the center of the universe."

I wondered what he meant by that. As we approached closer and closer, I perceived that the pole had a cross beam near the top and a man seemed to be tied to it. "Is that Jesus on the Cross?" I asked my guiding companion.

"Yes," he answered. "Though used as an instrument of death, the Cross became the instrument of life. As it was used to assist the Son of Man to conquer sin and death by sacrifice, so it became the very tree of life with Jesus himself becoming the fruit."

I laughed, wondering if my Angel was speaking in riddles on purpose. "How can Jesus be the fruit? He's not edible."

"Jesus was not man but Spirit and yet became man for your sake. Likewise, can he not make himself heavenly mystical food for you and your kind to consume if he sees it as good for you?"

I thought for a moment and then said, "Well that makes sense. But I don't understand why he would want us to consume him. Isn't cannibalism forbidden by God?"

"Yes of course it is. Jesus has you consume him, not by cannibalism, but mystically so that he becomes more and more a part of you, and then you are more and more a part of his body. Humans, unlike Angels, are physical beings of the senses so you need to experience faith through the senses. God knowing this set up the Blessed Sacrament in the way of eating and drinking—two things that bring so much joy to the hearts of men."

"I see. So, if I want to become more like Jesus, I must eat this fruit?"

"Precisely!"

"But would I lose my own identity? Would I forget who I was, if I became more and more like Christ?"

"No, my friend. You keep your own personality and identity but at the same time become an extension of Christ's mystical body. By doing so, you actually become more and more like your true self as well—since sin, vice and pining for error corrupt and distort the identities of men. Such a wonderful mystery has not been offered to us Angels, but only to mankind—for those who want it."

That made me feel bad for the Angels, wondering why God would give such a blessing to us and not them. "Does that not make you resentful? I'm sorry that we seemed to get the better deal."

"Don't be sorry. I already passed the test against sin—and having been sealed in grace, am now incapable of envy. There were unfortunately a number of us who resented both God and man for this unveiling mystery and became corrupted by their envy—just as some men hate God regardless of the love that he offers to them. I am grateful for what God has given me as well as for my brothers in the flesh. And you should be grateful as well."

I was deeply moved by his simple loving humility, and wished to hear more of his wisdom. "Well if I can become a better person by taking this fruit, how do I get some?"

"During every Mass around the world a great miracle happens, and has ever since the dawn of the age of the church, and will until the end of time. The priest, having been consecrated for such a purpose, calls down Jesus to become the appearance of the bread and wine presented. It is like when Heaven provided Abraham with the sacrifice to offer back up to God."

Amazement almost beyond belief gripped me. "So, you are telling me that the fruit of the tree of life, Jesus himself, comes to us as the Eucharist during every Mass, even at my local parish church?"

"Yes! Absolutely."

I might not have believed it had I not known that Angels could not lie. I still did not fully understand but was so glad to know that Jesus was some-how physically present in my own local parish for my own benefit. I had been looking for miracles to prove the existence of God, yet there was one happening every day in my own neighborhood. What I had been looking for had been hidden in plain sight my whole life. Why did no one tell me?

We were but a few minutes walk from the Cross. Jesus, with a crown of thorns on his head, looked badly beaten. I could barely look at him. Not only because his appearance was so sad, but because I felt partially responsible for his condition. It was as if I had nailed him to the wooden Cross myself.

"Why did he have to go through all that?" I asked my guide, feeling guilty at not knowing how to relieve his pain.

"He died for the sins of mankind—not for us Angels; since we know and see much more clearly than you, that any rejection of God by us could not be redeemed. Mankind however fell away from God partially in ignorance."

"But why such a painful death?" I asked, wondering why Jesus could not have died in a less horrendous way.

"Some say that only one drop of blood from Jesus would be enough to redeem mankind. Regardless, Jesus wished to lead his followers by example and show what he was willing to go through voluntarily for mankind. Now you have his example to look up to when you go through suffering for him."

"I see," I said, not feeling very consoled. I was glad to learn the reason for Jesus' suffering, but knowing that my sins were partially responsible for his pain made me regret every one of them all the more. I resolved to try harder to avoid them in the future; at least if I had a future anymore.

As I approached the Cross, I noticed that the kneeling person covered in black veils and robes was a young-looking lady. She had her arms crossed reverently in front of her breast. Although I could see deep pain and sorrow in her eyes, she had no tears. Her heart seemed completely devoted to the Son of God on the Cross. "Is she Jesus' Mother?" I asked.

"Yes," replied my guide. "She is the Blessed Virgin Mary. Because of her unique role in bringing Christ the King into this world at the Incarnation, she has been made Queen of both Heaven and Earth. It is the highest honor given to anyone of the human race, next only to Jesus himself. Just as she did during her earthly life, she always points people towards her Son."

Though very sad looking, Mary had great tenderness and kindness in her face. Remembering what the Angel said about becoming part of Christ's mystical body, I asked, "If we become one with Jesus, does that mean that Our Lady, Mary becomes our Mother as well?"

"Very astute of you," remarked the Angel.

I blushed. Perhaps because I felt that the compliments were undeserved. "Thank you!"

"And you as Jesus' brother can ask for Mary's intercession whenever you wish. She is always praying on behalf of mankind, but can help those who ask of her by the merits and sufferings of her Son even more. The same goes with petitioning all the Saints for help. Christians pray for each other while on earth. And since no one is dead in Christ, but alive in him, those brethren who have gone before you continue to pray for and assist you to help your journey toward Heaven."

"Now I am Jesus' brother as well? I thought I was part of his body?"

"It's a bit of a mystery but you are both. You become part of his body; you are also his brother; and being the Son of mankind, he becomes your son too; yet since Jesus takes on the role of the second Adam, that makes him the Father of mankind as well."

I was beginning to get overwhelmed by this load of instruction. "So, you're saying that Jesus somehow is my Dad, son, brother, and yet a part of me with the mystical body?"

"Precisely. And don't forget that he is also your friend."

My mind was still trying to process all that teaching. "I think I will just stick to that one for now. I'm not denying those others, but friend is easier to remember than a thousand titles."

"Fair enough."

I thought for a moment and then asked, "If Jesus' death already happened, then why is the Blessed Virgin Mary still here in front of the Cross?"

"Keep in mind that, even though the Crucifixion happened in time, the Saints now being with Christ in Heaven, are outside of time. She is praying to her son on behalf of mankind, but simultaneously. She is interceding for each individual who asks for her help, and groups of people, mankind as a whole, and the church; as well as for each period of time during the age of the church."

"Wow! She sounds busy."

"Yes, well heavenly beings have no need for sleep or rest."

I could suddenly perceive someone reciting the Hail Mary. It sounded familiar. Like Nate's voice. Nate, still in his bed, appeared without warning beside the Blessed Virgin. He was praying the Rosary.

I was grateful to see him but confused as to why he was there. Did it mean that his sickness had got the better of him, and he was dying? I was deeply troubled, wondering how long I had been gone and had neglected my brother. "What's he doing here?" I demanded, as politely as I could in my anxious state of mind.

The Angel smiled in consolation, "Don't worry. He is taking his petitions to the Mother of God. He is praying for Brendan and you to have a safe return—as well as for Paul."

If I lived, I would have to remember to thank him. If Brendan's Angel was correct about our being in a crucial condition, I was sure I could use all the prayers that I could get.

"He prays for you often, you know?"

"He does?" I asked, pleasantly surprised.

"Indeed. When he noticed you doing your daily prayers, it inspired him to pray on a more regular basis. He looks up to you a lot."

I was flattered but did not really think there was much to look up to. "That's kind of funny because I look up to him, you know?"

"Well anyway," said the Angel, "we should move on soon."

"Wait. There's something that I need to do first." I felt bad for Mary, seeing how sad she looked; especially considering that it was my fault that Jesus had suffered on the Cross and endured undeserved punishment. Walking up to her, I gave her a consoling embrace. While holding onto my Heavenly Mother, I asked her to assist Brendan and Paul and particularly to help my brother, out of my gratitude for his prayers for me.

I heard a loud, gentle, yet grief-stricken voice coming from the Cross, say, "Son behold thy Mother. And Mother behold thy son."

Then Mary stood up and took a fabric necklace from her garment. It was two brown pieces of wool at opposite ends of the string. She placed it around my neck with one felt piece on my back and the other on my chest like a two-sided necklace. Mary spoke to me in the most caring but mournful voice that I have ever heard, "Those who console me during life I will console, especially at the hour of their death." She gave me a gentle kiss on the forehead then went back to kneeling in front of the Cross.

"Wow!" I said, so happy to have received a gift directly from the Mother of Jesus. "Thank you so much." Worried though that I had acted irreverently, I said one Hail Mary as I kissed the sacred present I had just received, and then went and kissed the Cross before letting my Angel know that I was ready to go.

I followed the Angel's lead as he genuflected to Christ before we continued walking into the snowy wasteland again.

"Charity is always rewarded," remarked my Angel.

Remembering what I wanted to ask from before, I said, "Perhaps my friend you would show me great charity by telling me where we are going."

Chapter 20

Flowers in the Tabernacle of His Heart

"The next stop is to meet the hidden Jesus," my Angel told me.

Well that was as clear as mud. What did he mean by that? As we continued to walk through the glittering snow, a building came into view with a tower and Cross on top. Once closer, I noticed how remarkably similar it looked to my own parish church, St. Nicholas'. "That looks just like my parish," I remarked.

"It is," said my Guardian Angel.

As we approached the building, I asked, "Well, what's it doing here?" But before he could answer, I realized it would likely go over my head like before, and not wanting to waste his time in explaining something that I could not understand, I said in an attempt to stop him: "Oh! Right, right, that whole time-mystery-dimensions thing."

I halted before we got to the steps of the church. My guardian took a few more steps and then paused to wait for me. There was something I had been meaning to ask my Angel during our walk but had not mustered up the courage to put to him. But I knew if I did not inquire about it, it would eat away at me and be an ongoing distraction from whatever I was supposed to be doing once inside the church. Also, I did not know how much longer my Angel would be visible to me, so I wanted to make sure that I asked my question while I could still hear his response. *It's now or never,* I supposed.

"Have you ever made a snow Angel?" I asked, thinking how amazing it would be to see an actual Angel create one.

Amused at the inquiry, the Angel laughed, "No, I haven't."

"Well come on then," I requested as I lay down on my back in the snow. "This'll be epic."

My Angel looked around, perhaps to see if anyone was watching, then joined me on the ground and we proceeded to make snow Angels. "This is beneath the dignity of a Blessed Spirit," the Angel joked.

"It was fun though. Right?" I asked as we got up to look at our incredible masterpieces of art.

"Yes actually. I can see why it appeals so much to humans. Now, shall we continue?" he asked, gesturing towards my Parish.

"Only if you are done messing around," I teased. I followed the Angel up the steps, so happy to have experienced making snow Angels with an actual Angel.

Entering the nave, I signed myself with Holy Water from the stoup and genuflected. Seeing my Angel genuflect without making use of the Holy Water, I asked, "Why did you not take Holy Water?"

"Sacramentals are for mankind, not for Angels. Signing yourself with Holy Water is to remind you of the promises of your baptism. Angels are not baptized, so there would be no need for us to remind ourselves of the fact."

"But I didn't make any promises," I whispered, not wanting to disturb the peaceful atmosphere of reverence. "I was only a baby."

"For those under the age of reason, parents make the promises on behalf of their children when they bring them into the family of God; then, when old enough, the baptized renew those same promises for themselves. You will do likewise if you are confirmed."

"Ah, I see," I said, feeling stupid for not making the connection before that the Sacrament of Confirmation was a confirming of the faith.

I looked around at all the Holy images in admiration. Though I had seen them many times before, I took them for granted then, and never gave them the deeper appreciation they deserved. I loved the stained-glass windows too, and saw them as a great mix between functionality (bringing light into the building) and sacred art.

My favorite glass portrait, which always drew my attention, was still the one closest to the doors on the right side. It was an image of St. Joseph and the Blessed Virgin Mary showing devotion to the child, Jesus, who himself was holding up his Sacred Heart in his left hand. His heart was decorated with a crown of thorns, a Cross, and a mesmerizing flame. The infant Jesus' other hand was giving a blessing to the one looking at the picture and reading the inscription. St. Joseph and St. Mary also held their hearts in hand with the flames leaning and pointing towards Jesus. Their other hand was placed over the breast. Likely the reason I admired it so much was because it reminded me strongly of Xmas, for it depicted the young Holy Family together in awe of each other. It always made me want to cry. In this case, tears of joy.

I walked gradually up the center aisle between the two ranks of pews, admiring the dancing flames on the candles lighted at the two side shrines on either side of the altar, a tall statue at each. My favorite was the statue of St. Nicholas on the right. He was the patron of our Parish. Dressed in a beautifully decorated red robe, he wore the tall pointed Bishop's hat and staff—called the mitre and the crozier—and had an open black sack that rested slightly on his oversized belly. From his kind yet worn face a gentle gaze radiated. And his jolly smile could not be hidden by his midsized white beard.

Hearing two people crying in one of the pews to my left, I lingered a little, hoping to see if I recognized them without appearing nosy. One glance and I ducked down in panic as quickly as I could and hid myself in the pew to the right. It was my parents. They were crying but seemed to be trying to pray between shockwaves of tears. The sound of their sobbing was abysmally humiliating to my ears from the great shame it caused me. I felt terrible. Mortified over having been the one to give Mom and Dad such grief by leaving home without their permission, and now for hiding from them—too embarrassed to show myself. I was grateful though for their prayers.

"It's okay," my Guardian Angel informed me. "They cannot see either you or me. You don't have to worry."

Well that took away half my fussing, but not the half that hated myself for bringing them to this dreadful state. I also felt guilty because part of me got a sick joy out of seeing them sorrowing over me, since it showed they actually cared about Nate and me. "I did not mean to cause them such anguish," I told my Angel, "but feeling unable to go to them for help about what was bothering me was the reason I needed to go on this journey to look for St Nick instead."

My Angel rested his hand on my shoulder. "Intentions are often good, which can decrease culpability," he said. "Yet a wrong action is still wrong. And your parents' deep pain is one of the results of your wrongdoing. On Judgement Day, everyone will see all the pain their offenses have caused others, along with the happiness brought about by their good deeds."

Feeling rather helpless after hearing that, knowing how many bad deeds I had done, I asked, "Then can any of us be saved from our transgressions?"

"That is the entire purpose of Christmas: to bring peace and salvation to those of goodwill and to inspire reformation of life among evil doers. With God, everything is possible."

"Well I do love Xmas," I said, as my Angel gave me his hand to help me up from the floor. As I left the pew, I genuflected twice before continuing forward; once for leaving and another to make up for neglecting to do so when I took a dive to the floor earlier. And I cringed slightly as I fought the urge to genuflect a third time.

I edged my way forward, appreciating the exquisiteness of the Tabernacle behind the altar. It was a locked golden coffer that every square inch of this sacred space pointed me towards. I knew it must be used for something important, but actually had no idea of what. Above the Tabernacle on the wall behind was a simple large wooden Crucifix. This time I remembered to genuflect before entering the pew in the front row. It was normally reserved for those in wheelchairs. I liked it because it was roomier. No one who needed it seemed to be there so I hoped the priest would not mind. But perhaps I should have asked first. I looked at my guardian Angel on my left, hoping that he might let me know if it was okay for me to be in the disabled pew. He had his hands together in prayer, pointed towards the altar. I followed his example and folded my hands similarly and faced forward.

I made the sign of the Cross and said an Our Father, Glory be, and Hail Mary to help me focus on heavenly things while I thought of what to pray about. Then I continued. "Jesus," I prayed, "I've hurt my parents, was careless with my brother's wellbeing, and neglected my friend in a way which could have ruined him. I know that I need to make these things right, but I don't know what to do. And now Brendan and I might be dying. It's all, all my fault. Is it too late to fix things? Is there anything I can do? Please help me, if you still can."

After praying for a few minutes, at a stroke I witnessed five strikingly gorgeous Angels appear on the altar. Two were kneeling on either side of the Tabernacle, both facing it with their arms crossed in lowly reverence. Another two stood adjacent to them bearing torches. One other was poised as a thurifer offering incense to the Lord. I could hear the words of my prayers coming from his thurible and ascending with the incense. Moments later and I could see the Blessed Spirits no longer. Was God showing me how my prayers are offered by the Angels? Or might I still be in the cave at this very moment hallucinating? Could this whole experience of visiting the North Pole be the result of almost freezing in the cave? Was my violent death in a nightmare foretelling my current predicament if in fact I am dying in a cave?

A gleaming funnel of light swirled out from the Tabernacle towards me. All I could do was watch in awe. The child Jesus, looking only a little younger than Nate, came forth with his arms stretched wide. The light shone through the wounds in his hands and glared off his remarkable purple robes. His crown of thorns dazzled even brighter than a normal crown. He smiled and gazed at me with such a kind face that I can only describe his look as one hundred percent charity towards not just mankind as a whole, but me in particular—as though he preferred only me.

As if drawn by a magnet the fanned flame in my heart was pulled towards his. I got up and began floating in the light as I traveled towards him. I embraced Jesus in my arms and heard him say, "Tommy, I can do no more to show how much I love you."

I closed my eyes for a moment. Never in my entire life had I felt more fulfilled. When I opened my eyelids, Jesus and I were standing together in a large dazzling flower garden, which ran riot with so many radiant colors that I realized I had never even seen some of them before.

Suddenly an inspirational thought for a prose reflection sprouted in my mind. Alas! I did not have my journal with me. I strove to keep the idea alive to remember later on. As I did, the very next moment my journal, complete with pen, appeared in my hand. Smiling at Christ with gratitude, I opened up my diary and began to write:

FURNACE OF RADIANT LOVE

by Tommy Jolmen

I hear it. The blazing fire that burns in the Tabernacle. Throughout the Nave it echoes, welcoming me as I enter in through the doors. The roaring of fire swells with the sound of Christ's Sacred Heart, beating as a drum for me. My soul cannot help but dance to the percussion, and to the melody of heavenly choirs singing in adoration of him. While my feet guide me through the Nave towards the Sanctuary, my own heart unites with his until they beat in unison. An intense radiating heat enkindles my body and soul with delight as I kneel before the altar. The fire's penetrating heat does not scare me. Well, just a little. Yet it is a good fear. The flame's radiance threatens to burn away every false thing that I hold dear. I know that I should not cling to earthly cares, yet I struggle to let go. May that battle in my soul continue until all that remains is an empty vessel; a container that He may fill to the brim and his all-consuming love incandesce me.

Grow my vessel O Sacred Heart of Christ, every moment of every day, so that my flask can hold a greater and greater volume of Your charity. And I wish to reciprocate that love with You and with others. May anything that holds us back from You not be able to remain in Your presence.

Divine Child of the Cross, let Your Sacred Heart, that burning furnace of charity, ever fan the flames of my own heart. Make our hearts as one, and grow mine so that in magnitude it may be able to experience more and more of Your embrace.

Not only do You love me, You like me too. And You don't just like me, You love me as well. But still more, not only do You both like and love me beyond anything I could understand, You also prefer me. And not merely when I am faithful. Even when I have betrayed You, the countless times, Your preferential love seeks me out and finds me, leaving me no choice but to return to Your mercy. My clouded judgement veiled my eyes from seeing Your glow. But You stepped in and removed the fog, and continue to expel it, so that my eyes may see crystal clear the fulness of who You really are.

My Daddy, brother, son, friend, companion, comrade, and spiritual lover. You are all that I need—everything and everyone. Yet You provide me with even more than I need, befriending me with companions that we may share ever more of Your love when together with You. Love is infinite! The more we experience and share Your love, the more it grows.

May I do more than like and love You. May I prefer Your company every moment of every day into eternity. Impossible as it is for me to desire You as much as you desire me, grant to me the graces needed to grow in that desire daily, hourly, by every minute of every day, until the gates of Heaven usher me into Your eternal charitable presence.

Sacred Heart of the Divine Child of the Cross, preserve us with Your countenance.

I closed the book, grateful for the time given to me to write the prose while the thoughts were still fresh in my mind.

"Thank you for the lovely words you wrote to me," Jesus said, now holding a walking staff with a globe and Cross on top, gesturing for me to walk beside him.

Down a brick path with countless rows of flowers stunning in their beauty on either side of us we began a slow pace. Each delightful plant bowed its head as the Lord passed by.

"What is this place?" Had I ever breathed in such fabulous odors from wonderful flowers like these? And all the light radiating around me was not only seen but felt as though it were pure love.

In the tenderest of voices, Jesus responded to me, "We are in the Tabernacle. All these flowers represent how happy it makes Me when the faithful come to console Me in My loneliness."

I picked up a handsome velvety purple flower and held it in my hand while a candy-plum type of aroma tickled my nose with delight; then I stooped to pick up another bloom from every row to try to have one of each—but in vain. "You are lonely, Jesus?" I asked, astounded that God could experience such an emotion.

"At times very much. Don't forget that even though I am God, My divinity does not take away in the slightest from My humanity, and I experience all human emotions and feelings."

"But why are You lonely?" I asked. "Don't You have the Saints and Angels in Heaven to keep you company?"

"Yes. I do."

"I'm confused" I said. "How can You be both happy and lonely?"

"To put it in terms that you can understand, coming to earth is experienced differently than being in Heaven. When I come back to earth as the Eucharist, I am bound to be here until consumed or destroyed."

"Does that mean that anytime You appear as bread and wine by the hands of a priest, You are no longer in Heaven?"

"Not quite. I am still in Heaven which is beyond time. Yet I am also bound here on earth in every Eucharistic host. I am fully present in both Heaven and earth."

"It's difficult for me to understand, but I think I am getting it. Explain then Your woes to me."

"Well, after becoming the Eucharist, I am put in the Tabernacle in reserve by the priest. I don't mind that at all, because it is worth being bound there for the chance that some person will come and visit me in order to be in My physical presence. Yet these days, most churches are empty throughout the day. And so, I stay there lonely, hoping for someone to console Me."

I felt terrible. Having been so lonely myself much of the time, I could relate to the feeling and felt bad for not having visited him more often. "I feel lonely sometimes too," I said.

"I know. And I'm sorry that you suffer. I am always with you even though you can't see Me. But those who show Me great consolation in visiting Me in My physical presence, even if only for a few minutes I will reward with extra consolation and love a hundredfold."

"That's amazing. If I survive, I promise that I will come and visit You more often at church." Then I realized that such a promise might sound as if I only wanted his reward, so I added, "I do not mean only because I want a reward. I meant that I am grateful that You are so charitable in rewarding others, and that You of all people don't deserve to be lonely."

"Thank you, Tommy. I look forward to your visiting me as much as I have looked forward to this current visitation. And likewise, thank you for consoling My Mother earlier when you saw her at the Cross. Those who console My Mother, I reward even more than those who console Me."

"Can I choose both though? Not for a reward by itself but because You both need assistance?"

"You have a very kind heart, Tommy—a rare thing in these dark times. You must try your best to keep it by acting on your kindness and not being corrupted by the world."

The bouquet of flowers in my hand was growing too large to hold and I did not know if I could fit one more flower in with the rest. "I promise to try, Jesus. But I'm so afraid that I will become corrupted. What if I live my whole life serving You and then do something stupid at my last moment? You see Jesus, I have these intrusive thoughts that I cannot seem to ignore. It is as if there are two people arguing inside my head sometimes. What if the evil one inside me wins out in the end?"

Jesus smiled in a consoling way. "This is a great mystery that cannot be fully understood by men On the one hand, one must persevere in being good until the end in order to obtain peace in the next life. On the other, I would never allow someone truly devoted to Me to perish in his last moments. Showing devotion, charity, and avoiding everything bad as a daily practice acts as a self-predestination. Just as living every day only for yourself can destine you to reprobation. And if you do falter, then return to Me quickly like the prodigal son mentioned in the Gospels. Living well is an investment in your hour of death, giving you the fuel to persevere in those final hours. Those who do not invest in their hour of death are taking a huge risk. They are depending on the prayers and good deeds of others. Others' prayers of course do help many people, but there is no guarantee for an individual in them. There are some who wait as long as possible to turn to Me. Then they find that their pride has tainted them so much that they have lost the ability to do so. So, seek Me now. This way I can help you both in the present and at the hour of death. Do you understand?"

To hear all those comforting words made me feel so much better, but I was still a little worried—concerned that I was double minded and unable to show true devotion to God. "But how do I know if my devotion to You is true and not false, to make sure that I do persevere?"

"It is simple. It must be done for the right reasons. Don't pray only to make yourself look good or treat Me like a genie. I love being asked to help, but remember that it is a request rather than a demand—that all My graces are a gift and undeserved. Don't undertake devotions for pompous reasons."

"Thank you, Jesus. That is very helpful to me. Do You mind if I ask another question?"

"Please do. I am here to help."

"Well, I want to show You love and devotion every day. But I am running blind. How do I know what I need to do to seek You properly? You see, I'm not very well educated in these matters."

"Love Me with all your heart, soul, and mind, and love your neighbor. And how do you do that on a more practical level? The answer is laid out plainly in the Gospels and the Tradition of the church. Read the Scriptures and the Catechism to better understand the faith. And find a faithful teacher to help you on the path. But here are the basics. Do your day and night-time prayers. Attend Mass on all days of obligation, unless there is a serious reason that you cannot. Participate often in the Sacraments of the church to receive heavenly graces; especially, receiving Me in the Eucharist when in a state of grace, and frequent confession. My burden is light and My yoke is easy."

"Thank you, Jesus. We have not attended Mass on Sundays as a family very often. What if my parents don't want me to go when I ask?"

"Until you are of the age to make such decisions for yourself, obey your parents in those matters. Then attend when you are older. I only expect the things you are capable of doing. If you are not allowed to attend, I cannot expect you to break one commandment to follow another. Yet in your case, if you ask your parents, they will let you come."

We arrived at a gleaming crystal bench on the path and I followed Jesus' lead in taking a seat for a rest.

"We are coming to the end of this meeting I'm afraid," said Jesus. "But I have enjoyed our time together and our chat. Please come back and see Me again. Even if you cannot perceive Me this way most of the time, I am still here none the less, fully present under the appearance of bread and wine. And even though I am here waiting for everyone and anyone, it does not take away from the fact that I am especially waiting for you. Every sheep is a personal friend. I am not a distant shepherd, but a personal and caring one. Please never forget that, Tommy."

I tried to hold back my tears. I was overwhelmed with emotion because I felt so at peace around Jesus in this wonderful place and wanted to stay much longer—but I did not want to be a pest either.

"It's okay," Jesus comforted me. "You can create a Tabernacle just like this one or even better in your own heart and welcome Me there." Jesus handed me a purple silk handkerchief with the syllables 'JMJ' on it, and I used it to wipe up my tears.

"Thank you for the gift, the words of wisdom, and Your loving friendship. I am so glad to have been able to meet You in person, and I will try to follow Your advice. And I have a present for You too." I handed Jesus my giant bouquet of flowers which seemed almost as big as He was. "I feel kind of silly giving You flowers from Your own garden, but I doubt there is any gift we can give You which does not originate in some form from God anyway."

"Thank you very much," Jesus said, taking in a whiff of the aroma from them. "That is very kind of you." Jesus stretched his arms out as if on a Cross and then embraced me once more. I closed my eyes in complete contentment and when I opened them, I was back on a kneeler in the pew.

Was I really inside the Tabernacle just now? What an awesome experience that was. I was glad to have had the chance to talk and walk with Jesus in person for a while but felt saddened by the fact that it had to end so soon. If we were beyond time, then why not be able to prolong it in scenarios like this? I suppose whatever the reason, God must have done it for my benefit.

I said a long personal prayer to thank Jesus for the wisdom, time, and love he had given me, and then recited a few formal petitions. Looking to my left at my Guardian Angel, I wondered if he had known where I had been or not. I was puzzled about where we were heading next.

Chapter 21

Those who Mourn

My Guardian Angel still seemed deep in prayer and I did not want to disturb him by asking where our next destination was. Instead, I decided to go and pay homage to St. Nicholas at his shrine, figuring that my Angel would let me know if it was time to leave when he saw fit. I said one more quick prayer in thanksgiving, did the sign of the Cross, and genuflected again as I left the pew.

It came to me at that moment what the real purpose of genuflecting in church was. It must be to show proper worship to Jesus as the Eucharist present in the Tabernacle. Even though I had always bent my knee out of habit, now that I knew Jesus was in the Tabernacle, I understood the reason why I was supposed to do so. For as long as I could remember, Nate and I had followed this practice when in church, so our parents must have taught it to us when we were very young. I had always genuflected out of respect, though I did not know the purpose for doing so until now, yet I was grateful to have learned the reason—especially having been taught by Jesus himself.

The St. Nicholas statue was taller than I was; enough so that I had to look up to see his face. The Saint looked extremely lifelike, especially his eyes. Remembering what I had been told about sacred images being windows into Heaven, I wondered if, when seeing them, we were looking at the actual countenance of the Saints—that it might indeed be a two-way window of sorts.

Taking the thin wooden stick, which reminded me of a giant toothpick, I lit the end of it from one of the blessed candles then proceeded to light a taper of my own. And after crossing myself, I recited a prayer to the Saint, "In the name of the Father, the Son, and the Holy Spirit: St. Nicholas, I heard that you are the patron of children and travelers. Luckily for me, I am both at the moment. Please help Nate, Brendan, Paul, and me to get home safely. And please bring consolation to our parents and help them to be merciful to us—unless that is selfish of me to ask. Pray that God may forgive our sins, especially mine for getting everyone into this mess. And lastly, please in particular help Brendan. He seems to have so many family afflictions and mental problems on his plate that I could not even imagine how to deal with if I were in the same shoes. In whatever way you can, please help my friend. And thank you for doing so. St. Nicholas, pray for us. Amen. +"

Going around the stand of candles, I crouched down to kiss the feet of St. Nicholas in gratitude for his intercession and assistance. But when I lifted my face back up and turned around, it seemed that I was no longer in the church. I was now in a large study, with shelves covering almost every square inch of the walls. The shelves were full of scrolls, books, and stacks of envelopes. An enormous sturdy maple wood desk rested in the center of the space.

Shadows brought into being by well-placed candles, which were the only visible illumination to enlighten my eyes, filled the dark room. Though dim, the area did not strike fear in me. Instead I felt welcomed, perhaps from all the desirable ambient lighting.

Where was I now? In this place, nothing seemed to surprise me anymore. Walking towards the desk, I admired the smell of aged paper mixed with the alluring scent of burning wax candles. My heart jumped at a sudden metal clanging sound that caught me off guard. Jolting my head towards the direction of the noise, I noticed a mail slot with a pile of letters underneath—freshly delivered.

Feeling silly for becoming scared by something as docile as mail, I turned my direction again to the intimidatingly-sized desk. It had a beautifully matching carved wooden chair tucked into it, an unusually large magnifying glass, a letter opener, an old-style feather quill pen and ink bottle, and several large piles of letters casually stacked together around the table.

There were also a few letters not in the piles scattered on the table. Perhaps they were ones that were about to be read or recently had been. One of them I immediately recognized. It was the one I got so upset about my parents reading and then posted myself. There was a second one close by that had my brother's name on it.

Curious as to what it might say, I considered reading it. Was it wrong to do so if the letter was already open, or would it still be an invasion of privacy? After debating with myself, curiosity got the better of me, and I took the letter out of the envelope to read. It was as follows:

NATE'S LETTER TO ST NICK:

December 1st, 1997.

My dear friend St Nicholas,

Currently I am enjoying a strawberry, vanilla, and banana milkshake. I have become very good at making the chalky flavored drink from whey powder taste better. Earlier it got a little cold and I had to put on a sweater. The changing weather reminded me to begin my annual letter to you. And so here we are.

I hope you are having a good year so far. I don't expect many presents this Xmas, but I still thought that there was no harm in asking. The thing that I would like more than anything else is more protein powder. Out of misguided concern for me, my parents wish to limit my intake of it, so I thought it best to ask you for some instead.

They do not understand the importance of it for me. Even though you are very large, I know you are active too with all the presents you need to deliver around the world. I'm guessing that is the reason for all the milk you drink.

I want to do a great deal of good by helping my family and friends, but I can only make a bigger difference for them if I get popular. Everyone knows who you are, and you are able to do a lot of charity because you are famous, so you must know what I am talking about.

The quickest way to become popular is by becoming an athlete. At least for me it is, since I have little musical talent. It's like my favorite movie—the one with the boxer who never gave up. He was an underdog. But once he made it, he was able to use the respect and influence he gained to be a really great help to both his loyal friends and his family. Technically he lost that fight, but he still became famous from it. If he had not put in so much effort, with everyone already expecting him to lose, he might have not gained long-term fame from the experience. And he did win fights in future matches.

I don't think I've been very bad this year, but I have not done much good either. I tried to though. I tried out for every team that I could, but the coaches all must be intimidated by my athletic ability and are afraid of my skills discouraging the other team-mates or causing resentment.

But they've got it all wrong. I would help the other players to improve and would encourage the team. Yet if I get even better, then the coaches will no longer be able to pretend that I suck at sports. That's why I need a lot more protein to help me get even stronger than I am.

My brother on the other hand has been really good this year. When I did not make the cross-country team, Tommy tried to make me feel better. I pretended not to be bothered by being turned down, but he knew better. Brothers I guess can't fool each other about such things. He mentioned to me that not making a team would not cause him to love me any the less and that he loves me the way I am. He was only being nice with that nonsense, but it still felt amazingly good to have him say so.

On the other hand, he has called me 'Yobro' many times, though much less recently. Anyway, don't let that get him on the naughty list. I'm sure I have said much worse to him. I can't remember any examples but take my word for it.

Anyway, I was going to ask you if you would bring something extra special for Tommy this year. I think it would help cheer him up. I don't understand what is bothering him so much at the moment, but he seems very sad. Sometimes I hear him crying at night in our room when he thinks I'm asleep. I want to ask him what is wrong but worry that I may embarrass him if I do.

He is also exhibiting some strange behavior which has got me worried about him. Almost every day during the summer Tommy would spend hours singing Xmas carols. It's his favorite thing to do, but I've never seen him doing it except in winter before. Once in a while I joined him so as not to be bored while waiting for him to come and play. If he ever stops playing games with me, then I will know for sure something is very wrong.

Perhaps you could give him a Bible as a gift. The only one he has is borrowed from the library. He used to read mine, which I did not mind, but Mom got really upset when she found out because it is a keepsake from my baptism and apparently not meant for reading. So, his own Bible would likely make Tommy ecstatic. Though that might be what I get him. I am sure that he will love whatever you bring for him.

He hates it when I tell him this, but I think Tommy might be a Saint— just like you. Seeing him pray and read the Scripture by choice inspires me to more devotions too.

Anyway, thanks for listening, St. Nick. I hope you don't have any trouble finding our house. And I promise not to try and stay up to catch you this year.

Your friend,
Nate Jolmen.

Although grateful for Nate's concern about me, I felt terrible for causing him to worry over me. Nearby Nate's letter, I noticed a note from another recognizable name. After putting my brother's memo back in the envelope, I picked up Brendan's letter to read:

BRENDAN'S LETTER TO ST NICHOLAS:

November 18th, 1997

Dear St Nick,

It's me, your faithful friend who writes to you every year. Since you see all, I must be upfront with you. I have not been good much of the time this year.

I know that I am not supposed to show emotion, but I can't seem to help it. I'm such a cry-baby! My Mom tells me often that Dad left because of my constant tears, and that if I ever want him to come back, I have to get control over my sobbing. And I want him to come back so badly, so I really am trying. Honest.

I am getting better though. Now I can at least wait until I am alone in my cage before crying. I am able to keep it together until Mom goes to sleep. I have even quietened down my tears. If I don't wake her the whole night, then she will leave me the basin in the cage in case I need to go before morning. But if I do wake her, she will remove it as punishment. It is a good incentive to help me remain calm. She knows me so well.

I don't mind though. I will endure any punishment if it helps change me so that Dad will come back.

I haven't been all bad. For good behavior, I often earned two nights a week being allowed to sleep outside the cage in my bed. And I pray every morning and night. If I have trouble sleeping, I pray even longer.

Anyway, I know I have been bad this year, but I hope that I have not crossed the line so much as to end up on the naughty list. I am grateful for the coal that you give me each year. But I was ecstatically grateful for last year's gift. Normally I find the coal in my stocking each morning, and that year was no different. But I also remember and am so grateful that you visited me in person. You woke me up while I was asleep in my cage and handed me my very first Bible. Then you gave me a blessing before leaving. I was so happy and have read from my present often—especially the Psalms, which are now my favorite. Even the fact that you visited me was a gift to me. I don't expect a personal visit again this year, knowing how busy you are. Yet if you can bring me another religious book to help me learn more about God, I would be blissfully thankful. If you can't though, I understand. And although it is not a request for something material, if you can help bring my Dad back, I would be the happiest kid alive. Merry Christmas.

Yours forever,
Brendan Nicholas J Mascent

Wow! That was amazing. Why did Brendan not tell me that he was visited personally by St. Nicholas? Maybe he thought it was a common thing. I will have to ask him about it if I ever get to see him again.

"That was a private letter!" I heard my own voice echo back to me, which I recognized from shouting at my parents before.

I looked around the room to see where the voice was coming from. It was right of course. I had tried to justify reading the letters by telling myself that since they were already open there was no harm done. Yet I knew inwardly that they were still private, and I had not been given permission to read them. I read them partially out of concern for my brother and friend, and partially out of mere curiosity. How hypocritical of me to do such a thing. I feel more understanding towards my parents now for having read my letter; still of course thinking that it was wrong but realizing that their intentions were out of great concern for me.

I dashed over to where the statue of St. Nicholas was to apologize for what I had done. Yet before I could open my mouth, I quickly realized that the figure was no longer there. Where had he gone? I never even noticed the figure had moved. Suddenly I heard a loud but welcoming chuckle. Jolting my head back towards the chair where it was coming from, I saw St. Nicholas pulling the chair out from the desk to have a seat. *He is real!*

Seeing the surprised look on my face caused the Saint to chuckle all the more; however, I did not feel as though I was being laughed at but laughed with. "Welcome!" St. Nicholas shouted, "Welcome!"

My shock turned to glee on seeing that he was not angry with me. And without thinking, I sprinted over to him and sat on his knee, putting my arms around him. Then abruptly, I tried to slip off his leg without his noticing, causing him to chuckle again.

"I'm sorry St. Nick," I tried to explain. "You see, I was so glad to see you that I reverted to the inner child and forgot that I was too old to sit on your lap."

St. Nicholas took a short break from his gentle chuckle to say, "I understand, Tommy. It's nice to see you. Remember that you must become a child to enter Heaven, so don't feel too silly about it."

"Where are we anyway?" I asked, having no idea whatsoever where we could be.

"We are inside my shrine, Tommy. All these prayers, letters, and petitions have made their way to me over these past 1,654 years, asking for my assistance—from children, sailors, travelers, repentant thieves, and all sorts of other people."

"Wow! You keep all these?"

"Of course. I can't throw out a prayer, now can I?"

"No, I suppose not. How did you become the Patron Saint of children?" I asked after thinking for a moment, having always wanted to know.

"During my earthly life there was a terrible famine. A villainous butcher slaughtered three innocent children with the atrocious intention of selling their remains as fake pork meat."

I gave the Saint an astonished look, not understanding how anyone could do such a thing.

"By God's grace I miraculously revived the three lads. And so, I became well known as an advocate for the innocent and the young."

"Wow! That's incredible. I've never heard that story before. I'm so happy that you were able to help those kids, and for helping all children."

"I love to help people. And that includes you, Tommy. I want you to know that I have received every letter and prayer that you ever sent me. Even though many people today are in ignorance of who I am, I still pay attention to their requests. 'Forgive them Father, for they know not what they do.' Isn't it amazing that in this faithless time you live in, people still write letters to a Saint? Those who wish to destroy the faith of mankind can never succeed in the end. Who thinks he can fight against God and win? There is hope for the world, you see."

"I'm glad you think so, St. Nick."

"The darker the world gets, the lighter those who bear the light become. Be the light, Tommy. Don't let the darkness around about you snuff you out."

I wondered if perhaps Saints could not see the hearts of people the same way that God could, so I asked, "But St. Nick, can't you see that the darkness is not just around me but in me as well?"

"You have been given a great struggle, Tommy."

"Great?"

"Yes. Every struggle is a gift from God because it is meant to help you seek him."

"Really?" I was surprised to hear him say that pain could be a present.

"Tell me, Tommy. Have your struggles caused you to turn away from God?"

I thought for a moment. "I don't think so. I've held onto what little faith I possessed throughout my life in hope of not being overcome by my darkness."

"Exactly."

Thinking about those with worse problems who don't seek God, I said, "But some people do give into despair."

"Yes, and that is why trusting in God is a daily task. People can either turn towards God or away from him during life. Your struggles are there to help you, no matter how painful they seem. But it is still up to you to be a partner with the graces God has given you. Read the Sermon on the Mount in the Gospels, and you will see that those who are in pain in this life are favorably looked upon by God, while those who are excessively content are in grave danger of losing him. Fallen human nature needs pain as a constant reminder of what is most important in life. Too much comfort only blinds people and clouds their judgement, making them more and more selfish. If God has given you greater pain than some, be grateful for how special you are to him in order for him to do so."

"I understand what you are saying. But what if it becomes too much to bear? I am not very strong. What if I end up in the nuthouse? Can God heal me from my depression, acute anxiety, and intrusive thoughts if I have learned all the lessons that I can learn from them? I have gained more faith in God and understand things better now. So, I don't need it anymore."

"He may heal you and He may not. You can always learn more lessons and only God can be the judge of such things. You may have to struggle with this darkness your whole life, and if so, God has his reasons. Remember that to ask God to remove your current struggles is to ask him to replace them with others—and God knowing more than you or I do is perfectly well aware what you can bear or cannot. I am not able to promise that you will not suffer terribly in the future. Yet I can promise that God will never send you more than you can handle, even if it does not seem that way. And all your distress can be offered up to God as a living sacrifice. You may be stronger than you think. This life is full of sorrows, but don't forget that God will wipe away every tear from your eyes in the days when the lion will lie down peacefully beside the lamb and they will eat together."

What he said made sense to me. But it was still difficult to bear. I winced. Depression and uncontrollable intrusive thoughts, although I've dealt with them my whole life, have recently been escalating and could become worse. Suffering from them for the remainder of my life terrified and overwhelmed me. This time I did not even bother holding back my tears. What would be the point in putting up a front with someone from Heaven?

I crouched down to the floor and buried my face in St. Nick's robe as I wept, and he patted me on the head with his hands.

"It's okay. Listen, Tommy. Don't fret. I will be there for you always even though you normally can't see me. All the Angels, Saints, and especially God himself are there for you as well, in addition to your faithful earthly friends. Continue to seek God and ask for my aid and I promise always to help you, your family, and your friends. Life can be hard, but never give up. Always keep hope in your heart. You are not, never have been, and never will be alone—regardless of how lonely you may feel at times. The Good News does not cease to be grand from changing human sentiments. I love you, Tommy. And don't forget to be joyous in your heart, even when feeling down." He chuckled cheerily again.

"I love you too, St. Nick," I said as I wiped my tears with his robe and then got up from where I was crouching, only to see that I was back in the church facing the St. Nick statue. "And thank you, old friend."

Chapter 22

Reminiscences among the Trees

Turning away from the statue of St. Nicholas and back to the pew, I noticed my parents leaving the nave. They seemed anxious, and in a rush, causing me to wonder where they were heading so impetuously. Worried about them, I felt the need to find out where they were going. My Guardian Angel sauntered over to me and told me that it was time for us to leave. Perhaps he would be privy to Mom and Dad's destination.

As we left the church, I asked my guide, "Where were my parents heading? They seemed to be in a hurry."

"We'll talk about that afterwards," replied the Angel, as we started back into the vast land of snow.

"After what?" I asked, excited and worried at the same time by what it could possibly be. The exhilarating fresh winter air tried to cheer me up, but could not take away the anxiety I felt over my parents. Not that the church had felt stuffy; in fact, I loved the atmosphere inside. But experiencing the fresh outdoor open air after being a while indoors always made the experience new.

The coniferous trees round about, covered in fluffy snow, made me glad. I liked snow of course. Even on its own. But the sight of nothing but snow for miles is not very interesting. I preferred seeing the mysterious precipitation in multiple settings—on rooftops, bushes, benches, and coating branches. I was the more grateful to see trees now from the absence of any during the major part of my walk in the chamber. Here and there we passed by groves of timber and off in the distance an entire forest awaited us. I looked forward to the change in scenery.

As we passed by the first few trees, however, the strangest thing happened. A memory appeared with startlingly intense vividness before me. Following it, in front of each cluster of trees, other fresh and keen recollections came to life one by one. More bewildering still, I somehow experienced each single memory both from the outside and within itself, as if I were still simultaneously part of it. My conscience was speaking audibly to my entire being. I could feel each feeling of guilt or joy at my core witnessed to by raking up the memory. In some way I was at the same time also shown how my actions had affected others directly and indirectly.

"What was all that about?" I asked my guide when the first shock of the experience passed off.

"You must now see your entire life up to the point of the cave," said my Angel.

Now that I had a faint idea of what all those trees represented for me, I was no longer looking forward to entering the woods. Remembering what Dad had told me once—that our whole lives flash before our eyes when we die—I began to panic and tremble as I walked along, not knowing if I was ready in the slightest for the encounter. "Does this mean that I'm going to die for sure? Today? Right now?"

"We will get to that later," my Angel remarked noncommittally, either because he was not allowed to tell me or because he was not himself sure.

Recalling my parents rushing out of church in a panic, I pondered the likelihood that they had received bad news about my condition. Maybe they were on their way to say their goodbyes to me. I felt terrible for doing this to them, causing them such great worry over me. And now I would not even get a chance to say goodbye to them.

As we got closer to the forest, I slackened my pace in an effort to delay the inevitable. When only about a hundred meters away, I stopped where I was and gulped. "I'm not ready," I explained. "Do I have to do this?"

"I'm afraid so," said the Angel. "We all must account for our deeds—all of mankind and every Angel."

Why were the trees still getting closer when I had stopped moving? I could not tell whether I was being pulled by an invisible force towards them or they were advancing relentlessly on me. Or maybe even both. Regardless, I was going to have to face myself and I dreaded the likely end—seeing myself in perpetual despair in the dark void.

My Angel attempted to console me, saying, "Don't forget, you are loved, and never truly alone."

I was grateful to him for trying to comfort me. Finally gathering up the courage, I took the first step into the dark forest of dreadful memories. I could no longer see my Guardian Angel, but hoped that he was still nearby even if invisible. Someway, every moment of my life now passed clearly by me. I perceived it both internally and externally; in linear record and yet all at the same time. It was as if I experienced over a decade of time in just a few seconds and somehow without missing even one minor detail.

Not only did I witness each tiny moment of my life on a surface level, but every deed and thought in depth too; as well as what each action and inaction had caused to others around me, directly and indirectly. It was as if I was being judged by my own conscience rather than by God, with my Creator being more a witness for the case against me than the judge. I am sure that God still is my judge but that perhaps he only confirms what my own conscience clearly shows me to be already guilty of.

Made known to me too was every suggestion that my Guardian Angel had ever whispered into my ear. Both at the times that I listened to him and the all too many occasions I ignored his gentle reproofs and neglected his benevolent wisdom. How faithful my Angel and God himself had remained to me deeply inspired me. Regardless of the ridiculous number of times that I would have deserved just that, they never gave me up.

Seeing even the smallest of my errors made me cringe, for it showed so clearly how I could have chosen better. Though my good deeds were far fewer, they each seemed to cover a great multitude of bad ones, which brought me great consolation—reminding me that a selfless act of love was worth much more in weight than a wrong one. I knew that if I was ever sent back to earth, I would be more careful about everything I did; and that I desired greatly to be slower to speak, and to listen more cautiously to others rather than just hear them speak.

The greatest lesson I learned was that we are all our brother's keepers, not only for our immediate family and friends first, but for everyone who comes into our lives. And also, that we are all deeply connected and all our good and bad behavior in some way has an effect on the entire world. Seeing not only the normal visible things in everyday life but the invisible, I was reminded of how the veil between Heaven and earth, the living and the dead, this life and the world to come is so very thin.

The end of the woods of recollection was now in view. My first and last memory passed by just as all the others did, when I exited the forest, walking by the final tree of recall. I was left in awful terror, fear and trembling, yet never in all my life had I felt so loved and embraced.

Suddenly the chamber I was in, which had met its usefulness, dissolved; and what surrounded me now I could only describe as pure light and charity.

It was as if nothing mattered and yet everything did matter at the same time—an unexplainable paradox. I was overwhelmed with ecstasy—a blissful joy penetrated the very core of my being. Was I in the pure presence of God?

"You have an important choice to make, Tommy." said a piercing voice of love which penetrated to the deepest marrow of my bones.

"Okay," I said, not knowing of any way to hide from pure light and love and realizing that this was not something that I could get out of.

"You have to choose between returning to earth to live out the remainder of your life or else staying here in eternity," the voice commanded, but without a hint of pressure.

"You are giving me the choice? Really?" I asked, surprised that someone as indecisive as I was would be trusted with so important a matter. What if I made the wrong decision? Was there even a right decision in a case like this? Or would both options be correct?

The silver cord that I noticed earlier, connecting me to my body, became visible again, heading downwards into a newly opened spiritual gateway—though I could not see precisely where it led.

Wondering what state my eternity would be, I asked, "If I choose to stay, would I be with you or would I suffer that unspeakable deadly abyss?"

"Before losing consciousness, you took advantage of the graces provided to you by Christ's sacrifice and merits, by making a perfect contrition. Those who ask receive, and those who forgive are forgiven. Having done both by daily prayer and final perseverance in addition to Mary having pleaded on your behalf, all your sins have been pardoned. Though a temporary time of purging would have to be undergone before you could enter Heaven."

Wow! To be offered Paradise. I was overjoyed. This would be a very difficult decision to make though. Somehow, I had made it into Heaven, so I should not lightly give up that chance—lest I return to my body and do something stupid and lose God in the end. On the other hand, based on what Jesus said to me when I was in the Tabernacle, staying on the narrow path is fairly straightforward if I try my best. But what about Nate, Brendan, and Paul, as well as my parents and other friends? Would they be okay without me? Or are Brendan and Nate being given this same choice right now too?

If they were stuck on earth while I went to Heaven, I would feel bad for leaving them there. Yet if I chose to go back to earth and found out that they were in Heaven, it would also be a huge disappointment; not because of envy, but from my not being there with them.

Thinking that knowledge of these factors might help my decision, I asked, "Is Brendan also being given the same choice as I am, or am I the only one? And how is Nate doing?"

"This is a decision you have to make on your own," the awe-inspiring voice said. "You must decide without knowing that."

I had no idea why I was not to be privy to such knowledge, but I was not about to argue vainly with pure light. What a hard decision. Perhaps in a poor attempt to stall, I asked, "What is this cord that attaches me to my body all about?"

The gentle yet steadfast voice assured me, "The cord keeps souls attached to the body, so that even when traveling in the spirit, it can find its way back home. However, once this cord is severed, the separation between soul and body becomes permanent until the Resurrection at the end of time, when all human spirits will be returned to their bodies."

How much time did I have to decide? If we were outside time at that moment, did that mean that I had an endless period in which to make a decision? And what would an infinite amount of time even be without time as a reference? Would an endless span of days make impossible decision-making easier, or would it make me even more indecisive—prolonging the determination?

Either way, whether I had the equivalent of a hundred years to think it over or but a few minutes, I needed to decide. I had learned so much on this journey and I would never get a chance to apply the lessons if I did not return to my body. Even if I might be disappointed to return to earth and find that my friend and brother were dead, the thought of risking leaving them on the earthly plain while I enjoyed Heaven would be a much greater heartbreak. Granting the fact that I could not be upset once in Heaven because of leaving others on earth, since by its very definition Paradise is perfect happiness, I would still feel bad about the idea here and now. I thought therefore that the answer was obvious. While I would love to go to Heaven, it was my duty to be present for my family and friends as best I could.

"I've made my decision," I said, hoping that it was the right one. "If I have access to Heaven while on earth, based on what I learned, I can do a bit of both—being around for those on earth who need me, while still accessing Heaven until I can go there permanently at the end of my life."

"I understand," said the terrifyingly beautiful voice.

Without warning I was pulled swiftly into the open portal then traveled through a dark tunnel with a bright light at the end. I saw a hospital room, glimpsing it too quickly to perceive much, and then woke up in an unfamiliar place. Though the light from my last location had been much brighter than this place, this light was slightly painful to my eyes. I placed my hands in front of my pupils to protect them from the brightness until they could get more used to it.

Chapter 23

A New Brother

February 3/1998.

It has been about a month since going on our adventure. Or as parents like to call it, running away from home. I think I will make a journal entry soon to record the full details of the trip to make sure that I never forget, but for now I just wanted to give an update.

Neither Brendan nor I were expected to live when we were found. But somehow, we came through, spending several weeks recovering in the hospital. We were admitted for severe hypothermia after the search team found us, thanks in large part to Paul's efforts. I have learned that once someone stops shivering during hypothermia, he can begin to feel overheated and start removing his clothing. That would explain what Brendan must have experienced by the time I found him in the cave.

I am grateful to be alive, and thankful for all the wisdom that I learned on the trip. I am now confident that even though I often feel alone and at times appear alone, I never actually am. God and his invisible friends, as well as my earthly ones are all connected to me—always by their prayers and love, and frequently by their presence. When I feel alone in a crowd, I remind myself that there is at least one invisible Angel for each one of the people, and then I recall God's loving-presence—so that even when I seem to be among strangers, I know that I am among friends.

At first, I was not sure if my spiritual journey with my Guardian Angel and St. Nicholas, and actually being present with Jesus in the Tabernacle, was a true near-death experience or only an intensely vivid dream. I did want to believe it had actually happened, but had my doubts. Eventually I realized that I was still wearing the wool scapular which the Mother of God gave to me, and still possessed the purple handkerchief from Jesus to wipe away my tears with. And later I noticed that the prose I had written for Jesus, when visiting him in the Tabernacle garden, had actually been recorded supernaturally in the journal that I left at home. With those three material witnesses, I no longer had any doubt that the experience was real. My only dilemma was whom I should tell it to and whom I should not.

Speaking of the prose from the journal, I was so happy finally to have found an audience for my poetry and prose. Knowing that the Child Jesus, author of the universe, was and is grateful for my writing encourages me to overcome any insecurity about whether mere mortals like it or not.

Nate told me during a hospital visit that the old Hermit, Francis Dominic, must have been the spirit who came to the cabin to add the logs to the fire place. He entered Nate's room and prayed with him when he was sick in bed. Considering what I have been privileged to have seen, I don't doubt it for a second. I guess the holy man wanted to show us his Christian hospitality for as long as we stayed in his abode, even from beyond the grave.

The body of the Hermit is being turned over to the Diocese. They are going to investigate him to see if there may be a cause for his canonization. It is apparently an in-depth process and the investigation starts at the local level. Nate is fairly confident that Francis is a Saint, whether he will be canonized or not—and so am I convinced, but it would be great if he ended up being raised to the altars. I am fairly certain that it was due mostly to his favor with God that I experienced so many graces while staying at his abode.

Today is unique because there are two big events taking place. And, however you look at it, a strange combination they make. In the afternoon there is a funeral and in the evening a birthday party. I would not have combined two such events on the same day, but that is what has happened. The adults perhaps thought a birthday party would take our minds off the death, but who knows?

Although Brendan's Mom was confirmed dead from alcohol poisoning while we were still recovering at the hospital, they wanted to postpone the funeral so that Brendan could attend. His Mother's remains were cremated. That way they could wait 'till after the funeral to bury her. Neither Nate nor Paul nor I knew Brendan's Mom, and from the one time I heard her voice I did not think I would have wished to, but we still wanted to go to the funeral to support our friend in his time of need. It is good for our own souls when we *pray for God to grant rest to the dead, even if it is a prayer for someone we may not have liked. I have not yet had a chance to see how Brendan is taking all this today, but he seems to be managing okay on the surface.*

The whereabouts of Brendan's Dad are still unknown. With the evidence of neglect and abuse being clear, he would not likely be allowed to have custody of his son even if he did return. I don't understand how parents can hate their own kids. Brendan had no other family willing to take him in and it seemed probable that he would be placed in foster care. After Nate and I both nagged our parents every chance we could get, however, they gave in to our demands. Or maybe they were genuinely touched by his plight. Either way, Mom and Dad offered to look after Brendan so that he would not need to become a Ward of the Crown. After a probationary period to make sure everything is working out, we will be able to send in the paperwork and adopt him as a member of the family. Nate and I could not be happier about gaining Brendan as a brother and I think our parents have taken a liking to him as well.

As part of the hospital's protocol, when all the markings that he had on the soles of his feet were found, Brendan had to stay under psychological observation before he was released, to make sure that he was no longer a danger to himself. My family visited him several times during his stay as an in-patient.

The facility informed us of things to keep an eye on, since he would be staying with us. They had been testing him for Post-Traumatic Stress Disorder (PTSD), which he might have got from all the abuse and trauma from his family. Apparently, the mind can learn to shut down to protect itself when it is exposed to too much trauma. One of the symptoms we are supposed to watch out for is to see if he has any more blackouts. When something triggers a traumatic memory, it can cause the mind to blackout or have a flashback, or have recourse to some other form of escape.

I think this may be what happened to him when he zoned out after Paul grabbed him and he began reciting the Psalter from heart. He did tell me that the Psalms used to bring him so much comfort when he read them in the cage, and that he read them a lot. Perhaps, his mind went to the Psalms as a method of bringing him solace in a situation of too much stress. I'm not really sure. But I'm glad that he is getting help and I hope that he gets better or at least learns to cope well.

Going to the hospital made me realize something. Although mental institutions can seem scary, as regular hospitals and dental offices do, they exist to help—not hide people society thinks are crazy. Most patients are not locked up for life, but are released when better. And some do get better. Perhaps seeing how Brendan received some much-needed help persuaded my change of mind too.

I still think I may end up institutionalized one day. But I no longer fear it in the same way. If I ever have to be, then I should be grateful to such places for giving me the support I would need. And I am certain that my loved ones would not abandon me there, but would visit me often—just as we did with Brendan. Now that he has been released, Brendan is still required to attend weekly therapy sessions for an unspecified period of time—which is the adults' way of saying 'until we say so'. I am not complaining about it though. It seems good for him.

I have to talk to Brendan about my spiritual quest and ask him what happened during his, but I have been waiting for a good opportunity. I did not want to bring it up while he was in the hospital. It occurred to me that speaking about visiting the spirit world might prolong our release date, and I did not want to take the chance.

I have already told Nate who enjoyed every minute of the story and demanded each detail—worrying that I might have left something out. I'm glad he believes me and does not seem to be resentful that he did not get to meet St. Nick in person like he wanted. I think he sees us as a team and thinks that whatever I experienced was for both of us. He always has a positive outlook on such things. If the roles were reversed, I don't think I would have held any ill will towards him either, but I certainly would have been jealous at the very least.

Before telling Paul, I wanted to wait until school started again to make sure that he did not go back on his word to me and use the story to make fun of me, turning all my classmates against me. On the first day back, Paul went up to the front of the classroom. I was worried that he was going to expose my adventure to all my peers and paint it in a bad light. It may have been mean of me to have doubts about trusting him, but it is hard to break the pattern of experience.

Instead of ridiculing me though, he simply recited a beautiful poem about his Grandma, in solidarity with his promise to me from long ago. Now when I say 'beautiful', I only mean that he spoke the words from a sincere heart. I feel bad for thinking this, but his poetry writing skills could use some work. Anyway, he then told everyone that poetry was cool and that no one had better dare laugh at him or any other poet. I was pleasantly surprised and wondered if he had written the poem before or after the trip.

Without thinking it through, I stood up by myself and began clapping, in hope of starting a chain reaction. I did, but not the clapping one I intended. Instead, everyone, other than Paul, looked at me and laughed for over five minutes, while I slowly sank back down on my chair in blushful shame. Even when a friend tries to get himself mocked in self-chastisement for previous misbehavior, somehow, I am the one who still ends up as the target.

Paul at least appreciated my gesture. He sat back down beside me and thanked me for clapping and apologized for unintentionally causing me to be a laughing-stock again. Since I thought more about supporting him than of the consequences of doing so, I did not see him as the reason. Either way I was thankful for the apology. I did however feel resentful towards my peers for continuing to see a need to mock me. May God remove such bitterness from my heart.

Now that I know I can trust Paul, I will tell him the full story sometime. I don't think he will believe me, which perhaps is what causes my hesitation, but he will not likely use the story to exploit me. And I think he deserves to know, since he came with us the whole way, not to mention saved our lives.

I also have to attend weekly therapy. Not by order of the hospital, but of my parents. I am grateful for this being my only punishment. I thought that Mom and Dad were going to kill Nate and me, in a manner of speaking, but was pleasantly surprised that they mostly let us off the hook. They actually apologized to us and admitted that our behavior was likely a reaction to their neglect. I don't know what that means but I am grateful nonetheless not to be grounded for the rest of my life. Apparently, my sessions are not punishment but preventative—and though I am not sure I entirely believe that, I would not trade the sentence for another penalty.

Actually, I have come to enjoy and look forward to therapy, granting that I would never admit that fact to Mom and Dad. Nate had kept the card from the priest with the psychology degree and recommended his offer to see me. His name is Father Raphael. My parents were delighted, probably because he was cheaper than other options. I was a little hesitant at first, not knowing if he would tell my parents everything I said—but we talked about that very issue at one of my first sessions. As I noticed that he was not blabbing what I said in confidence, I started telling him everything. I even told him about my spiritual experience during near death—and he believed me.

I have come to trust him and he gives me great advice. My mental problems have not been fixed by going to therapy, but I have to admit that it has assisted me in coping better with them. Having someone to listen to and understand me, and not simply pretend to, yet without having to worry about overburdening him, is very helpful.

Based on Father's recommendation, I was assessed and found out that I suffered from Obsessive-Compulsive-Disorder (OCD)—a mental disorder. No one knows yet what causes it. Most people have unwanted thoughts and ideas and deal with them by ignoring them. For whatever reason, my unwanted thoughts cannot be ignored in the same way, so I am stuck with having to face off against intensely intrusive ones most people would dismiss as silly. Feeling that I have to do things to prevent my loved ones from dying or getting hurt, needing to touch objects, worrying that inanimate objects might be sentient, an overly scrupulous conscience, and the crippling anxiety that comes with it are all apparently related to this condition. I had always worried that I was double-minded; and in a sense I am, but at least now I know there is a reason for it brought about from the symptoms.

On the one hand I felt worse when diagnosed. It was as though the experts were confirming there had been something terribly wrong with me all along. On the other, it helped me to feel normal; because it is normal for someone with OCD to have all those problems. And so, if I have OCD, then I can expect to have the same sorts of issues. Knowing that I am this way helps me to cope with it better.

Father gave me some really great advice when we talked about my diagnosis. Though I cannot ignore the intrusive thought patterns, I don't have to argue with them directly. He gave me a method to try which has worked about two thirds of the time, at least with the bigger ones. If I get an obsessive thought—for example, that I need to touch the floor three times so that Nate does not get hurt—instead of arguing against it or giving in, I can come up with a short repetitive prayer to say instead.

I have been trying out one that I found in a prayer book: "Jesus, Mary, and Joseph, I love ye, save souls." I find it helpful because it takes the focus off of me and puts it on God and others. It does not always work. Sometimes a thought catches me off guard as something that I feel I have to argue with. Basically, I often feel that if I don't argue with the thoughts, then I am accepting them by default. On occasion there is such an emotional reaction to the thought that I face it head on. Often rage or sadness that such a thought could come from me brings me to forget that it was not my fault or something that I could help. But I am slowly changing that with this helpful tool. I only have to remind myself now and then that not engaging is not the same as accepting.

After talking with Father about it in one of our sessions, I am thinking about sitting down with my parents and having a talk with them—a prospect which makes me sound like a parent wanting to discipline his child. I am not ready to tell them everything yet, but maybe one or two things would help. After all, I cannot expect them to be there for me if they do not know what I need. I am supposed to do it before my next session, but I think I will wait a week or two more.

Nate, Brendan, and I are also taking classes together to be confirmed. Paul is considering doing so as well, but wants to think it over. And Mom and Dad are now taking us to church every week; perhaps because they saw what the lack of spiritual fulfillment for someone like me did to my psyche. Either way, I am grateful. And I did not end up even having to ask them to do it. We also, to Nate's and my delight, have taken up the practice of praying the Rosary as a family every night.

The other big event today is Nate's birthday. Brendan and I are planning on walking to the corner store early to shop for a birthday present and wait for Paul to meet us there. Then we will pick up Nate to head over to the funeral. Nate will likely demand that he accompany us to the shop and will not understand my refusal to let him. But we have no choice but to disappoint him. I am not trying to be mean, but Brendan and I plan on looking for a gift and will not want him to see what we bought—though I haven't the faintest idea yet what to get him.

He has no interest in protein powder anymore. Even if he did, I would not buy it for him. Surprisingly, he has given up the pursuit of athleticism altogether now that he has found a new interest. Nate and I did both agree, though, to go on morning walks together so that we can both stay fit—or at least get into shape, that is. I am extremely grateful that we are walking rather than jogging. Brendan is going to start joining us too, for it was recommended to him from mental health experts that it would do well for him to adopt a fitness routine.

Nate's original intention was to become athletic to help others; family and friends especially. He thought athleticism was the easiest way to achieve fame and fortune. But after seeing how much Brendan and I improved from weekly therapy, he decided, as another way to assist people, to focus on studying human behavior instead of seeking fame. I think he may now want to be a therapist himself when he grows up.

I am glad to see him putting his energy into something he seems to have a natural talent for (he has such a positive attitude and is so good at studying), rather than what maybe one day he will admit he was terrible at. I'm worried however that he is going to start looking for guinea pigs to test his learning on. This fear does not come out of paranoia. He asked me if I could be his test patient once he knew more. And I could not say no to my brother's glittering puppy eyes.

On a side note, I deeply regret introducing Nate to the word 'Walk-er!', for my brother has been relentless in using it ever since—sometimes in a fitting way, other times not. He used it once when I forgot to take out the trash when it was my turn, which would work. But then he also mentions it whenever I need to retie my shoe laces. I honestly cannot tell if he is doing it on purpose to annoy me or if he just really likes the word. If he does not give it up soon, I fear that a phrase I have loved will now become hated. But I digress.

Anyway, I should get going and try to pick out that gift, mourn at a funeral, then celebrate a birthday. What a strange combination of events today brings. Until my next entry, good day journal.

Chapter 24

Paying for Friendship

Brendan and I walked side by side on the pavement heading to the corner store a few blocks away. My stomach grumbled. I hoped it was not as loud as I perceived it to be. Not that I had any reason to think Brendan would embarrass me in public about it, but it still made me feel insecure. My stomach always made loud grotesque noises when I got hungry. With the crunch of our feet on the freshly fallen snow I hoped at least it was less noticeable while we walked on the street. It was most humiliating when the noise happened in class right before lunch. All I could do in such a situation was hope that people did not know the sound was coming from me. If I asked them if they did know, then they would find out even if they never knew to begin with.

"I'm really hungry," Brendan said to me only a moment after another growl came from my stomach.

Did that mean he could hear it and was trying to show solidarity so that I would feel less mortified? Or perhaps he was only mentioning being famished himself without reference to my racking hunger.

"How about you?" asked Brendan.

If he had heard the stomach clamor then he would already know that I was hungry. Good, then. That meant he must be ignorant of the matter. Unless he was only asking in order to pretend that he did not know, so that I would not feel self-conscious about it. "Yes," I replied, "me too."

"My stomach's growling," Brendan complained.

He must've known then. He was pretending to have the same problem to try and make me feel better. Or maybe he was just being very open. "Well let's pick up something from the corner store to eat on the way back in addition to the snacks for the party."

"Sounds good to me."

If Brendan was sincerely hungry, that was a good sign. I've heard that people sometimes lose their appetite when overwhelmed. I'd wanted to ask him how he was dealing with his Mom's death, but didn't know how to bring it up. I had no wish to stir up a hornets' nest if he was not ready to talk about it. I hoped he would bring it up when he needed to if he didn't mention it first. I thought I would ask him about it after the funeral and party. That way I wouldn't risk causing him extra tension right before his Mother's funeral— in case the conversation became too emotional for him.

Leaning back against the outer store window, I waited for Brendan to re-emerge from the shop. Earlier, when we reached the cash register, Brendan informed me he had forgotten something and asked me to wait outside for him. I wondered what it was that he needed.

It had not felt that cold walking to the plaza, but when I stopped moving, I began to take notice of the frigid air, and hoped Brendan would not be much longer. I stared at a 'for rent' sign on the store window across the parking lot, remembering the times that my family and I shopped there. It used to be a dollar store. Everything was cheap and Nate and I had a marvelous time looking through the toys and other products. My heart sank. It was too bad it had to close. I knew things must change, but I never handled alteration well—at least the negative kind. Some change was good, such as making new friends and trying out a new theme park. But stores having to close was not one of them.

A gentle breeze caressed my face, trying to make me forget my nostalgic woes. But to no avail. Though I appreciated the effort, I could not take my mind off it. And perhaps resentful over my refusal to be consoled, the wind became irrational—speeding up and slowing down as it saw fit, until it settled on being heavy.

Brendan walked out of the shop and looked around 'till he saw me. Then we walked on, Brendan leading the way at an astounding pace.

"Wait for me," I said as I ran a few steps to catch up.

"Oh, sorry," Brendan said as he slowed down, "I didn't realize how fast I was going."

We were heading towards the park where we were to wait for Paul. Though some of the snow covering the ground was fluffy and fresh, it did not hide the old completely. It was that unfortunate time of winter when much of the snow had become gross-looking and corrupted by black slush. I much preferred the fresh snow of earlier in the year.

I put my hand in my pocket to see how much money I had left and could only feel a few coins. I had spent most of my allowance money on chips, soda pop, and other snacks, but Mom would reimburse me when I got home, since it was for the birthday party later on. We had had no luck finding Nate a present. We should have gone to the mall for more options rather than to a plaza with only a few stores.

"So, what did you forget?" I asked Brendan, glancing at the white grocery bag he was carrying which seemed to be empty. "I can give the receipt to Mom and she'll reimburse you for it if it's for the party. As long as it's a reasonable amount of course."

Brendan did not say anything. "Are you alright?" I asked, wondering if he was off in his own world again.

Still nothing. "Brendan!" I shouted, wishing that I had yelled a little less loudly than I did.

"Oh sorry," Brendan replied, finally. "I spaced out for a moment."

"No worries. I was wondering what you went back to purchase. And if you kept the receipt, Mom might reimburse you." I immediately regretted using the 'Mom' word. It was probably too soon for Brendan to feel comfortable calling her that, but I hoped he had not noticed I said it.

After a short pause, Brendan responded, "It was candy. I already ate it though. And the cashier kept the receipt."

"That was smart of you to eat it so quickly. I would probably have snatched a piece otherwise. Well no use hanging onto that empty bag then. Just put it in my bag." I held up my grocery bag slightly.

"Hold on a second, I have to fix my boot lace." As we stopped, Brendan crouched down facing away from me. But while he pretended to fix his lace, I could hear him rummaging through the bag, probably trying to hide the contents in his coat.

"I was only kidding about snatching your candy, you know? You don't have to pretend you already ate it. We all have a favorite candy that's too good to share."

"I don't know what you are talking about," Brendan said as he stood up and handed me the empty bag.

"Alright," I answered, not understanding why he felt the need to hide candy. As I placed the empty bag in with the groceries, I noticed that it was not entirely empty. There was a receipt inside. I thought he told me that he had left the receipt at the store. I said, in a slightly irritated tone, "You know that you can trust me, right, Brendan?"

"Of course," answered Brendan as we trailed along towards the park again.

Not understanding the reason why he was deceiving me, I said in a concerned voice, "Well if you don't want to tell me, then that's up to you. But you should go to confession for lying."

"Among other things," he mumbled sorrowfully.

That comment really worried me. What did he mean by it? I pulled the receipt out of the bag and said, "You said the receipt was left at the store. You can either tell me what you bought, or I can read it for myself—but you might feel better if you came clean."

Brendan looked down at the ground and said, "I shouldn't have lied to you. I'm sorry. I hate lying. I'm not the lying type."

"I know," I said. "So why are you doing it?"

"I thought you wouldn't understand, so I tried to keep it from you. You can look at the receipt if you want, but it's too difficult for me to say out loud."

"Alright I understand," I said, un-crinkling the receipt to read what was listed. It was a pack of disposable razors. "Why didn't you ask me for help?" I asked, very annoyed that he was suffering so greatly in secret.

"Because I was doing better. And I am. It was solely for today. The funeral is too much. She was always on to me about crying. I can't show disrespect to her by sobbing on the day of her funeral. I understand now that she was wrong about all that stuff, and that I should not suppress my emotions long term.

"My Angel was right: that it's okay for me to get sad and cry, and that I don't have to hold back my tears. But one day can't hurt. It's only once more that I need it. Understand?"

I was so happy that he had opened up and given me an honest answer. I understood how difficult this day must be for him. Trying to cheer him up with a joke, I said, "Listen, addiction is like a good bag of chips."

"What?" Brendan asked, looking confused.

"With addiction, you can't just have one. It's never enough to be satisfied."

"You're right," he said. "But I still need it today. I'm struggling so badly. Please look the other way. And I promise to never to do it again, okay?"

"You already promised that."

Brendan sighed, "I did, didn't I?"

"I am here for you. Whatever it is that you need. But I cannot let you hurt yourself or I would be the worst friend ever."

"I get it," Brendan said. "In that case pretend this conversation never happened and you won't know anything about it. No one will ever find out that you knew, even if I'm caught."

"That's not what I meant."

"Yeah I know. That was my last-ditch effort. Can you blame me for trying?"

"Yes, I can. But I won't."

"You won't tell anyone, though will you? I mean, I would understand if you did. And it's the responsible thing to do. But they'll send me back to the hospital, and who knows when they would release me? If I ever try again then by all means tell. But this one time, leave it between us, okay? Please."

He was reminding me of my own fear of being institutionalized. Feeling pity for him, I said, "I'll tell you what. If you hand over to me what you bought, I will do the irresponsible thing this once and not tell anyone."

Brendan thought a few moments then took the package of razors from his inner coat pocket to hand over to me. I put them in my own jacket as Brendan agreed, "Deal!"

"Thank you," I said, relieved to see him regaining his senses.

"No, thank you," Brendan said. "If you told Nate, he would make me his patient guinea pig the moment he got the chance."

"Well you know the real reason why Nate is becoming a therapist don't you?"

"No why?"

"Because he lacks patience. And if he becomes certified, he gets all the patients that he needs."

Brendan stared blankly at me. "I don't get it."

"You know: pa . . . tients . . . tience . . . It's a play on words."

"Ah okay," Brendan acknowledged, "That's actually clever."

"Thank you," I said, amused with myself for coming up with it.

Passing the park. I noticed a group of my classmates hanging out there about a frisbee toss away. They saw us pass by. One of them came running over to catch up to us. It was Jarod Famean. We stopped to see what he wanted.

"Hey guys!" Jarod said as he approached us with a smile. "I didn't expect to see you guys here."

Jarod was not usually that nice to me. I would not say he was normally mean either, but I had never seen him act like this before. Maybe he was in a really good mood today.

"Hey Jarod," I said as he gave us both a high five.

He rested his hands on his knees for a moment while he caught his breath. Though he had a fairly muscular build for his age, he seemed to be out of shape somehow. "You're the new guy, right?" he asked Brendan.

"Not really," Brendan responded. "I was born more than a decade ago."

I could never tell if Brendan took things literally on purpose or if he was actually being serious. "No," I laughed, "he means new at our school."

"Anyway," Jarod added, "you guys should come down and hang out with us for a bit. Come on. It'll be fun."

Brendan looked at me for reassurance and I nodded. We both followed Jarod towards the crowd.

"But we can only stay for a few minutes since we are waiting for someone," I told him.

Jarod said in a negative tone, "Whoa, you guys are popular all of a sudden."

Was he being sarcastic? I couldn't tell and I did not want to accuse him of it in case he was not. That might destroy my first opportunity to hang out with Jarod and his friends outside school. I had tried so many times over the last few years to join them at recess and they always had a new reason for not letting me join in. Even for after school and weekends, I would get the same kind of answer. I wondered what had made him finally change his mind. Perhaps they thought Brendan was cool and asked me only because I was with him.

As we approached the gang of seven kids—five guys and two girls—I saw that four of them were from my class but I did not recognize the other three. They each greeted us kindly and made us feel welcome. After a few minutes of chatting, Jarod casually tried to grab my grocery bag, likely thinking that it was up for the taking.

When I resisted, he asked, "Those snacks are for everyone, right, Tom?"

"No, sorry guys," I answered. "They're not. These snacks are for my brother's party. He probably wouldn't mind if you came, but you'll have to wait until then to have any."

"Look man," Jarod asserted, "we don't want to go to your brother's lame party, alright?"

"It's not lame at all," Brendan insisted. "There will be pin the tail on the donkey, piñatas, games, and family friendly movies!"

At that, the whole group of them seemed to laugh in unison. I was on Brendan's side in thinking the party was cool, but I knew he wasn't selling it very well. I pressed my teeth hard together for a moment to stop myself from laughing at what Brendan had said too. It was the timing of it that I found amusing not what he said, and I did not want to mock one of my best friends. I could only hope that Brendan did not notice how hard it was for me to keep from joining in the laughter.

"Well, listen little man," Jarod said to Brendan, "that may be cool and everything, but we have some place else we have to be. And we're very hungry. How about sharing some of those snacks with us? You can go back to the store and get more for the party. Or you can give us money to go and get some ourselves."

"Don't you get an allowance, Jarod?" I asked, not liking the direction in which this conversation was going.

Jarod coughed into his hand to clear his throat. He seemed to be getting more upset with me. "Why do you think we invited you down here? You guys really think you are cool enough to hang out with us?"

"What do you mean?" I asked, wondering where this was leading.

Jarod got right in my face and I backed up a few steps, intimidated by his arrogant manner.

"Listen man, I'm going to show you compassion and tell it to you straight up for once," he threatened. "You are a loser and a freak. Why do you think no one wants to hang out with you at school? Huh? And if this little guy is spending time with you then he must be one of your kind too. How do you think lame people become cool? Do you think it happens by accident? No. A cool person takes them under his wing, like a mentor—and shows them how it's done. I can do that for you. And as much as you are a freak in middle school, how much worse will high school be without someone like me watching out for you? I'll let both of you into our group here for a probationary period, but in return for that awesome favor, you can't expect to come in for free. You'll have to provide something of value in return to make it worth our while. You can start with giving us your snacks. Okay? That's a good deal, right?"

Brendan put his hands in his pockets to pull out some change. "How much would it cost us to be your friends?"

Poor Brendan. He was such an innocent that he would not hesitate to gain more friends even if it meant having to pay for them. He did not realize the dishonesty of so ridiculous a notion.

The whole group laughed again. "You see," said Jarod, "this guy gets it."

My heart picked up its pace frantically. "Put the money away, Brendan," I instructed him as politely as I could, trying my best not to let my negative feelings veer towards him. I was peeved that this group would take advantage of such an innocent. "You can't buy friendship," I added.

Every time I thought I had overcome my gullibility and naivety, I found myself easily tricked again. Why was I so readily deceived? I knew these kids never hung out with me, but I still thought we were friends. Sure, they teased me, but companions do that to each other. Now I found out that all my peers had always considered me a loser and a freak. I suppose I could not blame them, for I am a little eccentric at times—most times even. But how could I have been an outcast the whole time and not even realized it? Now my incompetence had put both Brendan and me into a humiliating situation. How could I get out of it? The group didn't seem the type to let us leave without taking what they wanted. Could we outrun them? Jarod seemed out of shape, but I wasn't sure about the rest of them. My hands and back were drenched in sweat.

"Well," Jarod argued, "you may not be able to buy it, but you can still pay your friends to teach you to be cool."

That statement was the last straw. I could not hold in my anger anymore and handed Brendan the grocery bag. "How can I pay you to teach us what you don't know?" I yelled at the top of my lungs. "None of you know the first thing about being cool if you think it requires payment to learn! And how dare you try and take advantage of Brendan like that too. You're a bunch of neurotic self-centered sociopathic con artists, who would steal candy from a child without a second thought; prevent Scouts from helping old ladies across the street; and not even give the time of day to their own Grandmother!" In my ire, I grabbed hold of Jarod's jacket collar and held onto it until my sanity returned, as it suddenly occurred to me what I had just done. Then slowly I let go of the jacket and brushed it off with my hand and gave a nervous laugh. "I'm sorry guys, I did not mean any of that."

Jarod took an intimidating step towards me and I lost my balance and fell backwards into the snow. "It's been a while since we've seen Spazky. I was wondering when you would freak out at everyone again. This time there is no teacher or anyone here to protect you."

"Get out of here, Brendan," I warned, hoping to save at least one of us from being beaten up.

Brendan tapped Jarod on the shoulder. Having got his attention, he said to him, "Did your Mom die?"

I don't think I will ever know what is going on in Brendan's mind. His full attention now on Brendan, Jarod grabbed him by the front of his jacket, making him flinch and said, "You're an even bigger freak than your friend. Now what were you saying about my Mom?"

"Please don't hurt him!" I begged as I scrambled to get up off the ground.

Realizing that the expected punch seemed postponed Brendan opened his eyes again. "If your Mom died," he said speaking to Jarod, "it would explain why you were so upset; but everything would be okay because you have all these friends to support you."

Jarod let Brendan go for a moment and looked back at me. "Is your friend 'special' or something? What on earth is he talking about?"

Not seeing how to explain away Brendan's statement, I tried to account for it as best I could, keeping Jarod's short patience in mind: "We are about to head to a funeral for Brendan's Mom. He's trying to relate his feelings to your suffering, I think."

"Now I feel terrible," said Jarod, starting to pace back and forth. "I can't beat someone up who just lost his Mom." Then he looked at me. "You still have both your parents, though. Right?"

Jarod's gang laughed in harmony again as if they were all well-rehearsed yes-men with no will of their own.

"Hey Jarod!" Paul Revell, coming from the other side of the park, called out nonchalantly as he suddenly appeared and walked up. "Are you guys ready to go?" he asked turning to us and pretending that nothing was happening.

I was paying so much attention to Jarod that I did not even notice Paul's approach. "Yes," I said, grateful for his arrival and good timing. "Come on, Brendan. Let's go."

"Paul can't always protect you," Jarod said, spitefully, as Brendan and I walked up to Paul with the bags of groceries.

Paul turned his head around towards Jarod and gave him a cold look. "Do I have to make a point today?" he asked.

"Na," said Jarod kicking the snow with his boot and putting his hands in his pockets, "I was just joking around. See you guys at school."

"Thank you, Paul," I said as we left the park to head back to my house. "We were goners without you."

"Agreed," added Brendan. "Thanks for being so intimidating."

Paul laughed, "If I didn't know any better, I would feel insulted by that statement. But you're welcome."

My heart rate was still agitated and now seemed to be skipping beats— my chest getting tighter and tighter, causing my lungs some difficulty in breathing. I was concerned that I might be having a heart attack but did not want to worry the others over what was more likely to be paranoid hypochondria. I still could not believe that I was seen as a loser among my peers. Objectively, I knew that I had real friends both visible and invisible, so finding out such a thing should not have bothered me. Yet my emotions and heart rate did not seem to be listening to my reasoning.

What bothered me even more was being patronized and pitied by the lot of them. As if they felt bad for me for not fitting in, and perniciously offering their false sense of friendship. Was the whole school really laughing at me? Now even the wind felt sorry for me, dying down to give me a moment's peace.

My hands were tingling and starting to get numb, which filled me with unease since numbness was a symptom I had never before experienced. Ever since being released from the hospital, I had not had any of the old episodes. Why did they have to start up again today of all days?

I was supposed to be there for my friend in his time of need. To be by his side for his Mom's funeral. And now I was making it all about me by having an hysterical attack. I had to get it under control this instant.

The left side of my face started to feel a numb sensation which was also new and I began twitching just under my right eye and above my lip. Perhaps I was having a stroke. This was also supposed to be my brother's day. I didn't want him being scared over me on his birthday. I should be by his side to celebrate, but instead I was selfishly taking the spotlight from him by bringing about this preposterous situation. Nate is another year older today and one year closer to moving out and not being near me anymore. Perhaps that was what was distressing me so badly. But I could not let it. I needed to recover quickly from this panic-stricken mania.

I was losing my focus and felt clumsy, wobbling slightly as I walked. Maybe it was all three issues combined into one that had triggered a veritable storm in my nervous system. Or maybe my body had not fully recovered from the hypothermia and was no longer working properly. Whatever the reason, I felt dizzy and confused and sat down on the ground, not wanting to wait until I fell and hurt myself.

I could sense that hideous foggy persona of death from my old nightmare once more lurking in the shadows, hoping for me to give up. I knew that I was likely delusional again, but what if this time I was not? You only need to be wrong once about something being real or not if it intends to hurt you. It slunk slowly closer and closer until it hovered over my shoulder.

I hugged my knees to my chest and rocked back and forth. I couldn't remember any of the prayers, and that scared me even more since they were not hard to recite; so I said the simplest one I could think of over and over again to take my mind off things, "Lord have mercy!" it went. "Lord have mercy!" The shadowy delusion recoiled and retreated a little, but I could still sense him close by.

At first, I hadn't noticed that Brendan and Paul were standing near me asking what was wrong. I may even have forgotten for a moment that I was with them.

"You stay here with him," I heard Paul say to Brendan. "I'm going to run and get Nate, to see if he might know better what to do."

"No . . .," I said, trying to add more before Paul could leave but found I was not able to without making a great effort. I did not want them to bring Nate, hoping to keep him ignorant of this absurd episode so as not to worry him on his birthday.

Brendan was sitting beside me with his arm around me, trying to comfort me by telling me everything was okay. I seized my knees in my two hands and clenched my right leg as hard as I could. Then when I needed a break, I did the same with the left, attempting to get feeling back in my hands and distract myself from the paranoia of confusion plaguing my mind.

I should not feel afraid or anxious about anything, I kept trying to tell myself; especially considering what I had been privileged to see during my adventure. But my feelings refused to heed my logical arguments. The leg gripping seemed to be working and returning my focus but when I noticed a couple of people walk by us, I became frantic again, wondering what the neighbors must think of me.

Paul returned with Nate and they both crouched down near me, Nate being directly in front.

"I'm sorry Nate," I managed to say after a much greater effort than it should take to say so simple a sentence.

"It's alright," Nate comforted me.

"I've ruined your birthday," I confessed apologetically.

"Nonsense," Nate again reassured me.

"And I couldn't find a present for you in time."

Nate thought for a moment, then tried to make me laugh with his usual wit. "It's alright. Your presence is the only present I need. The joke would not have worked though if you had said gift, so you can blame yourself for the bad jest."

I laughed as Brendan gave Nate a high five which I assumed was his approval of my brother's style of humor. Nate took my hand and told me to squeeze it as hard as I could. Paul filled him in on what had happened, and after pondering his words for a few moments, Nate said, "I think you are having a panic attack, which is not dangerous. Even though it feels as if you are in grave peril, you are completely safe. The worst that can happen is that you will tire yourself out after a few hours of feeling great dread. Understand?"

I nodded, partially consoled and partially dreading the possibility of having to experience the ludicrous situation for several hours. Nate seemed to know what he was talking about though. Either that or he was confidently misinformed. His assurance was very comforting to me.

"Listen very carefully, okay?" Nate said with conviction.

I nodded again.

"What does my hand feel like?"

I thought for a moment. Although my mind had slowed down, it seemed to be working better now. "Cold," I answered.

"Good," Nate said without hesitation. "And what color is the sky?"

I looked up at the sky, wondering if Nate might be playing a cruel joke on me with such nonsensical questions. "Blue . . . no, wait. Grey." I corrected myself, giving a quicker answer that time.

"Great. And what are your favorite color and food?"

I was beginning to get a little frustrated, wondering what Nate was up to. "Purple pizza . . . I mean purple and pizza." I laughed. "What's with all these ridiculous and weird questions?"

"Don't worry," Nate replied, "just one more. What's your favorite thing to do?"

"Spending time with all of you guys. Why?"

"Well that's nice of you to say. So, you are doing your favorite thing right now," Nate replied. "How do you feel?"

Now that he mentioned it, I did feel better. I was still a little dazed from brain fog but my head no longer felt it was over-firing with too many thoughts. The murky shadow seemed gone for now. Feeling had returned to my hands. "How did you do that?" I asked Nate. "I feel much better."

"It's simple. Your brain was overworking from fear, so I distracted you with simple non-fear-based questions to take your mind off it—not too easy or too difficult. That way you would need to use other parts of your brain without feeling overwhelmed by it."

"Wow!" I admitted, quite impressed yet not fully understanding what he was saying. "Where did you learn all that? Can I do that on my own if it happens again?"

Nate smiled as he helped me up. "I'll tell you what. Tomorrow I can go over some techniques with you that you can do on your own in case it happens to you again."

Once we were sure that I was stable, the four of us began walking towards my home while Nate explained to me what a panic attack was.

"You see, if you were being chased by a tiger or a trash panda . . ."

"Hold on. A what?" I cut Nate off.

"Trash panda. A.K.A. racoon."

"Oh okay, continue. Sorry."

"Well if you are being chased by a possum with rabies . . ."

"A possum with rabies?" I interjected again.

"What about a tree rat?" asked Brendan.

"Sure," Nate replied. "Or any kind of dangerous animal. You end up getting an adrenaline rush. It's your body's way of dealing with an immediate threat. Once the threat is over, your body returns to normal. The problem with a panic or anxiety attack is that you end up experiencing that same danger mode in your body when there is no actual peril. With no real risk, it is very confusing and scary because your body senses a hazard but you don't know what the danger is. It's a fluke. But you can't die from it even though it can feel as if you are dying."

"I think you will make a great therapist one day," I said.

"I think he already is," added Brendan.

"You really seem to know your stuff," Paul acknowledged. "It's great that you found something you are good at."

"That's the problem," Nate joked in a solemn tone. "When you are good at everything, it is so much more difficult to pick which thing you want to do the most."

"How do you manage?" Brendan asked Nate, either sarcastically or sincerely—I can never tell.

"Day by day," Nate laughed.

As we headed back to get the house ready for the party and dress for the funeral, I inwardly thanked God for all He had done for me. Especially bringing Nate, Brendan, and Paul into my life. Knowing that there are false friendships out there where people only use each other for their own gain, I was very happy to have three favorite trustworthy comrades, even if I could not tell how long I might be able to have their friendship. The worry of this time passing still overwhelmed me at times, but I did not want to allow it entirely to cripple my ability to enjoy the present. I think it really is true that if I seek God first, all other needs will be met for me, even good and true companions.

Chapter 25

Contemplations

TOM'S JOURNAL:

February 3/1998.

*T*oday was a long day. But I now have a few moments to myself. After reflecting on my adventure with Nate, Brendan, and Paul, I have some thoughts about it that I want to make sure to write down before I forget them:

   With the wisdom with which God has for some reason graced me—certainly not for anything virtuous about me that I can tell—I am cautiously optimistic about what each day may bring. And although I do not look forward to the sorrows and sufferings that may come, it helps me cope with all my struggles to think of the day when all suffering will end—when the lion will eat grass with the lamb—and I can enjoy endless happiness with my friends and family, both visible and invisible—though I suppose on that day, the invisible would become visible. Anyway. I was still heartbroken by the enlightenment of my status that Jarod 'compassionately' shared with me, but I reminded myself of the wisdom my Angel imparted to me: that I was loved, and never truly alone. I don't need everyone to like me in order to know that I am loved by many.

   Even though I intended to go on a journey to find St. Nicholas and to discover proof for God, it seems that St. Nick and Jesus were on an adventure to find me—and I am glad that they did so. It is interesting to ponder that St. Nick, who began his journey during his earthly life so many centuries ago, still *continues his traveling now with all the people he keeps helping from beyond the veil of Heaven; and each of us who gains his assistance becomes part of that journey. And this truth applies to all the Saints and the people they help. Each group of Patrons and those they aid join their adventures together in Christ, the chief cornerstone of every Saint—how incredible that is!*

Goodbye journal.